STRAY DOG

STRAY DOG

Gavin Murtagh

Book Guild Publishing
Sussex, England

First published in Great Britain in 2007 by
The Book Guild
Pavilion View
19 New Road
Brighton, East Sussex
BN1 1UF

Typesetting in Baskerville by
Keyboard Services, Luton, Bedfordshire

Printed in Great Britain by
CPI Antony Rowe

A catalogue record for this book is available from
The British Library

ISBN 978 1 84624 141 3

Preface

Every now and then someone comes along to change a situation. Sometimes it is for the better, and on other occasions, for the worse. Rudy Metthewson was not your usual average kid. 'Rebel Rudy' didn't join in with the main group, preferring to stand to one side, observing. Always deeply contemplative, watching closely the actions of contemporary behaviour. Wondering why those others found bullying so attractive. Why it always appeared a human trait to seek out another individual and proceed to initiate all kinds of punishments at the whim of the bullying sect. But Rudy could also see beyond the childhood skirmishes. He could see that his future would be forever blighted by the majority view of right and wrong. What others considered acceptable always appeared to clash with his sensibilities. But Rudy had already made up his mind about these problems. Why Rudy felt this way was not yet fully apparent; the reasons lay submerged in his deep subconscious. What might be considered by some to be dark secrets from long ago were to more spiritually enlightened souls a sign of real hope for salvation that there would come a day when the meek and good of this earth would find succour by the mysterious power inherent in this bloodline – a hidden power passed down through centuries by Russian ancestors: Stanislav Aleksei Vostrikov, through to Aleksei Vasiliy Rudikov, and on to Rudy Metthewson. This was his real family connection, the secret identity of which had been well hidden for so long and for good purpose, as most who sought ultimate power would stop at nothing to gain the knowledge now inherited by one so young. But Rudy was not without considerable protection and, as will be seen, anyone upsetting this bond would pay a price. Let no-one underestimate the powers of the individual mind. Some are blessed with a natural spiritual power far in excess of any unnatural adversary. Clark Kent might have been 'Superman' in comic book form, but Rudy might just be the real thing.

1

High on the hilltop, covered with deep green forest, birds and animals sought sanctuary within the cool recesses from the unrelenting sun, as high above, in the cloudless sky, an eagle soared, scouring the distant fields for prey, the magnificent bird showing complete disinterest in the human activity below. A small dog that had been barking and running around as people danced now lay panting beneath the shade of a tree. Gradually the dancers sat down forming a circle, leaving a single girl dancing in the middle, tantalisingly, slowly twisting and swaying in time with the tune played on the accordion by a member of her family, a favourite uncle, Sergei. Another relative, Ivan, who had been dancing a little too energetically, sat at the gathering shielding his eyes from the hot sun, whilst mopping his balding pate. Squinting against the sunlight, he noticed a young man enjoying the spectacle in front of him and cried out, 'Aleksei! Put away that slathering tongue, it is putting off the rest of the audience!' Aleksei took no notice and concentrated on the movements of the girl.

Another man, elderly in years, took up the shout, laughing now with the others. 'She is not yet your wife, Aleksei, and I might beat you to her!' The congregation howled with laughter at the sight of the eighty-seven-year-old Stanislav rising stiffly to his feet and turning in a slow circle, gesturing his arms toward the eighteen-year-old Elena, who had, throughout it all, ignored the banter, keeping her eyes on her prey. Aleksei too would not be distracted, his eyes now fixed on those of his Elena. Never had he been so happy as at this very moment.

Elena Zvadsky, lithe of body and fierce and passionate of mind, captivated the senses of Aleksei, who still could not believe that such a spirited young woman would have eyes only for him. He felt enormous pride. His elation was heightened by the quickening movements and obvious promise of a sparkling display, as Elena began to pirouette. But as she danced closer Elena's movements slowed again and her eyes began to lose their sparkle. She suddenly looked afraid as her attention was caught by something moving in the distance behind Aleksei. She stopped dancing and stood absolutely still, riveted to the spot, anxiously watching as trucks appeared along the road towards the village. The rest of the crowd also stood silently staring at the slow moving convoy. One of the trucks halted close by and a young officer got out and walked quickly up to the gathering.

The congregation had enjoyed a glorious day thus far. The hot sunny weather had been perfect for the festivities and all were cheerful, enjoying brief respite from the troubles that had befallen their country since the revolution in 1917. Ten years on and Russia was in the grip of the Bolshevik terror campaign. A party of these Bolsheviks, the 'majority', had just arrived at their domain to remind these villagers of the reality facing them all. The young officer could not have been more than twenty-five years of age, his youthful good looks spoilt by a scowling face. His stance was confident as he looked arrogantly at the concerned faces of the gathering. He smiled cruelly.

'Good day, comrades. Nothing at all for you to be concerned about. We are on our way to pick up a few people who have, unfortunately, acted in a manner which leads us to believe they are a danger to the security of this region and thus the Soviet homeland.'

2

Having imparted his news the officer turned to go.

One in the congregation was not satisfied with this explanation.

'Forgive me for asking, but what kind of things have these people been up to? I can't say I have heard anything such as you mention happening in this region.' Old Stanislav's shrewd gaze was now on the young man who turned to face him. The soldier's eyes narrowed and his hand hovered over the holster strapped to his belt.

'Comrade, I think it wise not to ask too many questions. You appear to have lived a long life, free from worries. I would not wish this to change for you or any of you others. Just accept that some are considered enemies of the people and are being removed to a place where they can make up for their crimes.'

The soldier again made to leave.

'The labour camps.'

The whisper spread through the picnic party.

Having heard the whispering the officer turned to face them again wearing that cruel smile.

'Yes, you are correct. Not places I would recommend to anyone wishing to lead a quiet life. The work is quite hard and the leisure time very little, so I hear. The prospect usually terrifies those selected to work in these camps, but that of course is why they were designed in the first place, was it not?'

The officer's face broke out into a wide grin, but this was soon replaced by a scowl on hearing Stanislav's words.

'You are only young and have the experience of someone so young. I was there in the Crimea as a fourteen-year-old boy. I fought on the Eastern Front in 1914. Yes, I have lived a long life, but free from worries? I can still hear the sound of battle and smell the terrible stench of death. All those dear comrades who died...'

Stanislav did not finish his sentence but his look of

contempt left the officer in no doubt of the old man's feelings. Olga, her face full of fear, stepped forward, taking her husband's arm, whilst searching for signs in the demeanour of the young soldier, attempting to gauge what to expect next. Aleksei also noticed this and stood in front of his grandparents as the officer stroked the button on his holster.

'My grandfather meant you no disrespect. He has seen so many distressing scenes it sometimes brings high emotion and he speaks of those times. And we have all had a little too much wine.'

Elena also reacted and stood beside Aleksei, trying to raise a smile to the officer. For a brief second this registered with him and he leered back, then, again noticing the contemptuous glare in Stanislav's eyes, he simply snorted by way of a reply and returned to the truck, which began slowly following the rest of the convoy into the village. The crowd could clearly see that some unfortunates had already been picked up and were now peering out of the backs of the vehicles. The expression on their faces, a mix of fear and resignation, was unmistakable.

Stanislav spat on the ground as he watched the procession leave. 'Bolsheviks. A curse on all of them.'

Aleksei looked alarmed and said, 'Be careful, Grandfather. There are many collaborators now who would pass on that comment to the police. And you have clearly made your impression on that officer, who will remember us. You would never survive if they took you.'

Stanislav chuckled grimly and turned to face his grandson. 'Aleksei, I am too old to care.' The old man turned to the rest of the congregation. 'But the rest of you must take care. Aleksei is right. There are those amongst our people who would sell others for just a rouble...'

Stanislav stopped talking as the sound of screams and shouts drifted over to them from those being taken for

4

transportation. A general feeling of helplessness struck them all as they looked solemnly towards the village. Aleksei put his arm around Elena who was shivering, even though the day was so hot. She looked up at him with tears in her eyes, but said nothing and looked back at the trucks now leaving towards the next habitation. Aleksei also felt cold ... and fearful.

Aleksei Vasiliy Rudikov had known Elena since he was a young boy of seven, when her family had arrived at their village to visit an aunt, and had decided to stay permanently. Although extremely shy and reserved, the young Aleksei had immediately shown his liking for the girl with flashing eyes and dark brown locks. Even then, as a five-year-old, she had alternated between styles of long and short hair. When her hair had grown to the tips of her shoulders, or sometimes even just a few inches, she had asked for it to be trimmed back, almost to the length of Aleksei's own. When he first noticed this he had felt too shy to ask her about it, but after the third occasion she had had it cut he had plucked up the courage to inquire. Elena had laughed at him; he had felt indignant and reverted to his normal silent self. She had noticed his embarrassment and watched him closely for several days. Even though she was so young and fairly reserved most of the time, Elena had another side to her that completely baffled Aleksei. She had suddenly grabbed him one day and had planted a kiss on his cheek and then run away. He had hesitated, then, on a sudden impulse, had chased after her. He searched high and low, but could find no sign of her. As he had trudged back to the village with sullen resignation she had suddenly appeared before him.

'It is because it gets very hot. If you had long hair in summer you would already know that, Aleksei.'

Aleksei had been taken aback by it all and for a moment

stood confused, wondering what she was referring to. Then he remembered.

'But why don't you tie your hair up at the back like the others do?'

'Because my having it cut annoys you, and I like sometimes annoying you.'

At that she had run off again, leaving Aleksei totally confused.

But, as time went on, Aleksei lost some of his reserve, for he was blessed with good vision and reactions, and his confidence grew. His prowess with a rifle was evident by the catch he would return with after a day's shooting with his father and grandfather. Aleksei always enjoyed these trips, although he had felt some degree of discomfort as he had seen increasing signs in his grandfather, Stanislav, of his not really enjoying the company of the man who had married his daughter. Vasiliy Rudikov was a very complex man. He was thought to have had an affair with a woman in the next village; not only that – it was rumoured that he was also involved with the woman's husband!

Stanislav Aleksei Vostrikov was built like a mountain bear and growled like one: six feet four inches, with large hands and grizzly, rugged features, reddened by his many years spent in the outdoors, but this appearance belied a good nature and warm heart. Those he liked enjoyed his benevolent nature; those he disliked were frozen out. He had made concessions and promised to try to get on with Vasiliy Rudikov only because of entreaties from both Olga, his wife, and their daughter, Yuliya, who, despite her husband's infidelities, still loved him and wanted the relationship to endure. Aleksei had an older brother, Yuriy, three years his senior, but neither brother really had any time for the other. Yuriy took after their father, in both looks and temperament, whilst Aleksei

6

took after his mother, a fact that had not gone unnoticed by Stanislav who, though he tried not show it too much, doted on the boy. Olga had chided her husband on many occasions, telling him he should devote as much time to Yuriy as he did to Aleksei, but she knew deep down the reason for the imbalance. Stanislav had always wanted a son, but only Yuliya had come along, so, in the old man's eyes, Aleksei was the son he had longed for. She was also aware of something else that tied them together, a secret few others knew about, even Aleksei himself, until one day Stanislav had found him looking into a small mirror he always carried with him. He had used this whilst they were on their hunting trips, as a signalling device and even to light fires by deflecting the rays of the sun. On this occasion Aleksei, at that time a healthy ten-year-old, frowned as he looked at his reflection in the glass.

'What is it, my boy? What is it you see in the mirror that displeases you?'

Aleksei had jumped, not realising Stanislav was there. He did not want to say what it was that bothered him.

'Nothing, Grandpapa. Just a few ugly spots. That's all.'

The old man squatted down to Aleksei's height and peered at the boy's face.

'Nothing like you say. There are no blemishes to be seen. So what is it really, my boy, that concerns you?'

Aleksei looked down. 'My eyes, Grandpapa. Why are my eyes as they are?'

Stanislav looked into the mirror. 'You mean the darkness in your eyes?'

Aleksei nodded. 'Not just that though, why are my eyes different from everyone else's?'

Aleksei had been referring to the hint of an almond shape, similar to those of people in the Far East. The old man had grunted in acknowledgement.

'Time to tell you a story, my boy, but you must never discuss this with anyone else – is that clear?'

Aleksei's eyes were wide open as he nodded his agreement.

'You have eyes as you have because you are special. Not just to your family, but also to a greater family going back well into the distance of all time. Your ancestors and you are genetically and spiritually connected in a way that gives you a certain amount of power. But this power is not for you to use just for your own benefit. It does not work like that. It is there for protection, and for other reasons I cannot go into right now – maybe another time.'

Aleksei looked shocked. 'What kind of powers are you talking about, Grandpapa?'

Stanislav looked at him for a moment. 'You have a special eye and instinct for shooting, do you not?'

'You mean, that is my power?'

'Just part of it, but enough for you to be going on with for now. I will tell you more when the time is right, but you must promise me you will say nothing of this to anyone. Not to your parents, your brother, not even to Elena. You must swear to me an oath on this, Aleksei.'

Aleksei looked back at his grandfather. 'I swear this on the lives of all I hold dear. I will say nothing of what you have told me to anyone else.'

Stanislav chuckled deeply. 'That is good then. One more thing though I will tell you, as you have asked. Your eyes are probably shaped like that because of the genetics of our bloodline. It is said we are distantly related to the Mongols. Apparently, long ago, a shaman foretold that our line was blessed with certain powers that would be passed on through the ages. It is your turn now, as it was mine before. Grandfather to grandson, each generation the same. Your grandson will inherit from you. But I must not say any more for now. I can see you have many questions for me, but they must wait for when the time is right, do you understand?'

Hiding his disappointment, Aleksei replied, 'I understand, Grandpapa.' He felt frustrated as he wished to ask his grandfather more questions, but he could see the old man was getting up to go. 'Thank you for telling me that much, Grandpapa.'

As he stood, Stanislav turned to face Aleksei. The old man took on a strange look and his eyes began to change from the normal grey to red, like coals on a fire. Aleksei felt something bearing down on him, making his head spin as the pressure increased. Then he passed out. Waking, a while later, Aleksei found himself alone. He tried to recollect what he had been doing before he slept, but his mind was fuzzy and his memory blank. He looked down at the mirror and slowly recalled something of a conversation he had with his grandfather, an oath he had sworn over a secret. Then he heard the voice – a voice in his mind he would get used to hearing over the years, a soft comforting voice that warned him, as his grandfather had, that protection of the secret was paramount to all considerations.

By fourteen, Aleksei was a strapping five feet ten inches tall, with features any girl would find handsome. His dark brown eyes were his main feature, having a deepness that captivated many. But to counter this recently found confidence, in the meantime, Elena had found another playmate – a girlfriend, Raisa. The two of them appeared inseparable. Aleksei had not been aware that this was a natural transition and fretted weeks, until one day Elena came upon him and gave him a kiss which they hoped would cement their relationship forever.

But that hope had been dashed a few days after the trucks had passed through their village. Elena's family had heard a rumour and decided to make a sudden break for it, slipping out of the village late one night. They had told no-one, not even Stanislav's family, who had secretly gathered to discuss this unexpected development. Aleksei, in no mood for such a meeting, ran to the secret spot where he and Elena usually met, away from prying eyes of other villagers. He had not seen or heard from her in those past few days, but that was not unusual, because she often had to go on errands to the town, which took up her time. And sometimes she would stay overnight, or for a couple of days at the houses of other friends or relatives. Running full pelt and gasping for air, Aleksei found the tree they used as a place to leave messages to each other. He breathed heavily as he reached inside the hole and found a small packet. His heart pounded now, more from anxiety than from the efforts of the running. He opened the package carefully. Inside, he found a letter and a smaller envelope that contained a small cross on a chain. Aleksei's vision blurred as he blinked back tears, reading Elena's note.

Dearest Aleksei,
I wish I were there standing beside you at this moment so you could hold me as only you can. My heart is broken. I was forbidden to make any visits to you as I would surely have stayed and not gone with my family. We are all in danger of being the next on their list so the decision was to go. When we reach safety I will of course write to you and let you know where we are. Please wear this cross to remind you of your loving Elena.
Until we can be together again I will wear your ring always for you are to be my husband. God has already blessed us.
My love always
Elena
21st July 1927

Overcome with emotion, the heartbroken twenty-year-old fell to his knees and sobbed. 'Where are you, my Elena, will I ever see you again?'

Aleksei sat for a very long time as he remembered all of the times with his Elena. He was inconsolable and would thereafter refuse to discuss his feelings with anyone else, as much as his family tried to give some reassurance. Aeksei would return often to that secret place and, sitting by the tree, each time would be fingering the cross around his neck trying not to lose his memory of her. He also was hoping each time to find another letter from her, hidden inside the tree, but of course he knew it was a pointless exercise; she was never coming back. But he needed to do something that admitted some slight glimmer of hope of contact, for he required it to keep his spirits alive and to retain his sanity.

As it transpired, Aleksei did receive some correspondence from Elena during the following years, but she always appeared distant and careful with her words. She refused to divulge where she was at any given time, saying that it was best not reveal her whereabouts in case the letters were intercepted. Aleksei felt extremely dismayed at not being able to reply, but at least he had some small comfort in the knowledge that she was still alive and safe. However, this situation was soon to change dramatically as the last letter he had received in September 1935, had been written hurriedly and posted from a town just outside Kiev. It was written in another's hand which he did not recognise, and said that Elena had been caught and made to sign up into the Red Army. Aleksei had not received any other correspondence from her since that time. The following year, much to the dismay of his family, Aleksei decided to become a conscript, reasoning that it might be the only way he would be able to find Elena. When his commanding officer discovered his prowess with a rifle,

Aleksei was sent on special courses to train as a sniper. In his spare time he continued to ask questions of army comrades and conduct searches for his beloved, but it was as if she had disappeared from the face of the earth.

Then one day as Aleksei sat on a step inside the army barracks, smoking a cigarette, pondering on matters, an officer appeared beside him. Aleksei thought he recognised him from somewhere in the past, but before Aleksei could place the face the officer barked at him.

'Extinguish that cigarette and stand to attention in front of an officer.'

Aleksei glared back at the man as he slowly got to his feet and stubbed the cigarette out with his foot.

'So we meet again, Aleksei Vasiliy Rudikov.'

The scowl on the officer's face immediately prompted recollection in Aleksei – the young man from the trucks that day at his village.

'Yes, I see you recognise me now. It was a long time ago, but I always remember a face. But I did not introduce myself properly then. I am Captain Maksim Surnyaev and you are to join my company.'

Aleksei felt a sudden sense of concern as he listened to this, remembering how he had sensed the same danger when confronting this man all those years ago. Captain Surnyaev would still have been a fairly handsome man, but his propensity to scowl so often over the years had left a permanent imprint on his features, cancelling any sign of pleasantness. His build was slight, so he made up for this by wearing a uniform jacket with padded shoulders. But his thin neck and spindly legs were not so easy to build up or hide and the total effect was somewhat comic. Surnyaev's blue eyes bored deeply into Aleksei. He appeared to be guessing what Aleksei was thinking.

'So, comrade, as I can see from your face you do remember our little encounter and you may also be wondering if I knew your name even then? The answer would be, of course, yes I knew this, and more. Your family and friends were being kept under a lot of discreet surveillance. I must add I do not understand why my reports were not acted upon. You seem to have lived a charmed life so far, but I warn you, here and now, you will have to curb that tongue of yours and the many wanderings, whenever your spirit so desires. You will act under my orders and obey at all times. Is that clear, comrade?'

Aleksei felt himself tense, but immediately freed his mind of all thoughts as his grandfather, Stanilsav, had taught him long ago. It was not a time to release the phenomenon, certainly not to be witnessed by this man, who appeared to know too much about his family already.

'Is that clear, comrade?' the captain repeated, this time more gruffly.

Aleksei sighed quietly. 'As you please, Captain.'

Captain Surnyaev snorted, reminding Aleksei again of that day. 'You snipers seem to be a law unto yourselves as far as the army command is concerned, but I am warning you, Aleksei Vasiliy Rudikov, if you fall out of line with me I will ensure you are put in a place you will find far from your liking. Is that clear?'

'Yes sir.'

Captain Surnyaev chuckled dryly. 'That is better. So what of this lady you are trying to find. Is she the lovely girl who smiled at me? Elena Zvadsky, I believe, was her name, yes?'

Aleksei became rigid again, wondering what this man had up his sleeve. He replied hesitantly.

'You know of Elena Zvadsky? You know where she is?'

Surnyaev chuckled again. 'There is little I do not know about the movements around me.'

'You mean she is here, close by?'

Aleksei, in his excitement, for a brief moment, forgot of whom he was asking the question. But as he watched for any sign of hope of an answer from the captain, he could clearly sense it was becoming a game to him.

'Maybe if I find your attitude to discipline improving I will think about allowing you some contact, but for the time being you will act only under my orders.'

Aleksei felt shell-shocked. Captain Surnyaev had made it clear he was in control and Aleksei would not have an easy time of it. Now, to make matters worse, he also had knowledge of the whereabouts of Elena. Deep inside, Aleksei let out a silent scream of pain. So near, so very near, yet so far. The mental chains imposed by Captain Surnyaev would surely make it even harder for him to find his Elena. If he were to disobey and found her, he would run the risk of being shot, or incarcerated. His situation was impossible. The man grunted and turned to go. Aleksei watched him depart, silently swearing an oath that if this man continued to interfere with his search for Elena he would find his nemesis in Aleksei Vasiliy Rudikov.

2

Stalingrad 1942. The Soviets had paid a very heavy price for trusting, then misjudging, the intentions of Nazi Germany. Hitler's sights were now on defeating the Russians and the future looked bleak as yet another city shuddered under the bombardment of the Nazi *blitzkrieg*. Thousands, if not millions, of Russians had already perished in the defence of their country.

In this once beautiful city, now reduced to broken buildings and rubble, Aleksei held his position with rifle aimed. Five hours had passed, but he patiently waited, his gun sights on a particular building. He knew he was there. He could feel he was there. He would not give up until he had him.

Beside him was a fellow sniper, Oleg, which was unusual as Aleksei preferred to act alone. This other soldier was now becoming impatient.

Scratching himself, he moaned at his partner, 'Come on, Aleksei, give it up. There is no-one there. Let's get out of here.'

The sound of gunfire and shells exploding surrounded them, but Aleksei remained where he was. He remained silent and calm, as he always did when stalking his next victim. His compatriot sighed heavily and crouched down again, training his own weapon on the building Aleksei had identified earlier. As he did so, Aleksei let out a short breath.

'There!'

Through his sights he saw for a fraction of a second

15

the image of the German sniper. He waited a moment longer and the image was there again; Aleksei immediately fired a shot. His comrade now had the same spot on the building in his own sights. There was a brief moment before a rifle appeared through the gap in the broken window. Both men tensed, waiting expectantly for the return fire, but the rifle dipped and fell down outside the building. Staggering after it came the German sniper who fell onto the windowsill, blood oozing from a wound to his head. Both Aleksei and Oleg fired into the German's body, which plummeted to the ground.

'I think you might say he is dead and finished, eh Aleksei?' Oleg had a huge grin on his face. 'But how did you know he was there? You are a very spooky man, my friend.'

Aleksei stretched and groaned. 'Perhaps we can have a night's sleep at last.'

But his relief was tempered by a fact that he knew his sleep would be disrupted by a combination of dreams of the good times with Elena and the sorrow of what had happened to her since.

Unspecified Gulag, summer 1947.

'Prisoner 222339834 Aleksei Vasiliy Rudikov, you have a visitor!'

Aleksei sat on the ground in a corner with the heavy regulation blanket over his head. The cell was equipped with bunks for at least eight prisoners, but for the past week now he had been the only inmate; all the others had gradually disappeared. He vaguely heard the rattle of key in the lock and the sound of the solid door opening on squeaking hinges, disturbing his reverie. Aleksei had, as usual, been thinking of things from his past and shivered as he looked up from his seated position on the stone floor toward the doorway at the familiar face of the guard peering in. Then an army officer pushed past him and entered the cell, followed by a soldier, holding a rifle.

'Aleksei Vasiliy ... comrade "Lyosha" ... I am glad to meet you at last.'

The officer waited for an answer.

Aleksei looked sideways at the wall as he spoke. 'Lyosha is for my friends, General. I fear you will not prove to be a friend.'

The man in the full uniform of a colonel of the Soviet Red Army looked unperturbed by this slight and sat down on the chair provided for him by another guard.

'As you will appreciate from your army experience, Aleksei Vasiliy Rudikov, you are addressing not a general but a colonel of the glorious victorious Soviets. I am Colonel Vladimir Dmitriy Guznischev. I am called here merely to check on your progress and ask you why you have been so difficult for us to deal with since that time ago. Your own involvement was, without any doubt, so important in our eternal struggle with the Nazi tyranny. The Great Patriotic War.'

Aleksei turned to look at the colonel. 'I do not remember you at Stalingrad, Colonel. Were you then at Kursk? Maybe at Leningrad?' Hearing this question, the soldier guarding the cell looked curiously at the colonel. Guznischev seemed a little perturbed at first, then shrugged and forced a laugh.

'I was in so many places ... you may not have had the pleasure, Aleksei...'

Aleksei ignored the reply and asked of the soldier, 'And you? Your family must be aware of how you have managed to find such a venerated position, guarding one who doesn't even know where he was during the war?'

The guard who had been standing to attention relaxed as he glanced quizzically at the colonel.

17

'Stand to attention, soldier!' the colonel roared, appreciating just how much Aleksei had made an impression on the young man.

Aleksei said wearily, 'Colonel, you ask me about my own involvement in your war. Not our war, Colonel, your war. Josef Stalin. His war. But our war did not begin with Hitler, Colonel. It began a long time ago with Lenin and his wonderful vision. A wonderful vision that involved the labour camps and the transportations of all those poor so-called enemies of the people. Is not that how the zeki were described, as the Bolsheviks and their terror took hold of the truth? I too had heard of all the terrible things that the zeks were supposed to have done and how they were a threat to the motherland. I was led to believe that they all deserved their punishment, but I have lived amongst them these past two years and have a very different tale to tell you, comrade Colonel Guznischev.'

The Colonel stiffened. He sat for a short while deliberating, then spoke.

'Comrade Rudikov, what you are saying is a crime against the state, but that you appreciate already, as is the use of my addressing you as "comrade". This title would never be afforded any of the other zeks. Not even some guards are thus addressed.' The colonel chuckled, looking around at the guards in the doorway, who scowled back. 'We would prefer you to have been a hero and to be able to show you off to the rest of the Soviet Nation. You performed miracles with your expertise with a rifle.'

'You have come a long way, Colonel. From Moscow? Is that where you all skulked away from the action when the rest of us faced such terrible times? And now you ask me to be a hero? A hero to do with what? The war has not ended for some of us, Colonel. Stalin has made certain of that. What difference is there between Josef Stalin and Hitler? Both exterminated undesirables and

18

Stalin continues to do so. All those brothers and sisters, mothers with babies, fathers, grandparents – all of them Soviets, Colonel – some heroes who fought the Nazi tyranny only to find an even more sinister tyrant leading the Soviet Republics. No, I do not wish to be a part of your scheming. Life is hard here, but at least I have my conscience to warm me, comrade. But you would not understand what I am talking about.'

'I think I understand fully what you are saying, Aleksei Rudikov, but I have not come here to debate this issue with you. No, there is something else that you have alerted us to, apart from your views of Josef Stalin. And even he might still forgive you if you are able to assist us now. I am informed that you have continuous dreams of, and conversations with, the spirit world, and that some of your extraordinary powers have seriously disturbed the other inmates. They even requested to be moved and, of course, we did not disappoint them ... all the way to Siberia.'

The colonel laughed heartily at this. Aleksei pulled the blanket from his head and looked closely at Colonel Guznischev as he spoke.

'Then you believe in life after death, comrade Colonel?'

The colonel's expression changed.

'You would be surprised comrade, if I were to tell you of what experiments we have conducted involving mind control. But with you it is different. Your mind appears to be naturally tuned to the other voids and dimensions. What you could achieve for our glorious nation could be beyond our dreams.'

Aleksei looked at the colonel, then at the soldier, who was now staring down at him.

'Would you not like a chair to sit on, comrade Rudikov?'

The colonel looked around and gestured to a guard who grunted and brought another chair into the cell.

Aleksei watched the movement, but remained sitting on the floor. 'I would rather sit here than rise to your level, Colonel. Down here I am at least closer to my natural motherland. It is not her fault that others use her for corrupt purposes.'

Colonel Guznischev sighed heavily. 'I am getting a little impatient with you comrade. I am here to try and help you back to a status you should have attained with your glorious war record. But you are making it very difficult for me to pass on any recommendation to the politburo. There are some other countries who would covet our resources, and we have to consider ways of protecting our nation.'

'America? This suspicious encounter with a country that was supposed to be an ally a few years ago?' Aleksei pulled the cover back over his head.

'You are well-informed comrade, as I would expect you to be. But I must warn you that if you refuse we will have no alternative but to round up other members of your family. And they will be taken to the harshest of camps, whilst you sit in isolation, thinking about them, and this chance you had to save them.'

Aleksei shot to his feet, dropping the blanket on the floor. He was taut, and full of anger, his dark brown eyes glinting with menace. He felt an enormous surge rising within. The soldier had raised his weapon to point straight at Aleksei, while the other two guards, already alerted by the prisoner's movements, entered the cell, armed with large coshes. The colonel remained seated, appearing confident that his safety was assured.

Aleksei trained his full attention on the two guards, who were now fast approaching his position. Both looked, momentarily, at the colonel for instructions but he merely shrugged back at them. Taking this as a sign of consent, both rushed forward, with coshes held high above their heads, about to strike the prisoner. Aleksei did not flinch as they struck, but both missed their target. Standing back in amazement, they looked at each other questioningly. The two then returned to gaze at the prisoner, who had by this time, sat down in the corner. The guards came at Aleksei again, but this time they suddenly stopped and turned instead to face each other. Each began to hurl insults at the other and, with eyes bulging, the guards systematically, rained blows down on each other. Blood splattered across walls, as the bludgeoning became ferocious, until one guard, with his head split wide open, fell to the ground. Throughout this fight the colonel sat impassively, looking down upon Aleksei, who was watching the gruesome scene unfold, with a look of curiosity.

The colonel noticed this and said, 'Well, Aleksei? You wished them to do that to me ... me ... is that not so? You actually willed it to be so, yes?'

Aleksei, his curiosity now heightened, heard the colonel's words, but remained silent, as he was still observing the guard choking and gurgling in his death throes. The other guard stood over his compatriot, with an expression of complete bewilderment, now appearing to come out of a trance. He shook his head and began to cry, as the realisation of what he had done began to sink in. He glanced around at the colonel, but did not have time to ask a question, as the soldier raised his rifle. The guard threw up an arm in protest, but the soldier fired a shot that finished the argument.

'Do not be concerned for these two, Aleksei Rudikov. They are vermin, just as the other inmates are considered to be, but we give the guards the belief that they are well thought of and superior to their prisoners, and all works well. Magnificent logic, do you not think?'

The colonel began to laugh, then stopped abruptly as he heard the sounds of footsteps – other guards, alerted by the gunshot. Colonel Guznischev motioned to the soldier, who walked outside of the cell and barked orders at the approaching guards.

'This is now an area forbidden to you. The Colonel and I have the matter under complete control, so return to whatever duties you were doing. If we need assistance, we will call for it. Now go!'

The sounds of the shuffling footsteps departing were evidence of the guards' complete obedience to orders. The soldier returned.

'Yegor Strashnikov, I am very pleased with your handling of this. Tell me, would you have shot our friend Aleksei here?'

'Of course, Colonel.'

'And would you have felt badly about shooting a hero of the Soviets?'

The young man looked flustered for a moment then stood to attention and replied, 'I have no feelings one way or the other, Colonel.'

Guznischev laughed. 'A good reply. I can see you will go far with that kind of attitude. Now please return to the entrance and ensure no-one is within hearing distance.'

The soldier understood and obeyed the order, clicking his heels before making for the doorway.

Colonel Guznischev looked down at Aleksei, who was peering back up at him from beneath the blanket. The two dead bodies of the guards lay between them.

'Comrade, you were right when you asked if I had come a long way. But this is not just in distance from Moscow – it also involves experience of the secret experimental departments of our government into the paranormal. You may appreciate that you have been watched closely, no?'

Aleksei continued to stare, but remained silent.

The colonel nodded his head slowly. 'I think that is so. Your unique ability as a sniper during the war, with superb sixth sense, even had the Nazis asking after you in wonderment. How you were able to figure out positions to cause the most damage to their hierarchy had them worried, I can tell you. Whatever plans they conceived, you appeared to be a step ahead all the time. Not just in Stalingrad, but many other places too. And then you would just disappear for weeks on end. You made no contact with your friends or family. That kind of devotion to duty, Aleksei, is the main reason we won that war. Not tanks. Not simply guns. Our minds were the key factor and this is why we must preserve them through this conflict with our new enemy, America.'

Aleksei sighed. 'I hear what you are saying Colonel, but how can I feel that it is my war? I like Americans and I can't see the threat they pose.'

The colonel felt something and sensed a thawing in the prisoner's attitude.

'Not ordinary American citizens, but their government, and financiers, are after our special resources: oil, gold and other precious metals that they covet and require to sustain their greed for power over all. They are afraid of Communism, which fuels the vehemence of their attacks on our own ideology. We wish you to join us in this battle against the corrupting influences of the Capitalists. The West.'

It was Aleksei's turn to chuckle now.

'Comrade Colonel, the corruption is endemic in both our cultures. The only question is, which is the worst? I have sight, as you have already noted. But my visions are very different from yours. The people are more important than this petty conflict. Have we not suffered enough with the Nazi tyranny, the West and ourselves, to have to battle now with each other over a few spoils?'

'Not spoils, comrade, but important resources to keep our people from the bleak future of being a destitute nation, with starving families, whilst the West sits on its fat backside enjoying the fruits of victory. They would have no pity on us.'

Colonel Guznischev was becoming more familiar with the prisoner as he sensed a bridge forming between them.

'And my family? They will be allowed to return to their homes? Unmolested by the state, as long as I do your bidding?'

Aleksei looked straight into the colonel's eyes. Guznischev smiled and nodded.

'Comrade Rudikov, I should have appreciated that much, eh?' He chuckled softly, then continued. 'You already knew we had taken your family and friends as a precautionary measure, but they are at one of the best camps. And yes, they will be returned under that agreement of your compliance to our work. There is another thing you should know...'

'That you are also like me, a seer, with the same powers. This is how you deflected my thoughts of harming you onto the guards.'

Aleksei stood now and walked over to a bunk bed. The colonel watched and waited until Aleksei lay down before he answered.

'Very good, comrade. I fear though I may not be quite as strong as you. I too have the abilities and that surge building inside me at times of stress, but I have some artificial parts to my make up, the result of the many experiments. But you, Aleksei, are the real thing, having the natural capacity, which is unbelievably rare and of so much worth to our studies.'

Aleksei sat up suddenly, his eyes wide. 'You wish to experiment on me? Is that what you are saying, Colonel?'

Colonel Guznischev noticed the effect on the prisoner and sensed he was perhaps revealing too much, too soon. Aleksei Rudikov lay back down again.

24

'Colonel, that thought fills me with disgust and dismay.'

'Then perhaps it needs to be discussed more. We will have to listen to what you have to say on the matter.' Guznischev looked closely for a positive reaction, but Aleksei was now showing nothing. The colonel deliberated for a moment, then said, 'I have also news of Elena Zvadsky.'

This did cause a reaction in the prisoner, who sprung up from the bed. But the sudden movement caused Aleksei to feel faint; his head swam with a combination of the shock and the earlier effort. He shook his head in an effort to clear his mind.

'But Elena is dead. She died at Stalingrad. Captain Surnyaev showed me the official papers.'

For the first time, the colonel actually appeared to be uncomfortable with what he had to impart.

'Not Elena, your intended wife ... but Elena Zvadsky ... your daughter.'

Aleksei's mouth hung open as he tried to find words of reply. He had no knowledge of Elena's having been pregnant and she had never mentioned it in her infrequent letters to him. All he knew was that part of her family had escaped, but that Elena had been caught and conscripted into the Red Army. Surnyaev had managed, successfully, to keep them apart and so the last he had heard of her was in 1942, fighting in Stalingrad, but he had not been able to find her when he returned to help with the liberation. All he had learned were rumours, a confused message that she had apparently died, but her body was never found. It had been rumoured she had been raped and killed by the Nazis, but Aleksei had refused to accept this, wanting to believe she had died courageously in defence of the city. The pain he still felt acutely was rising again, and tears formed in his eyes as he blinked back at the colonel.

'I am sorry this has been withheld from you comrade, but my superiors forbade it in case your reaction was unfavourable.'

As if in a trance, Aleksei muttered, 'Dearest Elena! She could not even bring herself to tell me of our child. But she would have known that I would have risked everything, even my life. I would have moved heaven and earth to be with them and she knew I would desert my post to do so. So my daughter is how old? Where are we now, 1947? Is she nineteen ... maybe twenty-years old?'

Colonel Guznischev paused again before he continued.

'Nineteen, I believe, comrade. Born in February 1928. Such a long time for you not to know, but I have other news. Elena gave her daughter into the guardianship of a friend, as she believed all her family had been arrested. This friend managed to find a way of transporting her to Britain, where she was adopted. This was about 1929 or 1930 I cannot be any more precise, as I have no more news from that point on.'

Aleksei stood motionless, the blood draining from his face. Then it suddenly caught up with him and he felt overcome. His face crumpled in agony and he could no longer contain himself. Burying his head in his hands, he wept bitterly.

In an office deep in the heart of the Pentagon, an aide put down the phone and sat in stunned silence. His boss had already entered the room and waited for his junior to pass on the information that had just been relayed. The aide still sat and stared into space, as his superior said impatiently, 'Well, John? what did he have? What did he say?'

John Mackay slowly shook his head and whistled. 'Mister Collins, have I news for you. That was Doug James. It appears one of our most experienced field agents is in direct contact with our Soviet friends. Seems, by all accounts, the Soviets are all excited over an experiment involving some kind of mind control. I know you will say we've heard all this before, but this time it appears they have the real thing...'

3

November, 1958, and ten-year-old Rudy Metthewson sat staring into his breakfast bowl, listening to the snap, crackle and pop emitted by the cereal, just as it always did, matching the advertising slogan. He sat perfectly still, apparently mesmerised by the noise and movement in the bowl. It seemed to reach somewhere deep inside his senses, making him feel warm and comforted – a strange sensation, provoked by the inanimate – and it reminded him of the sounds of many footsteps, walking on snowy ground, grinding and crunching the solidity of virgin snow into hardened ice.

His mother doted on him, perhaps just a little stiflingly so, but at this precise moment she was making angry sounds which brought him out of his trance.

'Rudy! For goodness sake get a move on. Staring into the bowl won't get your breakfast eaten and you will be late for school again.' Rudy still made no movement. 'Rudy, please, for heaven's sake, your headmaster will be telephoning me again and what do I tell him? He sits looking into his breakfast bowl every morning. What kind of mother will he think I am?'

Rudy looked up and, glancing sideways, gave a reply short and succinct. 'A Mum who has more patience than a saint, for heaven's sake.'

He didn't wait for an answer now, grabbing up the bowl and taking it off with him through the front door.

Helen Metthewson stood quite still, pondering his sudden reply. By the time she had gone to the front door, she found that Rudy had disappeared from sight. Helen shook her head slowly, then, with a heavy sigh, closed the door and returned to the kitchen. She poured herself another cup of tea and began to read the morning newspaper. The clock on the mantelpiece in the front room chimed softly in the background. Helen sighed to herself, knowing that Rudy had probably missed his bus, not being able to run to the stop with a bowl of breakfast cereal in his hands.

But by some miracle – or more likely, because it was late as usual – Rudy managed to catch the bus. The other passengers were intrigued, and amused, by the boy sitting alone, slowly working through the slopping bowl of cereal. The bus lurched a couple of times, but Rudy was ahead of this, having either taken a mouthful first or waiting for the bounce to subside before taking the next.

One concerned woman remarked to him, 'You will end up with terrible indigestion or, at worst, hiccups.'

Rudy gave her a large grin with teeth full of soaked crispy shapes. She gasped, and left her seat, muttering about the youth of today as she alighted at the next stop.

Now, having completed his meal, Rudy proceeded to wipe the bowl with his handkerchief. Then putting it into his satchel, he too made a move as the school was at the next stop. One or two of the other passengers exchanged glances and nods, seemingly of approval. For Rudy, though, his mood began to change as soon as his feet touched *terra firma* again. This time of the day he found daunting. But Rudy couldn't bear to explain to his mother why he left it to the last minute before making his way to school.

He stood for a short time outside the school gates – observing. Rudy spent a lot of time taking in all kinds of situations. Standing on the fringe of events, trying to puzzle out the many facets of human behaviour. This day, he could see already, had another slant on it for him to analyse.

Across the playground, a group had surrounded an unfortunate soul. Even from this distance, he could recognise all the participants, especially the kid being picked on and subjected to a verbal assault. The victim, a boy called Jimmy, had a peculiarity: his face always carried a smile. This was the reason for the bullying crowd surrounding him. Their intention was to remove it from his countenance.

Rudy felt sickened as, one after another, the boys began laying into their victim with slaps and punches. Gradually, Jimmy's face took on a cloudy look, but the smile remained. Soon, however, tears streamed down his cheeks and the smile reverted to a grotesque white mask with blue lips. Jimmy collapsed onto his hands and knees sobbing.

Rudy began striding across the tarmac towards the injured lad, but stopped in his tracks as the five bullies turned toward him. He then looked sideways, as if expecting something, whereupon a window in the headmaster's study suddenly shook, then shattered, bringing a face full of rage peering through the broken glass. The five were now off on their toes, apparently an admission of guilt. Rudy would normally have felt a sense of achievement at this, but his demeanour changed abruptly on witnessing the furious head, Mr Langdale, rushing across the playground and remonstrating at the departing group. Then, pulling the distraught Jimmy to his feet, he continued his verbal assault.

'How dare you be involved in breaking my window?'

Jimmy viewed the headmaster with anguish and burst into more tears. Langdale began to drag the unfortunate boy towards the school building. In all of this commotion the headmaster had not seen Rudy, but this was not an oversight on the headmaster's part. At times like this,

Rudy's high emotion produced an effect which allowed him to sidestep the normal parameters of this world. The shattered window bore testimony to this. But on this occasion only a fraction of his total power was on show, whilst in such a state of being. Rudy was aware of some transformation if he was threatened or became angry and that he had certain powers and control over situations, as if his thought patterns were able to reach beyond the norm and the physical would bend to his command.

So Mr Langdale had not missed Rudy, as Rudy was not visible to normal sight. He only saw what Rudy wanted him to see!

Langdale suddenly stopped in his tracks, allowing Jimmy to catch up. Jimmy's knees were now grazed and bloodied from being dragged across the gravel, but the frozen figure of the headmaster was now facing the image of Rudy, apparently hovering some six inches from the ground, this being sufficient height for Rudy to be on eye-to-eye terms with Langdale. In a split second Rudy imparted and departed. Others were now emerging from the building, including the school nurse, Miss Cullen, an Irish lady of formidable disposition.

Langdale shuddered and shook himself, trying to recover his senses. He quickly turned and, noticing the crumpled heap behind him, instinctively knelt down to help Jimmy to his feet as Miss Cullen reached the scene.

'And I should think so, headmaster. Be sure this lad was not involved in the breaking of your window. How could you not see that for yourself? Jesus! Where are your wits man? First of all he's beaten and bullied by those five young thugs, who *did* manage to shatter your peace. Then you subject him to further unnecessary punishment. Shame on you!'

Langdale began to splutter words of protest but Miss Cullen, becoming increasingly annoyed, shot him a further contemptuous look and he realised he was not going to win. He mumbled an apology. Langdale, for all his bombast, appeared to have taken the criticism on the chin.

'And I should think so headmaster.'

Miss Cullen kept her expression, not wishing to let him see how surprised she was at his climb-down. As she escorted the now relieved Jimmy she said quietly to herself, 'I swear I saw another lad here. That Rudy. My bones tell me a thing about that one.' She shook herself out of this uncharacteristic reverie, then nurse and invalid set out to the sanctuary of the sick room.

Meanwhile, Rudy sat at his desk staring across at one of his classmates, one of the bullies, who was now nervously looking about in expectation of the worst. He met Rudy's eyes for a fraction of a second, which was enough for the next episode.

The boy scribbled furiously in an exercise book and then, to everyone's surprise, suddenly got up, scraping the leg of his chair loudly on the floor. He rushed forward to the front of the class and, to the astonishment of the class tutor, offered the opened book to her. One other person in the classroom knew exactly what the message scribbled in the book had contained, so it was no surprise to Rudy when boy and teacher left the room. Other classmates were muttering all around him, but Rudy did not respond to anything being said. He knew that the message now on paper was on its way to the headmaster's office. It would contain admissions about the broken window and the sustained attacks of bullying – not only those on Jimmy, but on others who would be embarrassed to be thought of as similar targets and would not like to admit to being so weak. It was peculiar how victims nearly always blamed themselves for their plight. Not today though. For the first time in his short life Rudy felt he had made a real impact He liked that feeling and had a desire to reach this plane of satisfaction again in the future.

Late that afternoon, when Rudy reached home again, he felt drained. The events of the day had caught up with him and he began to realise there was a downside to his earlier efforts. His mother had been busy preparing the evening tea when he walked through the door. She called a cheery greeting to him, but there had been no answer, only silence. Helen poked her head around the door just in time to see her son climbing the last step on the stairway.

'Rudy? Did you not hear me? Got your favourite tea tonight. Lasagne. Rudy?'

Helen followed his path. Rudy had entered his bedroom and closed the door. His mother now stood for a moment pondering the situation. She knew he had funny moods but this was different and she began to feel concerned. Not like him to be this quiet. He usually came back with one retort or another. But silence? This did not fit with Rudy at all.

She tip-toed to his bedroom door, listening for any sound, but the room was strangely silent. Helen made to knock on the door, but then stopped herself. Something made her uneasy. She suddenly felt quite unwell, a need to lie down, but she fought it off. Opening the door quietly she peeked inside the bedroom. Rudy lay on the bed still fully clothed, but fast asleep. She walked over to have a closer look, now very concerned. As she neared him, one eye suddenly opened, making her jump back slightly.

'Rudy, are you OK? You worried me. Is there something the matter?' Both his eyes were now open, but he seemed still far from awake. 'Rudy? Can you hear me at least? I am going to fetch the doctor.'

Helen turned and made her way back to the doorway, but froze as the voice behind her intoned a strange reply.

'Mum. This is my Mum. Lovely Mum. Always been my lovely Mum. Only Mum I ever had and ever want to have. But she is going to call the doctor. Doctor will come and take one look at Rudy. Rudy then be taken away. Never be allowed back again.'

Helen turned around. Her son was still talking in that strange way, but his lips were not moving. His eyes were closed. Helen began to get irritated.

'Is this some kind of game, Rudy? If it is I am not impressed. I'm getting very tired of it altogether. Do you want your tea or not?'

Still in the trancelike state, Rudy continued. 'No Mum, yes Mum. No, not a game. Games are for kids. Kids can be nasty. Hate bullies. Me? I am not impressed. Yes, I want my tea. Please.'

The last word made Helen feel even more certain that he was just play-acting.

'You said, "please". Are you awake really? Rudy, come on, I need to get back down to the kitchen to finish off.'

Adding to her annoyance Rudy began to snore quietly. She walked back over to him again and shook her head as she began to feel an awful strangeness, a feeling that seemed to flow right through her, down to her innermost being. What was wrong with him? She had witnessed odd behaviour in him in the past, but nothing like this. She had considered before that it might be the result of his not having a proper male rôle model since his father had walked out and abandoned them.

Jim Metthewson, a sullen bigoted man, had packed his suitcase one day in May 1950 and, without leaving a note or word of explanation with anyone, just disappeared. No-one had heard anything from him since. It had taken Helen a long time to get over the shock of his sudden departure, which had left her to cope alone with a boisterous two-year-old.

She had a suspicion that her step-parents had an idea why he had left, but they had never told her whilst they were alive, nor was anything mentioned in their wills or other papers. Both had suffered heart attacks within two months of each other in 1955. Arthur and Ivy Roper had adopted Helen in January 1930, shortly before her second birthday. Although they were both kind and attentive to her needs, Helen never really felt she could communicate with them, especially after she learned she had been adopted. This had been arranged for her eighth birthday as a surprise, something that Helen always wondered about, as it was far from the pleasant kind of surprise normally brought to a birthday party. But this was an example of how much the Ropers were out of touch with sentiment and a major reason why Helen felt she could never approach them over sensitive issues, like her adoption. When she fell pregnant, at the age of nineteen, a hastily arranged marriage had taken place in May 1947 to the father, Jim Metthewson, who was ten years her senior and whom Helen had known for a matter of only two weeks before losing her virginity to him whilst drunk. Her husband was morose and rarely showed Helen much affection. The sex, when it occurred, was perfunctory, not that Helen had any experience to compare it with, but by instinct she knew matters were far from right. Jim had been in the Royal Navy during the war, but had found it tough holding down a permanent job afterwards. Helen was not the only one who suffered his rejection. Rudy, since he had learned to walk, would often run to greet his father on his arrival after work, but Jim Metthewson would ignore his son, disappearing up the stairs to change and then, within a few minutes, leaving for an evening elsewhere, sometimes arriving home in the early hours of the morning, drunk and abusive. Helen had never told anyone about this behaviour, least of all her step-parents.

So she was not entirely unhappy that her husband had gone, even though it still rankled with her that he had left on the eve of their wedding anniversary.

She had often wondered about her origins, but even in death the Ropers had cheated her, having destroyed any papers that might have given her even the beginnings of an enquiry into her past and the discovery of her true ancestry.

Helen had moved when they had died, buying a small detached house in the same area with part of the not inconsiderable amount left to her in their will. The Ropers may not have given Helen much in the way of spiritual support and guidance in their lifetime, but they had provided financial security for her on their demise. When the solicitor revealed just how much this amounted to, Helen had been overcome, and shed a few tears, which had embarrassed her. Later that same day, Helen and an eight-year-old Rudy had visited the graveyard where her step-parents were buried and, having given thanks, Helen had been left wondering over something Rudy had said: 'I can feel them Mum, Nana and Poppa. They are happy now.'

All of this was in the mix of her emotions. Still haunting her were those men since, those other part-time, would-be surrogate fathers. Not one of them seemed to hang around for long. At no time did Rudy show any signs of discomfort over any of her paramours. He even said to her on one occasion that he didn't mind, as if he understood what loneliness felt like. For one so young he often came out with more sense than most adults. But at this precise moment he was not making any sense. Helen still thought she should call the doctor.

After reaching for the telephone, positioned in the downstairs lobby, Helen sat on the bottom step of the stairway then let out a short gasp, dropping the telephone at the same moment, as the figure in front of her began to speak.

'Want my tea now, Mum. That OK?'

The apparent spectre then wandered off into the kitchen.

Helen sat frozen to the spot for a moment, then slowly turned and looked back upstairs, wondering if she should go and check on her son, asleep in his bedroom. But if he were still there, would she ever come back down again? Helen decided to brave the climb. She paused for a few seconds outside her son's bedroom, then curiosity got the better of her. Peeking in again, she let out another short gasp. His bed was empty. Helen sat on that bed and considered. Then Rudy called upstairs. The sound of his voice brought her back to where she should be. But at the same time the nausea returned.

Rudy tucked into his favourite food. His mother sat motionless, staring into space.

'That was lovely, Mum. Thanks. Is there any more?'

Helen made no move to replenish his plate. So Rudy got to his to his feet, intending to help himself, but he stopped as he met instead a sudden awakening in his mother.

'What was that game you were playing earlier? And how did you get down here before me?'

She looked directly at her son. Rudy scratched his head with his free hand. 'Just want some more grub, Mum.'

His mother shook her head at him. 'Not good enough, Rudy. What is going on here? You are up there looking as if you are about to die and now, a few minutes later, wolfing down your tea.'

Rudy looked down. 'Mum, don't ask, please. Me. I am still me, Rudy your son. But ... But something happened to me today. Not sure myself what it was. Just felt all over the place. Then calmness. Saw them do what they did, so did what I did. Made them pay for what they did.

Then I came home. So tired. Heard you, Mum. Came back and here I am. Still hungry.'

Helen sat perfectly still, as if in her own trance, as Rudy helped himself to more of the fare. He had consumed half of his second helping before she managed to speak again.

'Who did what to you and why?'

'Not me. They were picking on Jimmy. You know, I told you about it before.'

Helen now stared at her son expectantly. 'And?'

Rudy put down his knife and fork. He realised by now that his mother would not accept anything less than a full explanation. But Rudy did not want to explain that far. Not now. Not yet.

'All right, Mum. But please don't get mad at me. I can't help it. It's just something that takes me over at times. Well, it used to take me over. But I can control it better now.'

He looked down at his plate as Helen's glare intensified.

'What takes you over? What are you talking about?'

Rudy began biting his lip. He remained silent for a while, gathering his thoughts. Helen remained sitting and staring at her son throughout. She could see that he was struggling with the answer, but she had no notion why Rudy found it so hard to explain. All this was about to change.

Rudy gulped as he began to speak again. As best he could he kept eye contact with his mother as he spoke, but he found himself unable to keep this up, as the anguish and strain began to show in her eyes. Rudy had to avert his gaze at the critical moment, not just because of the pain now etched across his mother's face, but because he wasn't absolutely sure whether the power now surging through him could be controlled sufficiently. His emotion was now taking him on another journey.

'The usual kids were pushing Jimmy around, trying to wipe the grin off his face. I got really annoyed when they punched him and made him cry, so I got them into trouble. I can make things happen, Mum. I broke Langdale's window. He thought it was them who done it. Then I got one of them to confess. Only had to have eye contact with him for a second and there he was scribbling a confession like there was no tomorrow.'

Helen stood up, but sat down again with a thump. She had begun to sway and Rudy rushed to her side. It took a few moments for her to recover, but as she found her vision again Helen gasped. Rudy's dinner plate had left the surface of the table, hovering a foot in the air above it. She turned to look at her son. Rudy just stared at the plate and as he lowered his head, so the plate descended to the table.

'Is that what you mean, Rudy? Is that what you can do?' Helen appeared to be still in a slight state of shock. Her words were delivered in automatic fashion, as if spoken by a machine.

'Sorry, Mum, I should have told you before. Then all of this wouldn't come as such a shock. I'm getting more powerful. I managed to break Langdale's window by just concentrating my thoughts on it. Like I did with the plate then. I seem to be able to make people do things too. Just by a short amount of eye contact. That's why I looked away from yours.'

Rudy began to feel concerned, as his mother continued to converse in a trancelike state.

'Think you might have been a little too late with that, Rudy. I feel very strange. Like I am somewhere else, but I know perfectly well I am still here. Have to get you some very dark glasses for times like this in future.'

At that Helen began to chuckle to herself.

'Come on, Mum, I will help you to the sofa. Have a lie down for a while. I will clear up.'

Rudy assisted his mother to her feet and into the front room.

She remarked as she lay down, 'Such a good boy you are. Having an awful dream that's all, isn't it?'

Rudy made no reply, just watching her as his she closed her eyes. Then he made his way to the kitchen to make good his promise.

As he washed the dishes his mind wandered. He was thinking over and over again about the position he now found himself in. Someone else knew his secret. Even if it were the one person in the world he would have shared it with anyway he still felt annoyed with himself for giving his mother such a fright. And that simple lapse in concentration would now open up all kinds of problems for him and he was sure he would have to face some pretty awkward questions. He would have to try and convince her somehow that he was in control and able to keep a short rein on his newly discovered powers.

After finishing the kitchen duties, Rudy made a pot of tea and carried a cup through to the front room. Helen had woken after her short nap. Thanking him and taking the cup, she took a sip. Rudy stood, waiting for the after effects.

'Had a very strange dream. Can't remember most of it but you were making this plate move around in the air. And what else? No can't remember. We had a strange conversation, but about what, I cannot recall.'

Helen continued to sip from her cup.

Should he tell her the truth, or would it be better to let her believe it had all been a dream? Rudy decided to leave it for now.

4

The following morning, Rudy felt tired and listless. He had not slept well, as he had been worrying over the events of the past few hours. He had still been fretting when he climbed into bed. He was concerned for his mother. Had he affected her memory? He hadn't meant to, but there had been eye contact, as there had been with Langdale and the others the previous day. Certainly their memories appeared to have been blanked.

Helen sat at the kitchen table, munching on a piece of toast, whilst flicking through the daily newspaper, spread out across the table. She looked up as Rudy ventured into the room.

'Rudy! You are white as a sheet. Are you all right?'

He looked back at her, still trying to gauge if she remembered any of the previous afternoon.

'Feel a bit sick. Didn't sleep too well. I'll be OK though.'

'Are you sure? Perhaps you should stay off school today. I will telephone Mr Langdale and explain if you like.'

Rudy shook his head vigorously.

'No, it's OK, Mum, I'll be all right.'

He did not want to miss today under any circumstances. Although he felt extreme trepidation at the very thought of what he might face when he arrived at school, he considered it would be a lot worse imagining what might be going on whilst being confined at home. He needed to attend school today and discover if there had, in fact, been any repercussions from the events of yesterday. Helen shrugged and began pouring milk onto

41

his favourite cereal. 'Sorry, Mum, can't face that at the moment.'

His mother frowned as she looked up at him. She knew well that his not wanting his breakfast was a clear sign of something wrong.

'I am not happy about this, Rudy. You never miss breakfast. What's up?'

He was on the spot. He decided it was time for his mother to undergo the ultimate test.

'Playground scuffle yesterday; I think there will be afters today. Don't want to miss it.'

'So how does this affect you? Who is involved?'

'Jimmy Anderson. He was picked on. Five of the school bullies beat him up yesterday. Langdale came out and caught them after one of them had smashed his window.'

Rudy waited for the reply, trembling inside.

'Are you in trouble too?'

'No Mum, I just saw what happened.'

She appeared to accept this explanation. Rudy vowed never to play mind games with his mother again. The colour gradually returned to his face and he felt up to eating a small helping of the crackling shapes.

'I worry for you sometimes, son. I really would like to know what goes on inside that head of yours.'

Rudy gave her a grin back. 'Too many mucky thoughts for that, Mum.'

'Rudy!' Then her face creased into a smile.

That actual day at school passed without any further comment. No-one appeared to be talking about it, mainly because Jimmy Anderson had not been in attendance. He had been kept away from school until the matter could be resolved. Langdale actually crossed Rudy's path on three occasions without a flicker of acknowledgement in his demeanour. The infamous five also paid Rudy no heed. The only tremor he felt came as he briefly sighted Miss

Cullen emerging from her medical room. She had shot him a glance and then continued on her way.

Rudy felt elated and disappointed at the same time. Pleased he hadn't had to answer any awkward questions, but rather put out that all his fancy magic had been lost on everyone. On this very point, however, he was soon to discover another truth that would shake him to the core.

Rudy again felt sleep evading him that second night. He tossed and turned, unable to find a comfortable position. Then, just as he drifted toward the twilight zone, something caused him to sit bolt upright. He blinked in his confused state and sleepiness towards the bottom of the bed. A yellow glow appeared with a shape inside. Gradually the shape took on form. As Rudy rubbed his eyes, he saw a girl of similar age to himself. Then, following her, other shapes appeared, forming into myriad personages. A veritable crowd had congregated.

Rudy again rubbed his eyes, as if this movement would cause the congregation to disappear. He began to feel frightened, but at the same moment the little girl appeared to sense this and held up a hand to him. Her lips made no movement, but Rudy could clearly hear her voice.

'Rudy, *Pri` viet. Me` nya za `vout,* Lorna. My name is Lorna. You feel afraid. I can feel it in you. But be not frightened. We are your friendly guides. You are part of us and we part of you. All of us here are family all wishing the same for you. For it is your turn now. You have the power this time. Use it for good as you did for Jimmy. But beware. You have already made mistakes. But you are aware of these yourself. You must be most careful with your thoughts. Control your thinking. Always be aware of your power. We will always be close. Not to interfere – that is not permitted – but to guide. We will always be there for your guidance. Sleep now. *Da svi` daniya,* Rudy.'

Rudy, though still afraid, sensed an enormous wave enveloping him. The fear began to drain away, replaced by feelings of utter calm and peace, as the personages returned to shapes, now flowing towards and through him. He felt a slight wind pass by him on each occasion, building up the total sense of serenity. Then all disappeared. The glow faded into nothing. He sat quite still for a moment, still enchanted by the experience. Then he lay down. Sleep came to him, deep and refreshing.

So deep was his sleep, it took several shakes from his mother the following morning to raise him to life again.

'Come on, Rudy, it's past eight o'clock. You will be late for sure today. Did you sneak some kind of sleeping pill in last night?'

He sat up and stretched his arms.

'Dreamed. Had a strange dream. A glow then shapes. The shapes turned into people. They spoke to me, some of it in a strange language. They must have put me back into the deep sleep. But I feel really better.'

Rudy rubbed his eyes and yawned.

Helen looked at him. 'Do you remember what they said to you?'

He began to wake up fast. She was asking questions again. He had to be careful. Rudy shook his head slowly.

'No, can't remember any of it. The voice. A girl about my age.'

He immediately regretted saying this, knowing it would bring another question from his mother.

'What did she look like? Anyone you could recognise?'

Helen had now become very interested. Again Rudy shook his head.

'It wasn't clear enough to remember, Mum.'

Helen folded her arms and appeared to hug herself tight. Sounding a little more excited, she said, 'Maybe you are psychic, Rudy. Perhaps a medium, a seer.'

Rudy looked confused at first. Then alarm took its place.

'I'm not mad, Mum. Not a psycho. I really did have the dream. I wish I hadn't said anything now. You will be taking me to the doctor next to have my head examined.'

He began to get out of bed, but Helen took his shoulders, lightly guiding him back to his sitting position.

'Not psycho, Rudy, psychic. A psychic sees things others can't. The beyond. And a medium can connect and communicate with those on the other side. Maybe, you are one of these.'

Helen spoke quietly and reassuringly but Rudy still looked thoroughly confused.

'I don't understand, Mum. On the other side of what?'

Helen considered this for a moment.

'When Nana died we all wished her peace in another place, didn't we?'

Rudy's brow furrowed but he nodded.

'Well, that is what is called the beyond, a place on the other side. I think maybe those who came to you are from the same place. Nothing to be afraid of.'

Rudy's mind began to wander and he blurted out, 'That's what she said. The girl. Not to be afraid.'

He looked up at his mother, immediately realising what he had said. He could sense what was coming next.

'Thought you said you didn't remember. Is there anything else now you can remember? It would be nice to know.'

He stared into space, now feeling curious. Not over what his mother had been asking, but even the fact she was still there despite his agitation. This usually stimulated the power and from this came the acts, through eye contact or concentration on the inanimate. All were missing.

'Rudy!'

He jumped.

'Sorry, son, but I am interested in this, always have been. Please, is there anything else? You would tell me wouldn't you?'

He observed her for a moment, wondering what he should say next. Then he felt a strange shift inside his mind. He thought one thing, at the same time as very different words came from his mouth. He would have to get used to this in the future.

'She said I was always to be a good boy for you, always to tell you the truth. I am telling you the truth now.'

As he completed this retort Rudy shuddered slightly. He knew he had said it, but the content hadn't been in his mind.

Helen looked hard at him. 'Rudy don't play games with me. What else was there?'

He looked back at her as innocently as he could.

'No use you giving me the butter in the mouth not melting experience, Rudy. I'm not happy with you at the moment. Maybe I should take you to the doctor after all.'

He looked up at her blinking and about to protest, but what he met made him smile back, as his mother chuckled. Helen hadn't quite finished though. She had ordered a taxi for his journey to school.

Rudy arrived just a few minutes late, but he managed to find his classroom and seat without any fuss. The form tutor had been dealing with the attendance register and someone had apparently called his name out for him. There were no side-glances from his classmates as he sat down. Neither was there a flicker of recognition at his sudden appearance from the form teacher, Mr Jamieson.

Rudy looked around himself. No-one made any eye contact with him, but he felt someone had waited for his arrival. A strange sensation but at the same time, now familiar to him. He left his seat, feeling himself drawn away and heading for the source, at the same time waiting to be called back by Mr Jamieson, but this did not transpire, so he continued on the peculiar path assigned him.

He closed the classroom door quietly behind him, looking back through the small window at the teacher and his classmates, but no-one appeared to have noticed his departure. He found himself walking further up the corridor towards another classroom. Glancing through the glass in the classroom door Rudy gasped. Seated in the classroom and looking back at him was the girl who had visited him that night in the dream. She then looked back at the form teacher, who was pointing to the blackboard, explaining the sentences chalked upon it. Rudy no longer knew what to do. He felt thoroughly confused as he wandered back to his own classroom, slipping back into the room, again without any sign from others of noticing his return. It was all strangely disconcerting to him, but at the same time he felt some slight reassurance. The girl had not abandoned him, even though his power had diminished so much he now considered himself to be practically normal.

Rudy brooded on the situation all through the school day. He had scanned the playground at break times but had not seen any more signs of the girl. The bell rang for the end of lessons and Rudy made his way towards the exit. As he passed through the school gates he met a very cheerful Jimmy Anderson.

'Hey, Rudy. My friend. Thanks for saving me from that lot.'

Rudy looked at Jimmy and gulped.

'What do you mean Jimmy?'

Jimmy Anderson had had to live with his impediment for so long he sometimes forgot how annoying it was to others who had had a bad day to see a boy grinning back at them. He always elected to wear his school cap tight over the top of his head, which only added to his comical appearance. Being also fairly tubby, he resembled Billy Bunter, even down to the public schoolboy's tight, squeaky voice. But Jimmy still had a heart of gold and that smile to go with it. And he had no intentions of lying either.

'I saw you look over to the window. Have to say Rudy, spectacular. Then when old Langers took me on that drag I saw you hovering in front of him. What's to do, Rudy? I've said nothing to anyone about it. I wanted to talk to you first.'

Before Rudy could answer a girl shoved past both of them and disappeared. Rudy still looking in the direction of the departure didn't at first understand the implications, until Jimmy spoke again.

'Ouch. She's a bitch. That hurt. Ermm ... what am I doing out here?' Jimmy turned in a complete circle finally resting his eyes on a now very interested Rudy. 'What was I saying, Rudy?'

'You said you were glad those bullies got what they deserved.' Rudy waited for this to remind Jimmy of what he had said but Jimmy's train of thought had disappeared. Shaking his head, Jimmy walked off in the direction of his parents' car, which had just arrived to collect him.

Rudy took this opportunity to speed off in the direction the girl had taken. He ran at full pelt, rounding a corner and nearly colliding with an old lady with a walking stick. She began to wobble unsteadily as he ran past. Looking over his shoulder at the frail spectacle, Rudy had two choices. He had just seen the girl some distance ahead of him. Rudy turned. Retracing his steps, he just managed to grab the lady before she toppled over. The woman leant heavily on the walking stick which, although thick and sturdy, began to bend under her weight. Rudy realised she was about to fall to one side and made a sharp movement to get under her. With all his might he held her up until she managed to right herself. Then he apologised.

48

Instead of thanking him the old lady began to take him to task over his mad dash around a blind corner.

'You silly young so and so, you almost knocked me over.'

But Rudy was looking back over his shoulder and saw that the girl was about to disappear in the distance.

Abandoning the old lady, he again made a dash after his quarry. Only then did she turn to watch him disappearing out of her sight. A broad smile broke out on her face and she raised her stick in tribute as her words rang out unheard. '*Spasibo. Udachi i khoroshego nastroeniya! Da svi` daniya*, Rudy!' (Thank you. Good luck and keep well! Good bye, see you next time!)

Rudy had made the right choice in saving the lady from the fall.

He saw the girl again as he sped around another corner, closing on her all the time, until he finally caught up with her.

'Hey! I want a word with you!' he shouted as he came close.

The girl turned in her tracks and Rudy let out a gasp. The face wasn't the one he had expected. Not the girl from earlier in the classroom, although she had looked the spitting image from behind.

'What are you shouting about now, you berk, Rudy?'

He recognised Tanya, someone he had heard had fancied him for some time. Rudy looked down, feeling highly embarrassed.

'Come to ask me for a date then?'

This made him shudder. He began to turn away, but then looked back, summoning up enough courage to ask her a question.

'That new girl in your class. What's her name and when did she start?'

She gave him a quizzical look. 'Well that's the worst chat-up line I've ever heard.'

49

'I don't understand.' he replied.

'Bet you don't. There isn't any new girl. Where did you get that from?'

He began to stammer, 'But ... I saw her earlier. Peeked ... through the glass ... the glass window to your class ... she looked back at me.'

Tanya put her nose in the air and sniffed with disdain.

'Dream on, Rudy. Thought you were odd, but now ... well, don't think there's any hope for you!'

At that, Tanya turned swiftly and was off. Rudy stood for a moment watching her depart, then he trudged back the couple of miles to his home in deep thought.

That evening, after a tea conducted in virtual silence, his mother at last spoke.

'Rudy, is there anything the matter? You seem to be brooding there.'

He looked up from his plate, fixing his mother with a stare that she found quite disconcerting. 'Rudy, please. Don't look like that at me. Just concerned that's all.'

'Going to bed, Mum. Sorry, I don't feel very well. I need another good rest.'

He got up from the table, gave her a quick peck on the cheek and disappeared up into his room.

Helen felt a sensation of sadness bordering on deep loss, like that she had experienced when she discovered that her mother had abandoned her when only a few months old. She had often wondered who she was and where she came from. She had a glimmer of a recollection of dreams she had from time to time when she was young. Now her own son was having dreams.

In his room, Rudy looked into the mirror on the wall, as if attempting to out-stare himself sufficiently to reveal what secrets lay hidden in the depths of his mind. Giving up, he sat down on his bed. He felt exasperated that he could not share his problems with anyone, especially his mother. Tears began to roll down his cheeks. Silently sobbing, he grabbed up a pillow; wrapping it in his arms he forced it against his chest for some comfort.

It began with the room taking on a luminescent brilliance. Rudy opened one eye, then he sat bolt upright. A shape within the main circle of light slowly formed into the girl. She sat cross-legged at the foot of his bed. Rudy blinked at her. Should he speak? He felt unable to, as if an invisible gag had been placed over his mouth.

A soft voice came to him. The girl's lips remained still but her eyes had an extra sparkle. 'Rudy! *Pri` viet*! I come to you this time to give a reassurance. You have passed another test of sorts. Your power, as you know, has been reduced. You were bound to get involved in scrapes every time your senses were disturbed. We have altered this level. That is why you feel different. The power is still there, Rudy, but it is changed for a purpose. Please still use your thoughts wisely and do not react unless severely provoked. That is all we ask. We will still be very close. You would ask if it was I in the classroom earlier. Well your mind is matched with mine and even part of your conscience too. I sometimes let you see what I want you to see. Do you understand, Rudy?'

Being absolutely spellbound by the aura and wonderment of the occasion Rudy could only manage a slight nod. The girl smiled in acknowledgement.

'I will return, but for now Rudy, *Pa` ka*... 'Bye.'

51

5

September 1960, and two years had passed peacefully enough in the Metthewson household. Rudy was now at a senior school studying for 'O' Level examinations, due in three years' time. Study had taken up the time he used to spend waiting for a glimpse of anything to match his earlier exploits. Rudy had accepted that Lorna's explanation of a change meant he would no longer dream as much as he had done. He had also started dating a girl from his school who had similar tastes to his in music, books and films.

During one visit to the cinema, Rudy had felt distracted, unable to concentrate on the film. His girlfriend, Julie, had asked him several times if he was OK. Finally, Rudy had given up on the film and asked her if they could leave; he felt something wasn't right at home. He had not told Julie of this, only that he was not feeling well. Julie had offered to walk with him to his house but he had declined her offer, saying he would be OK, so they parted when he had seen her safely onto her bus home.

Rudy could not shake off the earlier sensation of feeling that something was wrong. He was totally unaware of what he was about to find and that the witnessing of this terrible scene would bring a change in him overnight, shaping the adult yet to come. As soon as he arrived home his keen senses became heightened and he could see that something was not right. The house was in darkness. But he still hoped any problems he envisaged were in his own imagination. He let himself in by his own key, not wishing to disturb his mother and hoping she had decided on an early night.

Tip-toeing into the hall, he was about to ascend the stairway, when he heard slight sounds of whimpering coming from the front room. He cautiously opened the door. The sight before him made Rudy recoil in shock. In the corner of the room his mother squatted on her hands and knees. Her head bowed. Even in the near darkness Rudy could see his mother was injured. He reached for the wall switch and put the light on. Helen's clothing had been ripped to shreds, revealing much of her flesh, which was reddened and bruised. Spots of blood dripped to the floor as his mother raised her head and gave him pitiful look. She raised one hand to cover her face, hiding the cuts and bruises and stemming the flow of blood from her nose.

She took her hand away for a second and cried out, 'Rudy, please, no lights. Turn it off. Please.'

He immediately did as she asked. 'I'm going to ring for an ambulance, Mum.'

Helen staggered onto her feet.

'No, Rudy. No ambulance. No police. Nothing. Do you hear me? This is all my own fault. Just let me be on it. OK?'

As she said this she managed to stagger forward, gripping a chair by the table for support. Rudy went to help her but she brushed past him. He felt totally helpless as he listened to his mother grunting as she ascended the stairway and then heard her entering the bathroom, locking the door behind her. He heard her running a bath so went into the kitchen to brew a fresh pot of tea. He waited for some time but his mother did not return downstairs. She had disappeared into her bedroom instead, after her bath. Rudy quietly climbed the stairs, a cup of tea in hand. He knocked on his mother's bedroom door.

She called out, 'No Rudy, do not come in.'

Ignoring this he entered the room, placing the cup on a side table. He noticed immediately the change in his mother. Her face was white, contrasting with the bruises. Rudy had also brought up wet towels for her to place on her injuries but she shook her head.

'Just need to sleep.'

Her eyes began to droop.

But as she drifted into sleep she began to mutter quietly, 'All my own fault. Shouldn't have trusted that one. How dare he bring those two ... what did he think I...'

He rested a hand on her forehead as she continued to mutter this over and over again. After a time, she became quiet.

Rudy waited patiently, watching his mother slip into an ever deeper sleep. He then went to his own room and lay on the bed, still fully dressed. His mind was in a whirl as he contemplated everything. Sleep came to him fitfully as he could not get the image of his mother's injuries out of his mind. On several occasions he went out into the hallway and listened to his mother's gentle snores before returning to his bedroom. On the last occasion he finally managed to sleep and dreams came to him at the same time. He woke early the next morning with a start. Changing his clothes quickly, he knocked gently on his mother's bedroom door but there was no answer. He quietly opened the door and crept over to her bedside, noticing at the same time that she had been up sometime before he awoke, as she had obviously made herself a fresh cup of tea. She had only managed to drink half of this before entering a peaceful sleep again, aided by some pills. A pill pot sat on the table beside the cup. Rudy picked it up and examined it. It still contained sufficient pills for Rudy to be satisfied his mother had not over-dosed. Content now that she had reached a state where he could leave her, he made his way out of the house, ensuring the whole residence had been securely locked and also leaving a note to say he would be only a short time away.

Rudy had felt a slight surge inside as he walked towards the bus stop and at the same time he was reminded of the dreams he had had earlier which provided a mental image of the house he had in his sights. He travelled by bus to the other side of town, alighting at a stop close to the estate he had been shown. Never having had occasion to visit this part of town it was more intriguing for him and he wondered again about the dreams. Should he feel apprehensive? At this stage he did not really know what to expect next. But it was too late for any such thoughts as here he was standing on the pavement outside a house he knew to be the one. He walked up the front path, rang the doorbell and waited. No reply. Rudy stood back a few paces, looking up and down at the front of the premises. Not a flicker of occupation. But Rudy was on a mission. He was certain someone – *that* someone – was in there somewhere.

He walked to the side gate. Tried the handle but found it locked. Rudy looked up at the top. He was only five feet two, the gate at least seven foot high. Suddenly he felt another surge and instinctively leapt up. With fingers now on the top of the gate he pulled upwards. Legs sideways, he vaulted the gate and dropped down to the other side.

Once there he suddenly realised how vulnerable he was. Rudy shot up against a wall waiting for any movement. It appeared ahead of him. Rudy squinted as the sun shone in his face and saw that further up the back garden, a man was standing with his back to Rudy. One hand held a lighted cigarette, the other a massive sandwich, half-eaten. Obviously he was enjoying the morning sunshine

as he was shirtless. His frame was firm and muscular –
clearly he worked out regularly. Rudy thought perhaps he
was showing himself off to the neighbours. In any case
he was certainly an intimidating sight for anyone, let alone
a youngster.

The man turned sideways, apparently sensing an intruder.
Still munching on his last bite of the sandwich, he caught
sight of Rudy.

'How'd you get in here? You come to rob me, you little
git? Picked the wrong gaffe, haven't yah?'

He continued to chew, snorting with derision as Rudy
began to back off. His eyes now beginning to blaze, the
man suddenly rushed forward with his arm raised, about
to strike Rudy who stood absolutely still, feeling terrified.
The man swung a punch at his head but completely missed
his target. It was debatable who was the more surprised.
The man looked at his fist in amazement. Then he glared
at Rudy again.

'How'd you do that, sonny? That was me best right
hook I missed you wiv!'

Rudy did not reply. He just looked at him as the surge
inside began again.

The man tried hard to swallow his mouthful of food.
He had obviously more to say. But his throat had closed.
Much as he tried to swallow, the trapped food in the
closed hole refused to budge. His face now turning a
shade of purple, he tried to spit it out. Retching and
heaving the man dropped to his knees.

Rudy looked on with dispassionate eyes. He felt nothing
for him. The man looked up, his arms now flailing in a
desperate attempt to elicit aid from the youngster. Then
Rudy spoke.

'She is my mother. Do you understand?'

Whether the man heard or understood was immaterial
to Rudy. Saying it out loud satisfied him. The wretched

muscle man finally collapsed, succumbing to the end meant for him. Rudy stood by whilst his body went through the last twitches of life. He felt nothing but contempt. When he was satisfied life was extinct Rudy left for the next address.

Again in his mind's eye he saw the house. He felt confident he knew roughly where it stood. His senses told him it was situated only a couple of blocks away. Rudy found the house easily and waited. A short while later a car pulled up outside the address and two men went inside. Rudy nodded to himself. One stone, two birds.

An astonished face answered Rudy's knock on the front door.

'And what can I do for you, young man?

This uncharacteristic politeness brought another enquiring face into view.

'What are you on about, Arnie? Who's there?' When the other man noticed it was just a boy, he continued, 'What you being so polite for? Just a little kid ... or is this little kid here for ... our pleasure? Know what I mean?'

This man began to chortle.

'Come in, please. Don't mind him, he is so uncouth. What is it you wish from us?'

Arnie sucked in his cheeks on his thin face as he winked at Rudy, before turning to face the other man. 'You will be frightening our little friend here with your over-aggressiveness. He's probably a boy scout on a bob-a-job – is that right, son?'

Turning back to face Rudy, Arnie managed another sly wink. The other man glared at Arnie and then at Rudy. He was not much taller than the boy but everything else about him was menacing. His short-cropped blond hair sat on top of a large head, which accommodated bulbous blue eyes and a broken nose. The rest of his frame was firm and muscular, similar to that of the 'sandwich man', now deceased.

'What you bringing him in for? Ain't we got enough to worry about? She's probably called the cops already and given our description. We gotta scarper quick.' He winced as he put a hand on his crotch and rubbed it. 'That cow, she scratched me nuts. Still bleeding. Really feel like going back and giving her some more grief, but the cops will be there by now.'

'No chance of that. She was warned good and proper.' Arnie winked yet again at Rudy. 'Ignore him, please. What did you say you wanted from us?'

Rudy looked purposefully at the second man.

'Well? Got a tongue, have yah?'

Rudy spoke for the first time.

'So she was warned good and proper? How? That if she talked you would come back and take her son off somewhere bad?'

Arnie looked on curiously as he ran a hand through his black, slicked-back hair.

'How did you know that, I wonder, young man?'

'This one, your partner, reckons you ... Terry or Tel, isn't it? ... You and the other one did everything whilst *he* is innocent.' Rudy now looked at Arnie. 'Isn't that right?'

Arnie looked perplexed, but then he caught up with the insinuation.

'Oh yes, I see what you mean. Never touched the bitch. Outside all the time. Didn't want to get involved. You know?'

Terry, his eyes now bulging even more, spat.

'You fitting me up now, you queer shit. Just up your street. A bleedin' grass as well as a nonce.'

He made a sudden move for Arnie who wasn't prepared for it. He gurgled as Terry gripped his throat.

Struggling away from the grasp, Arnie choked as he cursed, 'Sod you, Tel. Don't you dare put your greasy mitts on me.'

A knife suddenly appeared in Terry's hands. His bulging stare caught Rudy's gaze for a fraction. Rudy nodded to him. Without a moment's hesitation Terry thrust the knife into Arnie's throat. Arnie looked shocked, and started to gag on the blood now seeping from the wound. He looked around the room in shock, resting his stare on Rudy, who again nodded.

Arnie yanked the knife from his throat, causing blood to spurt in a fountain but, apparently unperturbed by this, he staggered towards the now transfixed figure of Terry and embedded the dagger with a sharp cracking sound in his forehead just above the left eye. Tel let out a strangled scream, clutched at the weapon, and fell back clumsily into a chair.

Rudy stood and watched the final drops of life emptying out of both of them. Again, as at the previous address he watched dispassionately. Arnie was on his hands and knees facing the floor, which was covered by a deep pool of his own blood. Terry was in convulsions but managed to mouth silent obscenities at the boy.

Rudy would not let either rest easily. He would not let them go without prolonging their agony. He did not wish to recall the sight that had met his eyes when returning home, but the images flickered again disturbingly in his mind and he was reminded of why he was here at this house and why these men were suffering their fate. Both let out their final sighs as Rudy decided he'd had his fill.

Whilst waiting at the bus stop, a wave of anxiety poured over him. His mind became confused and he felt dazed. Someone asked him if he was all right and Rudy nodded back absently as he walked away. The resistance in his mind was dissolving, the shield was coming down and he began to have a great fear about what he had witnessed. It had been like an extension of the dream he had earlier, but he was fast coming to his senses and realising it had certainly been no dream. What he had seen had really happened. Then he heard a soft voice calling to him in his mind, a reassuring sign, and he calmed as he listened to her words. Lorna had been with him all through the previous evening and that morning. He was not to be concerned. What had to be done was done.

6

Rudy arrived home feeling drained. He had used up much of his capacity and now felt the urgent need to rest. But first he had to check on his mother. Ascending the stairway he could make out the faint sounds of gentle snoring, which gave him reason to smile for the first time for several hours. He entered her room and placed his hand again on her forehead. Her eyes momentarily opened but without focus, although she managed in her semi-unconscious state to recognise her son's touch.

'I love you my little Rudy. Such a tower of strength to his mum.' Then she went back into the deep sleep intended for her. Rudy bent down and kissed her swollen cheek lightly. Then he swiftly left her and rushed to his own room, seeking the solitude and space to let out his own agony. He fell onto the bed, buried his head in a pillow and wept bitter tears.

Helen remained housebound for the following two weeks. 'No visitors' were her express wishes. Rudy had telephoned his school explaining he had an attack of measles and that his mother would be sending a note in by post. The headmaster had begun to question why Rudy was ringing and not his mother when Helen had appeared out of the blue and taken over the call. Headmaster, mother and son all satisfied in one go. Helen soon unwittingly wiped the smile off her son's face though.

'I have been reading some of the backlog of newspapers. There's something very strange in one of them.'

Rudy's heart began pounding. He had already read the

report himself. He followed his mother back into the kitchen where several newspapers were strewn across the table. Helen pointed to one page and read aloud.

'It's headlined "Gruesome Discoveries". Today, after an anonymous tip-off, the bodies of Michael Birch, Arnold Crawford and Terry Blake were found at addresses on the Hilton Estate. It would appear Birch died from suffocation after choking on a food blockage whilst eating a sandwich. Crawford and Blake seemed to have had an altercation which resulted in each stabbing the other to death. A police spokesman has said, although enquiries into the deaths were continuing, they were not looking for anyone else in connection with the incidents which appeared unrelated.'

The article went on to mention the fact that Micky 'the Muscle' Birch, Arnold 'Arnie' Crawford and Terry 'the Torturer' Blake had all recently been released from prison on parole, after serving sentences for several offences, including conspiracy to rob, grievous bodily harm, aggravated assault, burglary and rape.

Rudy watched his mother quietly reading the rest of the article and noticed her look away briefly. Rudy knew the full extent of the assault on her reflected offences previously committed by the three men. They had been meant to suffer for their sins – he was convinced of it now. Helen looked up at Rudy.

'The date they were found was the day after I was attacked.' He looked down as she continued. 'Did you know? Of course you wouldn't. I had only just met him. So how could you know? And the other two ... dead as well ... I just can't take it in.'

'So it was them then? I did read it and I did wonder. Just out of prison...'

Rudy tried to sound sympathetic but Helen detected an edge to his voice, as if he were criticising.

'I know what you must be thinking of me and I don't blame you for that. I just haven't got a very good idea about men. I certainly picked a bad one there, but he appeared so nice. I know he was a bit rough around the edges, but aren't a lot of them? He came to work at the factory and chatted me up. He must have followed me home that afternoon without me knowing. And those other two smelly thugs...'

Her voice trailed off and she became silent again.

Rudy did not want to show his annoyance. It had been hard for him and he knew deep down that he was still angry and upset, but he also realised he couldn't help his mother whilst he felt this way.

'I didn't mean it to sound like criticism, Mum. It's not your fault Dad left us and if anyone's to blame for all of this then it's got to be him. He left you to fend for yourself and I hate him for that. I think he was a coward and, if so, it's best he left because I hate cowards, and bullies.'

Helen looked surprised.

'I have never heard you speak like this, Rudy. You really think that of your father? A coward?'

'I have always wondered why he left as he did. When I was younger I missed him so much and hoped he would suddenly appear and tickle me as he did all that time ago. That's all I really remember of him. Tickles. But every time you have been let down by a man since, I have thought of him. You obviously wondered why I never made a fuss over you being with any of the other men. Now you know how I feel. It was his rejection of us that has led to this and I truly hate him for that.'

His mother remained silent for a moment as she thought all this over. She was about to speak again, but Rudy hadn't finished.

Pointing at the newspaper he said, 'Bullies like those

men are everywhere and they were kids once and would have been like those bullies at my school. And they seem to get away with it most of the time because not enough people care about what's going on. But I do care and I'm not looking forward to leaving school and going to work because, from what I have seen already, there are plenty of bullies in charge in every type of job. Why do they always put bullies and cowards in charge of everyone else?'

Helen had not realised that her son had been that observant of such matters. She was feeling proud of his stance.

'I didn't realise you cared quite that much about it all.'

'I'm always watching other people and how they behave. It seems the wrong people are always picked on and that makes me angry. But this time it seems these men did get what they deserved and it's for the best all round because you didn't want a fuss mum. While they were alive you would never have been able to rest. You would have had to tell someone else eventually, especially the police, in order to find any protection. Then there would have been a court case, which I know you would have hated – so would have I. Now they will never bother you again, will they? And that is divine retribution.'

Helen shuddered.

'I never thought of it like that. But I still can't believe it happened so soon to them. Divine retribution?'

The Ropers had been a fairly religious couple and a smattering of this had been passed down to Helen, so when Rudy made his reply it immediately stung his mother.

'An eye for an eye, you mean, Mum?'

She looked aghast.

'No. No, that's not how divine retribution works.' Then she thought about it for a moment, considering what he had said and especially the position they both were in.

64

'Or maybe you are right. If this hadn't happened to me and if I hadn't felt so bloody full of anger and hatred, like you, for those three men, I wouldn't understand such as I do now. No. I think an eye for an eye will do.'

A knock on the front door interrupted any further conversation. Helen motioned for him to answer but not to let anyone in. Rudy opened the door to find one of Helen's workmates, Jill Brown, holding a bunch of flowers.

'Hello Rudy. Just popped around to see how your mum is. We have all missed her at the depot.'

Young as he was, Rudy knew by instinct what to say to Jill Brown and his mother discovered at that moment another facet of her son – just how quick witted an individual he could be, more than capable for a person of his age.

'Sorry, Mrs Brown, but she is asleep at the moment. She has been very poorly. It is very kind of you to call and I will tell her you did so. Can I get her to telephone you?'

Jill Brown was taken by surprise and hesitated for a moment, then thrust the flowers into Rudy's hands. Rummaging through her handbag to find pen and paper, she wrote a short note. Rudy thanked her and closed the door.

'Inspirational!' Helen whispered to him.

'I have my uses'.

Helen had felt awkward about missing so much time from her job at the factory. Even though the Ropers had left enough for her to be without money worries, Helen had her step-parents' work ethic and being at the factory had made her feel part of a community. She hadn't been entitled to sick pay, so she had not had to provide a doctor's note. But she was now glad of being able to speak with Jill on the telephone and have messages passed on to the management. In any case, Helen had been amazed at the rate of her own physical recovery, although the mental scars would take a lot longer to mend.

65

That same night Rudy had another visitation. The first thing Rudy noticed, apart from the usual brilliance of entry, was that the girl, Lorna, appeared to be growing at a rate matching his own. But her demeanour had changed and she no longer had the sparkle in her eyes. This had been replaced by a slightly steely glare. Her face wore a serious expression to match her eyes.

'*Zd` rastvuyte! Kak de` la*? But I can see that for myself. I am worn out too, Rudy. Traumatic. It is always a trauma dealing with entities like those three. You have now learned more than most do in a lifetime, or even two. Nothing else could have been done. Your mother's life would have been forever in danger. They would have returned to silence her. So it had to go the way it did. But there are many similar types in the world. So many are unmanageable as far as we are concerned. But because of their influence and unified aggression the world is run in part by idiots and cowards, as you have observed yourself. This is why we have to be very cunning and careful with our own power. Do you understand this, Rudy?'

He nodded.

'Good, because what might be coming up in the future will require your complete concentration and if others get a whiff of you and what you have in the way of powers, we could have a full-scale psychic riot on our hands. So be very wary now. Even our dealing with those three despicable men could have alerted more malign forces. Control your thoughts. Use your fine senses. Then we will always be able to give guidance and back up. Remember! Expect no protection from those others who would offer it. Many are in the same mould as those three were. They were behind smiling masks. Stand back from the limelight, unless it is absolutely necessary to involve yourself. Is that clear, Rudy?'

Again he nodded to her.

'I am sorry if I seem to have been over dramatising the situation. But it is important that you understand fully all the implications of your powers. I must go now. I have already exceeded my allotted time. Good fortune for you, Rudy. *Da svi` daniya!*'

The girl held up her hand, which Rudy returned with his own salute. A smile returned to her face and her eyes sparkled briefly. The light faded and she disappeared.

Rudy lay down and pondered on everything Lorna had told him. Much of it now made sense to him. But he felt a little uneasy regarding her view of his future. It sounded a very heavy existence, full of danger. But after these recent events Rudy had a harder shell now, and in the time to come many were to discover that fact. Another thing niggling at him was Lorna's use of a foreign language. He made a mental note to ask her what this signified on the next occasion they met.

7

July 1962, and some eighteen months on from the terrible events, fourteen-year-old Rudy was now waiting for the results of the rest of the mock 'O' level examinations. He had already gained some very good results in previous tests but ever since the trauma his mind had often been somewhere else. As a result he did not expect very good grades at all in the exams. His concentration wavered between what he was expected to learn here in this world and the many things he had experienced in the beyond. As time passed, the words of his guide, Lorna, made more sense. Rudy constantly looked for signs, but remembered Lorna's words: stay out of the limelight. This had always been easy for Rudy in the past but as he developed a sense of his own worth it became harder for him.

One hot and sunny summer afternoon in that mid-July, Rudy walked to Jimmy Anderson's house. Jimmy had proved to be a loyal and faithful friend since that time in the playground. Rudy valued his friendship and they got together quite often to talk over things in which they had a mutual interest. Jimmy had also felt he would flunk his exams but this did not bother him much as his parents had built up a very profitable business selling the newest inventions, including up-to-date washing machines. He would be expected to join the family business and eventually take it over when the time was right. Jimmy had a way about him, not just over the fact of his impediment. He really smiled for a purpose, as if he were a natural optimist.

It all added to Rudy's relaxed post-examination mood. He couldn't do anything about the results now, so what would be would be.

He first heard the whimpering as he turned the corner into a street close to where his friend, Jimmy, lived. A mob of youths had surrounded an old lady who now crouched on the pavement with hands above her head, pleading for them to leave her alone. The tone in her pleas, and especially the brogue, instantly identified itself to Rudy.

He watched as first a leg moved forward and kicked her to the ground, followed by another kick and a stamp on her head. The others now became brave enough to engage in the assault. Feet and fists rained down on the body of the unfortunate lady.

Rudy walked towards the crowd. One of them on the outside noticed his approach and cried out to the others. Knowing the presence of an onlooker could be a problem, a potential witness, most ceased their involvement and stared back at the intruder. The main party of five were still active in their assault. But even they stopped when they realised that something had caught the attention of the rest.

The woman began to raise herself from the ground, but one of the five turned and brutally kicked her down again. Rudy now recognised the main characters. The infamous five had returned and the lady on the pavement, now bleeding and bowed, was Miss Cullen.

'What are you doing here, you little shit? Thought you went off to be a priest.'

The group leader had made his move. The others began to chortle.

Rudy made no reply but pointed at the lady. The group's leader looked at him nonplussed. The rest were equally confused but when the leader finally decided to turn towards the lady he let out a cry of anguish. Miss Cullen was now on her feet. Blood poured down her forehead from the assaults. The look in her eyes had the congregation dancing – to her tune.

One good solid punch took out one of the five. He no longer owned his own front teeth. There followed a complete rout. How much blood Miss Cullen spilt compared to the efforts of Rudy became hard to gauge. No more than a few seconds had passed, but those who had not escaped bore the evidence of the violent retribution and lay on the pavement groaning in agony.

Rudy managed to persuade her away from the massacre into the quiet of her abode, instinctively finding the right address. With the door now closed behind them both sat on the floor panting. Miss Cullen looked across at her saviour.

'Rudy! For sure I thought I was about to meet my maker. You brave soul. But I knew that. Knew it all that time ago in the playground. Ta'ght it was me. The imagining. Now I know it was true.'

'Miss Cullen. Ma'am. Please don't ever say anything about this. It's not meant to be known – what I can do, that is.'

'Please call me Bernadette,' she said. 'Got to go and clean myself up now, Rudy. You were going somewhere, I take it, for you to be around here anyway. So off you go now. I will be all right.'

He looked alarmed for a moment and she saw the look.

'Rudy. This old lady is used to her solitude and needs her peace now. Thank you for all you did.'

She gave him a quick peck on the cheek and then disappeared upstairs. The stairway creaked as she ascended.

Back on the street Rudy pondered whether to make the planned visit to his friend, Jimmy. He decided otherwise; it was definitely time to go home. But something made him change his intended course. Rudy found himself heading back and approaching the place he wanted especially to avoid, the scene of the earlier skirmish. Ambulance crews were now in attendance, working alongside police officers. One or two were taking down particulars in notebooks. Rudy stood, uncertain of what he was doing here. Several of the injured youths looked at him as they were tended but none gave any sign of recognition. This fact registered with Rudy and he was glad that his powers appeared to be working sufficiently to affect their memories, but he felt a growing sense of unease.

Then from across the street, beyond the group of youths and their assistants, Rudy noticed a man looking at him. To Rudy he seemed a fairly old man, but also extremely fit, and dressed smartly in a black suit and green tie. His dark hair swept back over his head revealed deeply etched lines and tiny scars on his forehead. But it was his eyes Rudy concentrated on. They were as black as coal and there was something else, something emitting ... too late. Rudy suddenly felt a pain in his head. Images of a ping-pong ball bouncing around a court had his mind spinning, the object speeding up and bouncing in all kinds of directions. Following the movements in his mind made him very woozy. He felt sick and fell to his knees.

'Are you all right, son?'

Rudy began to regain his senses and, through the mist of his lost senses, saw a figure hovering over him. Then he realised the figure had a uniform, and his mind cleared very quickly.

'Were you involved in this fracas then, son? Are you injured too?'

The voice sounded caring but the face didn't match. A stern, sour expression came into focus as Rudy regained his proper sight. The policeman was still scribbling notes

71

in his book from the last youth he had talked to and was about to ask Rudy his details when a commotion behind grabbed his attention. A fight had broken out between one of the youths and an ambulance man. The copper facing Rudy did an about turn and ran to the aid of the stricken ambulance driver, cuffing the youth across the head, then bundling him to the ground, whilst another officer handcuffed him.

Rudy stood mesmerised watching the action. It was to him as if on film, playing out before his very eyes. But then he suddenly regained a little more of his senses. Remembering now the man across the street Rudy looked around him but there was no sign of the man. Rudy decided it was time to make a move. This was not a moment too soon as the copper was on his way back for a second attempt at gaining Rudy's particulars. He called after the disappearing figure of Rudy who was jogging away and slipping around a corner at the end of the street.

Rudy ran on for a distance. Then, when he felt it safe enough to do so, he stopped for a breather, looking about him at the same time. He blew hard, his general fitness still hampered by the effects of the funny turn he had experienced back at the scene of the fight.

Then Rudy saw him again. The man in the black suit and scarred forehead was now on the opposite side of the road. He was looking quickly left and right at the traffic, waiting for a gap in order to cross, but at the same time glancing at Rudy. The boy got the message and began running again.

Rudy made it around the next corner, upping his pace, but at the same time looking about him for an escape route. On glancing behind him he realised the man, who was now jogging after him, was gaining ground. The main shopping arcade was housed on that side of the road off the sidewalk, so the crowds were quite thick, hampering the man's pursuit. In his frustration he began to manhandle people out of his path, bringing shouts of annoyance from some. One actually squared up to him. A stout man in his sixties was no match for the fitness of someone a good ten years younger than him. The thump he took sent him rolling into the road, causing a car to screech to a halt inches from his frame.

Rudy witnessed this act as he glanced again over his shoulder and he became very frightened indeed. His heart began to thump and he began to feel a cold sweat of fear. He decided on a detour through one of the shops. A female sales assistant skipped out of his path as he sprinted down an aisle, deftly now avoiding a further chance of colliding into customers by a mazy path of sidestepping expertise.

But glancing back over his shoulder again he noticed the much less subtle approach of his pursuer, who was managing to barge his way through a number of people who were just recovering from the passage of the running youth. And still looking at the exiting youth they were totally unaware of the rampaging bull behind them.

Rudy ran through the back exit and found himself in an alleyway. He hesitated for a moment wondering which way to go next. Then he heard the yells becoming louder inside the shop and realised he hadn't time to make a decision. Instead, he was off again in the direction he had been facing. Rudy was tiring and feeling utter dismay, which mixed in with the fear made him despair, as he didn't know where he was going. Looking desperately around him as he ran, trying to find a place to hide, he suddenly noticed a smaller alleyway on his left and decided to take this path. Glancing back he could see the man had caught up again and was making strides towards him, which only increased the sense of his unbearable despair.

He felt totally helpless and could see no alternative to his being found in this alleyway, dead. His mum would never see him alive again. No, Rudy suddenly thought … he was not going to let it happen.

Rudy felt a slight surge inside and suddenly came to a halt, turning to face his potential assassin who came to a skidding halt at the same time. Rudy felt the surge increase as he faced the black menacing eyes. He also noticed a vein on the man's forehead throbbing as he recovered from the efforts of catching his quarry.

The man was about to speak as Rudy felt a greater surge inside. At the same time he felt an extreme confidence and lack of fear that certainly did not fit with the circumstances. But he could see a distinct change in the man's demeanour, as he recoiled, stepping slowly backwards away from Rudy, who knew that the man could see and feel what was happening and was afraid of it. Rudy felt another surge inside him, this time immense, apparently causing the man to shudder and hold his hands out as he backed away. The man suddenly turned and ran off, disappearing down another alleyway. Rudy was left feeling a little confused as the surges died down. He began to feel fearful again and aware of possible trickery. He walked tentatively to the end of the alleyway and, on looking both ways, saw no evidence of the man.

By this time a small crowd of concerned people who had witnessed the chase were approaching, having at last caught up. Rudy's first thought was that they would have been too late. They would now be discovering his dead and mangled body.

A middle-aged woman asked, 'Are you all right, sonny? Why was that horrible man chasing you?'

Rudy nodded his head, but at the same time he heard that soft voice inside his mind. A young girl's voice chiding him over his show of strength in such a public place.

Rudy broke out in a huge grin that perhaps was not what was expected of him under the circumstances. The confused shoppers looked at each other in surprise as he walked smiling past them.

'Someone has called the police so I think you should wait with us until they arrive.'

This completely removed the smile from his face.

'No need for the cops. It's all OK. I'm OK and I'm off.'

Rudy started jogging away up towards the High Street just as he saw a police car arrive. He darted up another alleyway and then managed to vanish into the shopping crowds. He sat on the bus home feeling drained and very tired. The realisation was sinking in of just how lucky he had been. He knew Lorna was not happy with him for yet another mistake. Nevertheless, he was aware she had assisted him again and whispered a thank you to her.

8

The journey had been long and Aleksei slumbered at last as he enjoyed the gentle swaying of the train carriage. But his enjoyment was interrupted by a dream. He had been in a field of corn playing hide and seek with his older brother, Yuriy. His grandfather, Stanislav, featured strongly in the dream and had been a distance away, gesturing as he often did and waving his arms at Aleksei. At first Aleksei had not wanted to approach the old man, feeling that he had betrayed his grandfather's memory. But as he got closer he noticed the huge grin on Stanislav's face and his arms out in welcoming embrace. Aleksei felt his face wet as he woke from his nap and realised he had been crying. He felt embarrassed as he looked across at Colonel Guznischev, who was staring curiously at him but said nothing. The soldier, Yegor Strashnikov, sat beside the interior door keeping watch, the three of them being the only occupants of the carriage.

Aleksei wiped his face with his sleeve and closed his eyes again. But this time sleep did not come to him, just thoughts. He remembered everything he had been told of Elena Zvadsky, mother and daughter, and tried to piece together more of the story from all he had known before this new information came to light. He realised he had known so very little up until now, 1947, but this new information had caused him to feel a sense of new hope that he might be able at least to trace his daughter. He realised it would not be easy, far from easy, in light of what was required of him in return for the release and protection of his family. He had considered that they would be pleased to be free again but perhaps not at the expense of his having to betray his ideals. He would not have done this under any other circumstances but what more could be done about it? He was trapped and under the control of the Bolshevik machine. He had considered that his grandfather, Stanislav, would have spun in his grave at the very thought of such betrayal. The old man had made it to ninety-eight years of age before succumbing to a bout of pneumonia in 1938, so thankfully he had not endured another world war, but Aleksei had sensed him close during this conflict. However, in the years since the war Aleksei had felt a distance between them, especially whilst housed in the labour camps, so this latest dream had been a relief to his senses and he felt it a good omen that his grandfather had returned so strongly to him. He smiled as he reflected on this; then, realising where he was he opened his eyes but the colonel appeared to be dozing. He watched the colonel for a short time until he felt convinced that he was asleep then Aleksei trained his sights on the soldier, Yegor Strashnikov. Although Strashnikov appeared to give one hundred per-cent of his attention to the corridor Aleksei sensed he could also see the two of them behind him. He wondered about this particular individual. What age would he be? Twenty? And had he been interfered with? Did he still have the mind he was born with or had the scientists experimented on him too? Aleksei decided to give up on this question for the time being but he felt sure that much more was going to be revealed in the coming weeks and months. Aleksei decided to close his eyes again and think of his two Elenas.

He pondered on so many questions – especially why Elena had not told him about her pregnancy. He considered the sentence in her letter left for him and that fateful day when her family decided to flee. He had read it over and over again and had been convinced that her words, 'God has already blessed us' were her way of telling him that she was expecting. But the very few letters she had written and sent to him since had not contained any mention of the baby, Elena. Maybe she had not wanted to admit to him, let alone herself, that she had given her away. He felt a sharp pain course through his mind as he considered this. In those subsequent letters Elena had described how her family had been forced to split up and that she had thought everyone had been captured. She herself had been conscripted into the Red Army and had fought during the war against the Nazis. They had tried to arrange a rendezvous but each time her unit was moved on the day before such a meeting could take place. Aleksei had even considered that this was an actual ploy in order to keep the two of them apart. If so, it had been a success on the part of whoever was controlling such things as the closest Aleksei and Elena had come to being together was at Stalingrad, in 1942. Every time Aleksei had finished an assignment he would disappear for a few hours, searching the city, trying to find her, but without success. Then he had heard an unconfirmed report that she had been killed, that she had been captured by a group of Germans who had raped her then slit her throat. Aleksei had been inconsolable for days after hearing this but it had not affected his ability with a rifle and he appeared from that time on to relish the opportunity of killing as many Nazis as possible.

But there was something else nagging at his mind over Elena. All those who were close to him in life and had passed over came back to him in his dreams at least once. Most of them came back again and again, but never Elena. This gave him hope that the report of her capture and subsequent death had been mistaken identity. Perhaps the woman involved had been someone who looked like Elena. He clung on to that hope day by day. And his daughter? Where would she be now and could she ever be traced? Britain was a small nation but large enough to have swallowed up his daughter, especially if she had been adopted and her name changed. He did not even have the name of Elena's friend who had arranged for her removal to those islands. But he promised himself he would use every opportunity to trace his daughter. Meanwhile he would also hope of news of his other Elena, never his wife, but blessed by God.

The train came to an abrupt halt. Colonel Guznischev opened his eyes and took a moment to focus. He really had been asleep. The soldier, Yegor, was on his feet and into the corridor in a flash, holding his rifle at the ready.

He returned shortly after and said, 'It is all right, Colonel Guznischev. It seems the train has been stopped in your honour. A car awaits you beside the track.'

The colonel stood stiffly his girth now more apparent, suggesting too much of the good life and not enough active service. As if reading Aleksei's thoughts, Colonel Guznischev hauled his great coat across his midriff and buttoned it.

He remarked absently, 'You are right, Yegor, it is an honour. A personal motorcade all the way from Moscow!'

As he said this, two unsmiling men in suits entered the carriage, motioning to Aleksei who rose to his feet. Each took an arm and marched him out to the waiting car.

Colonel Guznischev said, 'There, Aleksei Rudikov, you will see now how kind and lenient I have been with you so far. These two represent an awful truth to anyone not toeing the party line!'

He chortled as he climbed into the front passenger seat of one of the other cars. Yegor Strashnikov walked back to the army truck that had followed. The vehicles then proceeded from the railway trackside back onto the main road towards Moscow.

As they entered the capital city, Aleksei was immediately overwhelmed by the hustle and bustle of traffic and pedestrians all around him. After so long in solitude it was a shock to him. He had previously visited Moscow only once, on a school outing, and it had appeared like another world then. It did so now. This was the city where all the decisions were made so every resident was sure to be either a collaborator or a slave, or both. Aleksei had learned that much about Bolshevik policy. Isolate the individual so that no-one can trust another. Very clever – but only up to a point because with that attitude even the top man himself, Josef Stalin, would need to watch his back at all times.

The car he was travelling in came to a halt outside a large and gloomy building. The door flew open and Aleksei realised he was to have another escort. This time he was marched into the building and along long dusty corridors until the party reached a large office with a man sitting opposite them at a desk. The man looked up on hearing the approach of the escort. Aleksei met this man's eyes and uttered an oath under his breath, immediately recognising the commander of his old unit before and during the war. He had obviously found rapid promotion within the party's secret police system. He put down his pen and surveyed the prisoner.

'So, Aleksei Rudikov, we meet once again. I hope you will congratulate me on my promotion to colonel. The years have not been kind to you, I see – you have lost a lot of weight and muscle tone. They promised me you would be at least fed well.' He gave a short chuckle and continued. 'But now I find you have managed to convince someone that you do not belong amongst the enemies of the Soviet people.'

Aleksei glared at his detractor as he replied, 'Should I ask who it was that branded me as such? Someone who, to my knowledge, never held a weapon in any battle against the Nazis and now has ingratiated himself with the higher command so as to be afforded the rank of colonel? A person who openly accused me of deserting my post along with so many other comrades who fought valiantly for the motherland, and whose only reward was to end up in the camps. Why should this have happened, I ask, and where has he hidden ever since? I have the answer now in front of me.'

Colonel Surnyaev stood up and angrily slammed his fist down on the desk, his face flushed with anger.

'How dare you insult me like that! I should have you taken out and shot here and now.'

'That would not be wise, Colonel Surnyaev, as the order for the prisoner's release came from the very highest echelons of the party.'

Colonel Guznischev had emerged from his hiding place in the shadows after quietly listening to the conversation.

Surnyaev eyed his opposite number with contempt and suspicion as he replied.

'Oh, I see now, Colonel Guznischev, that he has won you over too.'

Colonel Guznischev reached into his coat pocket and withdrew a packet of cigarettes. He slowly took one out and lit it, puffing the first plume of smoke up towards the ceiling as he eyed Colonel Surnyaev.

'Colonel, you will obviously appreciate that we have a strict code of conduct in matters such as these. We have been taught how to respond when confronted with such a dilemma, no?'

Surnyaev seated himself again with his eyes still firmly on Aleksei Rudikov.

'Yes, I hear what you are saying Colonel Guznischev

81

but I cannot for the life of me understand why this miscreant is here after all he has said and done. His behaviour should have resulted in the death penalty.'

'Then you do not appreciate what is in front of you, Colonel Surnyaev. Take care. The prisoner possesses quite a lively mind. When activated it can deal out quite a shock.'

Colonel Guznischev chuckled as he looked at the two suited policemen either side of Aleksei. Both looked curiously at the prisoner, then at Colonel Guznischev.

'I do not understand what point you are making here, comrade Colonel.'

Surnyaev had picked up his pen again and began to fill in the form on his desk. At the same time the police escorts suddenly moved sideways as if propelled from their positions. Colonel Surnyaev looked up dumbfounded. Then the form he had been writing on rose from the desk, floated across the room and landed in Aleksei's hand. Aleksei then screwed the piece of paper into a ball and threw it back on to the colonel's desk.

'Do you believe in life after death, Colonel Surnyaev?' Aleksei asked.

Surnyaev looked perplexed. 'Life after death? Why do you ask?'

Aleksei looked left and right at his police escort who were showing signs of wariness. 'And you, or you?'

They shrugged back at him.

Colonel Guznischev intervened. 'Aleksei Rudikov, enough! We are expected elsewhere, so if you will excuse me, Colonel Surnyaev, I am sure you will be able to complete the paperwork without our presence...'

'I have not yet finished, comrade Colonel.'

Guznischev and Aleksei Rudikov had both made to depart but turned back again to face the police chief.

'Whatever trickery is being practised here I have lived

long enough to know a fraud. If you are stupid enough to believe in this stray dog then I truly worry for you, comrade Colonel Guznischev. Whatever happens I will never stand down from my original judgement of this deserter. I still think he should be shot.'

Colonel Guznischev's eyes narrowed as he replied, 'Then your judgement may not be as sound as you think, comrade. For the one who has primarily asked for his return is none other than the leader of the party.'

Surnyaev, his mouth hanging open, watched the colonel and prisoner as they made their way towards the inner chamber.

Both police escorts looked confused but one managed to speak.

'Excuse me, Colonel, but what is happening? It was like ... as if ... I were pushed with some force away from the prisoner ... yet his arms were firmly by his side.'

The other policeman nodded in agreement.

Colonel Surnyaev pondered the situation for a moment then replied, 'We have already been instructed not to speak about this matter but I hear and understand what you are saying. We must, of course, obey that instruction but at the same time we will watch this particular individual with a special interest. You agree?'

Both answered with a curt nod.

As they walked out of earshot Colonel Guznischev asked Aleksei, 'What would you have done if Colonel Surnyaev had taken out his revolver? He was pretty upset with having to deal with you again as it is, without being reminded by you of his past indiscretions.'

Aleksei Rudikov looked straight ahead. 'If he had done so there would have been only one with a bullet in his head, Colonel, and that would not have been either you or I.'

9

Deep in the bowels of the Pentagon during that year, 1947, several top-secret meetings were taking place. On this particular occasion the room was occupied by a dozen individuals, each having a specific job in the networking system set up to gain information for the defence of American interests against the threat now posed by the Soviets. Much of the work required extremes in covert operations never before undertaken and because of this the security classification of each member was the highest possible. Not even the President had access to the information gained by this secret group who were specially formed and funded by an unknown source, but one believed to comprise some of the richest men in the world. Strict secrecy was therefore essential.

At the head of the table sat Bill Collins who was responsible for the whole enterprise. He was quietly watching the others. Married to Martha for thirty-one years with five kids and seven grandchildren, he was a lay preacher at his local church. His brand of Christianity was fundamentalist. Fifty-one years of age, tall, lean and with a chin that appeared chiselled from granite, his outward appearance disguised a debilitating disorder that required medication, especially if he began to feel stressed. For this reason Collins delegated most of the work to his aide, John Mackay.

Mackay was a thirty-five-year-old Scot who had arrived on American shores with his elderly parents in 1940. His parents had been reluctant to make such a move but their son had convinced them that Hitler would succeed in invading the British Isles and that they would all suffer under German rule – particularly if the Nazis had discovered their Jewish origins hidden under a Scottish name. There was another factor he had purposely kept from them: he was about to be conscripted into the army. He was unsure right up to the last minute whether or not to tell them but decided it best for it to remain a secret. A secret to the grave as it turned out as both his parents had died within six months of each other in 1944, so neither had seen how the war had been won anyway. Mackay had never married and rumour had it that he had a partiality towards his own sex, the younger the better. His height was an extreme disadvantage to him amongst the other delegates. His five feet three inches meant that he preferred to be moving around most of the time rather than spend time alongside a six-footer, feeling just a wee bit out of his depth. At the moment he was sitting at his boss's right hand chewing on a sandwich taken from the not inconsiderable fare on the table. Eating was another of his problems, as was his consumption of alcohol. He was never seen at a convention without a glass in his hand but, surprisingly, he never appeared to get drunk. Bill Collins was a teetotaller, so would normally have had a dim view of his aide's fondness for liquor but John Mackay had never let him down yet so he was forgiven.

Sitting on Bill Collins' other hand was his other aide, Doug James, a wiry six-foot-two, forty-year-old Texan, who had sharpened his teeth in the oil industry. He could handle himself at any time the situation got rough and was the ideal candidate for the foreign assignments. The usual brashness of a Texan had passed Doug James by, as he was a quiet methodical worker who had a linguistic genius in him. He could pass himself off as a local in four languages, and could make himself understood in another half-a-dozen. James had been married but because of the travelling required in his work the relationship had seriously floundered and he had returned one day to find Maria gone with the children. The last he had heard she had found someone else and was living in California.

Further down the table were the four scientists, all brought over from Germany after the war, each of them having been handpicked by the consortium for their individual expertise. It was an acknowledged fact that these men were no better than those who had conducted experiments in the concentration camps, even though they denied being involved in any such activity, saying that all of those responsible for such terrible acts had been killed or taken by the Russians for their own purposes.

Last, but not least, were the five other American based aides who were responsible for sweeping up after the main players. Usually this involved silencing someone by any appropriate means. They were also involved with general day-to-day duties such as phone tapping, espionage, surveillance and anything deemed too secretive for the normal channels within the CIA and other security services.

The five were a cosmopolitan bunch: a Mexican, 'El Matador' Luis Alvarez Suarez; Dave Little from Iowa; a Swede, Harry Swenson; Bill Turner from Montreal and Klaus Zimmermann from Switzerland, although it was believed he was an Austrian by birth. All had high levels of psychic awareness, which had been increased by experimentation. The four ex-Nazi professors had spent a whole year experimenting on these five men and produced encouragingly positive results, although what had not been disclosed was the fact that another seven candidates had been discarded at various stages of experimentation. All these seven were to disappear in a convenient plane crash above the Pacific Ocean, having developed grotesque deformities as a result of the experimentation. However, much had been learned since, so the other five suffered only minor side effects, which were hard to detect anyway as each tended already to possess certain quirks, including psychopathic disorders. The biggest question was whether each could be trusted under the conditions of their employment. To make sure of this the scientists had implanted a device in each of them that would detonate if that individual ever thought of straying.

The Americans were desperate to keep ahead of the Russians in any field but especially in matters of paranormal activity. But the Russians had already made significant advances, assisted by their own capture of German scientists who had been transported back to the Soviet Union in order to assist Soviet scientists in conducting similar experimentation. On top of this the latest news had been a real bombshell. If true, it would set the Americans back even further in their efforts to match the Russians.

'Professor Muller, what do you make of this latest information from our Soviet mole?'

Hans Muller was by far and away the most adept scientist on the committee and his views were highly respected. He rose to his feet.

'Mr Collins, I have studied all the reports. I think the Soviets are making a great deal out of this, as they usually do, for reasons of propaganda. However, I have a suspicion that this time what they have is significant. During the war we were getting frequent messages from the front line that the Soviets had a soldier who appeared to have special abilities. He was employed as a sniper but not just an ordinary sniper – he appeared to have a sixth sense. He was always able to find where our most vital communications lay. He continually played havoc with all lines of communication by searching out and shooting the radio operators as well as the commanders. And our own snipers were in awe of him, believing him to be a

87

ghost. Not one sniper ever saw him, even though he killed so many of ours. We never learned his name but called him "stray dog" as he appeared to have no home.'

Bill Collins looked across to Doug James and said, 'Doug, can we be absolutely sure about what we are receiving from our Russian friend? I mean we have seen how much they have stretched the truth when trying to get one over on us.'

Doug James looked at Professor Muller. 'I am in agreement with Hans on this. This guy they have seems to be the real thing. It's scared a few of them by all accounts, even at the top level – and that is some performance, if true.'

Hans Muller nodded and continued, 'The report we received also mentions that this person was a prisoner sent to the labour camps after the war – he may be a dissident. Perhaps this is why they are using kid gloves on him; they are frightened that he might defect. But before we raise our hopes it also appears the Soviets have traced his family and issued him an ultimatum. That is not good news. We know what will happen, and so does he, if he does not do what they are asking of him. All I can do in my capacity is find a match for him.'

Bill Collins perked up. 'You think you can do that, Professor?'

'All I can promise is that we will all try our utmost to find some way of negating his influence. Our experiments are already at an advanced stage. As long as we can dispose of the failures, as we have done previously, I think we will find a positive result in the end.'

Bill Collins winced inside at this, even though he recognised it was for the security of his nation and all points west, but something about it severely clashed with his Christian beliefs.

John Mackay interjected tactfully, 'Hans, please remember there are some of us who have distanced ourselves from all knowledge of your experimental failures. Do whatever is required but please clear up afterwards, so nothing can be traced back. OK?'

Professor Muller nodded. He understood completely. Collins thought how perceptive he had been in employing John Mackay as his 'gofer'. He then stood up, which was a sign that the meeting had concluded. 'How's about we codename this fella "Stray Dog" as it seems he ain't got a home?' said Doug James as they all got their feet.

Bill Collins looked pleased. 'Like it Doug, yes I do like that. "Stray Dog" it is.'

10

It was 3.00 a.m. and Aleksei Rudikov could not sleep. He put on his dressing gown and left his sleeping quarters, wandering into the room that looked out over Red Square. The scene below was picturesque with lights reflecting off the snow. His mind had been spinning with all kinds of thoughts that had prevented sleep. Here he found himself in the one place he had often dreamed of since that visit as a child – the Kremlin, a place that, without doubt, housed some of those who had been instrumental in his incarceration in the camps. Thoughts of Elena, and their daughter, constantly nagged him. Time had not dimmed his feelings for the one he prayed would still be alive. He had learned now not to care about the time lost; he only wished for them to be together again. It was the only thing that kept him going.

His thoughts were rudely interrupted by a knock on the door. Aleksei turned as the door opened and Colonel Guznischev entered. He was still in full uniform.

'Aleksei Vasiliy Rudikov, please be at ease, my friend. I have someone with me who wishes to speak with you.'

The colonel moved to one side as another entered the room. Now standing before him was a face familiar, not from any previous meeting, but from countless posters and photographs.

Colonel Guznischev stood to attention as he announced, 'Aleksei Vasiliy Rudikov, please welcome Josef Vissarionovich Dzhugashvili, the General Secretary of the Party and leader of the Soviet Republic.'

Joseph Stalin eyed him curiously. Aleksei stepped back a pace. He felt naked. His eyes met those of his leader and found them searching his soul.

The glint in Joseph Stalin's eyes gradually softened and now Aleksei could see what others had seen and remarked upon – that Stalin possessed the eyes of an elderly grandparent, infinitely kind and solicitous for the wellbeing of his people. Surely the Soviet Republic was safe in his hands. Stalin spoke. 'Please be seated, Aleksei Vasiliy. I have some questions I wish personally to ask you.'

Stalin had a strong smell of drink about him but was not at all drunk. It was rumoured that he liked to party into the early hours of the morning and it appeared he had just left one of these functions. Aleksei seemed in a trance and it took the interruption of Colonel Guznischev to bring him out of his stupor.

'Aleksei Rudikov, find a seat!'

The words were barked as an order and Aleksei did as he was instructed. Stalin nodded to the colonel who moved back to guard the door. Stalin then sat down facing the perplexed Aleksei Rudikov.

'You look full of wonder, Aleksei. That someone so important is asking questions of you personally when I have a host of individuals to do this for me. Is that not so?'

Aleksei managed to say, 'It is an honour for me to be of service to you.'

Stalin turned to find Colonel Guznischev grinning at his protégé. The colonel was about to apologise but he waved it away.

'You have obviously taught him some etiquette in the time he has been under your wing.' Stalin then returned to Aleksei. 'Much has been said about you, comrade. I have lived a long life and am happy that I have my name forever imprinted on this great period in our history. But

91

I have dreams that make me feel unwell, Aleksei. Do you understand?'

Aleksei now saw a real vulnerability in the old man who had caused so many others to lose what little they had all that time ago and ever since. His mind began to settle and come together as he witnessed this surprising frailty in the leader of the Soviets.

Stalin noticed his curious stare and changed the subject. 'Did you ever meet the others out there? Vasili Zaitsev at Stalingrad? Erwin König? Maybe even Anatolij Chekhov?'

Both Zaitsev and Chekhov were now in Russian folklore after their exploits with a sniper's rifle. The German, König, had never been captured or killed as far as anyone knew. Despite his distinguished service, Aleksei Rudikov was officially an unknown as far as such glory was concerned. Such was the secretive nature of his duties, he had never been included in the list of wartime killing counts.

Aleksei paused for a moment, gathering his thoughts, then said, 'It will of course be known what my instructions were and why – to stay as well hidden as possible, not only from the Nazis but my own comrades as well. I preferred it that way anyway. Oleg was the only one who accompanied me at times and he was killed at Stalingrad. I never knowingly came across Chekhov and I steered well clear of Vasili Zaitsev as rumour had it he did not welcome any interference. I saw him, but he never saw me. As for Erwin König, who knows what happened to him?'

Stalin nodded his head slowly. 'It has been said that you shot König.'

Aleksei shrugged. 'I killed many Germans but I never asked them for their names.'

'The Germans have no record of anyone by the name of Erwin König. Could he have been running under a

92

code name, I wonder?' Stalin muttered a few more words to himself then continued, 'So why is it that after all that good work you unstitch it all by running away?'

Aleksei looked at Colonel Guznischev who shrugged back at him.

Stalin noticed this interchange and said, 'Is there something I do not know about this episode, Colonel?'

Guznischev replied, 'It was to do with a woman. He has been searching for her for years. Elena Zvadsky. She was conscripted into the army but their paths never crossed.'

Stalin sat forward in his chair, staring closely at Aleksei.

'So, all that for a woman. She must have been worth it for you to spend this time in a camp?'

'I was twenty and she eighteen. We were to be married but she went away with her family and I have not seen her since. It has been suggested that she was killed at Stalingrad but her body was never found. Colonel Guznischev also informs me that she had a daughter. *Our* daughter, I should say. Believed now to be adopted and living in Britain...' Aleksei trailed off as he stared into the distance.

Stalin's eyes glinted again as he broke into Aleksei's thoughts.

'You will not be running off again on this wild goose chase, I hope. We have much for you to do for us here. You have already been told that your family's welfare is in your hands? As long as you are of use to us they will benefit. Is that clear, Aleksei Rudikov?'

'I understand fully what is required of me.'

Aleksei may have said this convincingly but he could not be sure he would not run again if he thought that he could find a way to Elena.

Stalin got up from his chair and Aleksei did likewise. Colonel Guznischev walked forward to the door, waiting to open it, but Stalin turned back to face Aleksei.

He stared at him for a short while then observed, 'I hear you have tremendous abilities. Not another Grigori Yefimovich Rasputin, I hope.'

Stalin gave a short laugh. Aleksei looked grimly back at the old man who continued, 'I was wondering if you could see anything around me? What my fate might be? What these recurring dreams are telling me?'

Aleksei felt something. A strong sensation, but should he keep it to himself? He decided to buy some time.

'I feel something but I will need to dwell on it more before giving you an answer.'

Stalin's stony expression matched his retort. 'I think I see the answer already in your face, Aleksei Rudikov. Until we meet again then.' He began to walk out, followed by the colonel, but Aleksei had not finished.

'Excuse my impertinence, but you mentioned Rasputin.'

Stalin turned back curiously. 'There is something I wish to tell you. I know I should have mentioned this before but my grandfather knew Rasputin fairly well.'

Stalin moved forward and sat down in the chair again. Colonel Guznischev was shaking his head at the boldness of Aleksei Rudikov.

'I am all ears. Your grandfather knew Grigori well? This I know. Your grandfather was Stanislav Aleksei Vostrikov, was he not?'

Aleksei was shaken and could not speak. He just nodded his head. Stalin nodded back.

'Yes, it is a surprise to you comrade. Your grandfather was an army sniper. Did you know?'

'An army sniper! He never told me that, ever.'

Stalin stood again and said, 'Your grandfather saved my life. He did not have to. I knew his feelings about what we did. But he saw a potential assassin make a move for me and shot him through the head. My, how the Soviet State we know now might have been a lot different if the

94

assassin had been successful. Everything about the incident was hushed up because of who was involved and your grandfather went to his grave never mentioning it to anyone. But I am telling you this now because it is the reason you are here. I owed your grandfather a life and here you are alive. Please do not sully his memory. I would hate for you to fall foul of any of the committee after all that has been done for you.'

The old man's eyes were gleaming as he turned and walked out of the room.

Aleksei was left alone to ponder what he had just learned. He remembered what else he had sensed about the party leader. He had already learned that Stalin was considered only a part-educated Georgian who, as a youth, had been in a seminary but had left to join the Bolsheviks. Lenin was an intellectual but had taken a shine to Stalin and considered him more worthy to be the next in line for the leadership than any of the other intellectual party élite. But Aleksei sensed something over Stalin's past. It was well known that the Bolshevik élite were all atheists, but did Stalin still harbour religious feelings. Was there a strange kind of denial in him to have committed millions to a life worse than death? Was it guilt? Was superstition now weighing him down in old age, catching up with him and making him feel vulnerable enough to ask such a question of Aleksei? It was definitely not good news for Stalin or his supporters. Aleksei had clearly seen the demise of the Soviet leader in the near future, but he decided to keep this premonition secret from everyone else as there had been plenty of psychics in the past who had predicted events, then found themselves accused of plotting against someone or other and paid the penalty with their lives. Russian history was full of such incidents and Aleksei did not wish to become another such statistic.

Later that same day Aleksei had a visitor, a professor from the state laboratory where many of the experiments were undertaken. Professor Grigoriy Strekalovsky had five German scientists aiding him in his efforts to develop the perfect Soviet mind shield, an antidote to any counter-revolutionary. As the Americans had already discovered, the Nazis had been close to developing something that would have meant being able to create a perfect Aryan race capable of winning every war for the Germanic peoples. But now both Russia and the United States were using clandestine experiments to attempt exactly the same thing for themselves.

Professor Strekalovsky was a thin balding man of fifty-eight years who had seen, and been involved in, many changes over the years. He had benefited greatly from Stalin's régime and was held in high regard by the Politburo and General Committee. A trust not always afforded many in those dark days.

Stalin had met a resistance in Aleksei, which reminded him of that day Aleksei's grandfather, Stanislav, had remarked of his own lack of fear: 'You cannot kill someone who is already dead.' Stalin had quietly pondered these words, and they had worried him ever since. Could he ever admit to anyone just how superstitious he was and the voices that haunted his dreams? Worse, he had since allowed a mystic to predict his fate. And this had been the reason he had asked Aleksei such questions and, ever since, wished to know his power.

The Russian people would have been terrified if they had known of the secret ideological experiments now being conducted with a view to protecting their homelands from the capitalistic invasions of the West.

The professor began brightly. 'Good day, comrade. I have just to ask some simple questions before you are admitted to our laboratories.'

Professor Strekalovsky waited for Aleksei's reaction. There was none.

'Good. So we can expect your full cooperation? That you will help us in every way possible to ensure our experiments are successful?'

Again Aleksei made no sound or movement, but inside he could feel that surge. He tried to restrain it but his emotions were getting the better of him. He felt threatened and when he was angry it was easy for him to cause some kind of incident, as Colonel Guznischev had already witnessed.

Professor Strekalovsky had already anticipated the result of his antagonistic approach and looked away from Aleksei's eyes. An ashtray that had been sitting on a table suddenly rose and flew against a far wall with a crash. This brought Aleksei back from his reverie, just as a guard appeared through the doorway, pistol in hand.

The professor talked quietly. 'It is all right, thank you. We were only conducting a small experiment, is that not so, Aleksei?'

'Yes,' replied Aleksei, looking confused, and the guard retreated to the hallway.

Professor Strekalovsky remained silent for a short while watching Aleksei closely. He noticed that Aleksei's mind appeared still to be somewhere else. When their eyes met Aleksei looked straight through the professor.

'Aleksei what do you see at this very moment? Can you see anything?' he asked quietly.

Aleksei twitched slightly and then looked at the professor.

'I am no longer there. I am back here Professor Strekalovsky, in the room with you.'

'But where were you before, when you were moving the ashtray?' The professor was looking rather disappointed now as he had hoped to learn more of Aleksei's thoughts when he was in his trance.

97

'I will never divulge that professor. Wherever I am, and whomever I meet on the other side are for my own memory.' He glared at the professor.

Professor Strekalovsky remembered being earlier forewarned by Colonel Guznischev that Aleksei Rudikov would probably be the most awkward and frustrating case he and his team would ever have to handle. But he had never failed yet to get a positive result, even if the subject of the experiment were to be driven insane by his methods, or even lose his life. However, with all his experience and confidence in such matters something about this latest of his proposed investigations made Professor Strekalovsky feel uneasy. But he decided he would go ahead in his usual manner whatever the cost, for he knew Aleksei possessed something none of the others had had in any of his experiments before.

Aleksei watched the professor as he mulled over the situation. 'You would use experimentation to discover how my mind works? You might consider hypnotherapy, or hypnosis, but, I warn you, whatever and whoever assists me from the other side will not comply with your wishes, unless it is deemed to be for a good purpose. If you push too far then my mind will be deliberately blocked.'

Professor Strekalovsky tried not to show his exasperation because he wanted to appear confident in front of Aleksei, but he had already realised what a daunting exercise this was likely to become.

'I am just ordered to produce results, comrade. It matters not to me if the subject cannot withstand the experimentation. Plenty have been made to be sorry by refusing to co-operate. The camps have housed many who have failed us and ended up with minds that have been reduced to nothing, forever wandering around looking for what they will never find again until another comrade puts them out of their misery with a bullet. Is that what you want,

Aleksei? Do you remember the bargaining? Your family could all end up in that position again, in the camps, but with a different ending I promise you.'

Aleksei did not answer. The professor continued.

'And what of your extended family? Elena Zvadsky, her daughter and grandson?'

The professor looked closely for Aleksei's reaction after this reference to Elena and the revelation that there was a grandson. He was not disappointed with the effect. Aleksei was astonished.

'Grandson? I have not heard this before. Who says this and how do they know anyway?'

The professor sensed he had regained some ground and felt confident enough to expand.

'You have already been advised by Colonel Guznischev of how Elena Zvadsky had passed her daughter, *your* daughter should I say, to a friend before meeting her death at Stalingrad. Your daughter, Elena, was somehow taken to Britain where she was adopted in 1930 by a middle-aged couple named Roper. This is all information we have just discovered ourselves. So here we are now in January 1948. Your daughter was born in February 1928, which makes her nineteen years old. Her name now is Helen – very close to "Elena" – and we have all wondered why the Ropers should choose to call her that. But much of it is a mystery anyway. She was two months pregnant with your grandson when she married the father, James Metthewson, in May 1947.'

Aleksei shook his head slowly. 'Why are you telling me all of this, Professor Strekalovsky?'

'One thing that concerns me about you and has always concerned others too, is that all this information seems new to you. Why did they on the other side not tell you? That I do not understand.'

Aleksei took the point the professor was making. 'I will

have to ask them, if I am allowed to, but I do not think I need to anyway. They knew I would escape and try to find my daughter and her child.'

The professor had a smile on his face now. 'But if you co-operate there will be every chance that you will not need to escape. Afterwards, I am certain you will be allowed the freedom to find them yourself.'

Aleksei looked away as he replied. 'And if I were allowed to find them, how safe would we all be? We could all be disposed of together.'

'No, I don't think so, comrade. That would be a very expensive mistake.'

'What do you mean? How would it be a mistake?'

The professor measured his words. 'They have named your grandson, Rudy. Is it not a fact that the special power you seem to have passes through a generation to the next male? Grandfather to grandson?'

'Who said this and why? I would like to meet that person and ask him the same question.'

Professor Strekalovsky waited for Aleksei to focus back on him and then said, 'Another thing you may not be aware of is to do with your grandfather, Stanislav Vostrikov.'

'That he saved Josef Stalin's life? I know this already from his own lips.'

Aleksei again looked away from the disconcerting smile on the professor's face.

'I am aware of your conversation with our party leader, but no, it is not to do with his saving his life. I know you are now aware your grandfather was a sniper, as you were yourself. It was a great surprise, yes?'

'I was surprised my grandfather did not tell me of such great deeds. But that surprise is tempered by the knowledge that it was not his style to boast.'

Professor Strekalovsky sensed he had Aleksei now.

'Perhaps it is because he held so much more from you.'

100

'So much from me, but we were so close. I do not understand. Kept what from me?'

'You have already said that your mind is able to be blocked if other parties do not wish you to comply.'

'That is correct, but what has that to do with my grandfather?'

'Why is the information I am giving you not being blocked? Could this be for a purpose?'

'You mean my grandfather is the one who is blocking it all and wishes for me now to learn the truth and co-operate with you?' Aleksei felt angry at the mere suggestion.

Professor Strekalovsky's face was now a picture of contentment. 'I cannot interpret that in any other way, Aleksei. Your grandfather also had the powers that you have, albeit to a lesser degree. He was also sworn to keep the secret, even from you.'

Aleksei felt an enormous wave of distress pour over him. His grandfather had shared so much with him. Of course Stanislav had made known to him that he, Aleksei, possessed special gifts, but they had never been fully explained. Stanislav would only say, 'Be careful with them'. Now Aleksei realised his grandfather had meant for him to concentrate on the dreams. Aleksei heard the information the professor had divulged and understood at last that Stanislav had not been a part of Aleksei's dreams from the time when he had deserted the army in his search for his beloved Elena. Now he had returned in a dream as if to forgive him and ease his suffering at the camps. His grandfather had clearly been protecting him all that time and he now felt a new confidence growing inside.

The professor noted his respondent's shocked expression and continued, 'Stanislav was as cantankerous an old man as you could possibly find. But he had wisdom beyond most and a gift that the Bolsheviks craved, so he was forgiven most things – especially his views!'

101

Aleksei's eyes were wide open again. 'You mean he was collaborating with the Bolsheviks? I cannot believe this.'

The professor stood up and silently wandered over to a window overlooking the square.

Then he turned and said, 'Why do you think your family remained in your village? Did it not occur to you that others were being taken to the camps, but none of your relatives? Why not?'

Aleksei felt sick. No, he had never considered why his family had avoided the purges. He knew the reason now and his feelings for his grandfather were confused by the revelation.

'Do you blame Stanislav then? Would you not have done the same to protect your nearest and dearest, as you are being asked to do now?'

Aleksei felt defeated. The confidence he had felt earlier began to drain away. He could no longer argue the case with the professor because he suddenly realised he was right. But at the same time he realised that Stanislav, the grandfather he adored, had also been right. So what was left for him to do? Aleksei's grandfather had returned in the dream to warn him of this very day, he felt certain of that now. So all had to be revealed for him not to feel badly over a decision he was being asked to make. But something inside rebelled at the very thought of collaborating with this scientist.

Professor Strekalovsky knew instinctively that Aleksei was on the ropes and that one last punch would be the knock out.

'So Aleksei, you have much to consider. Your grandfather sacrificed his principles for you and your family and now you have the choice whether or not to save your family, including Elena, your daughter, and her child, your grandson.'

Aleksei clasped his hands together as he said, 'I am

one of the original proletariat, those considered only as breeders of children, who should be welcomed now by this nation of ours, since so many have died. I am going to pray that you are right about all of this, Professor Strekalovsky. If my grandfather sacrificed his principles then it looks as if I will have to do the same, especially if my grandson is to be the next target of your experimentation. I am only sorry that he will not be afforded the opportunity of knowing me, as I did my own grandfather as I grew from child to adult.'

He could still remember that occasion when he had felt a strange feeling inside and his grandfather had told him why. Stanislav had gone on to tell him to concentrate on what he was thinking about and that if he wished something to be, because of his thoughts, maybe it would come true. Aleksei had practised this over and over again with tremendous results, especially as a sniper, but he had also heeded his grandfather's instruction that he was not to divulge his secrets to anyone else. *Anyone!*

Professor Strekalovsky watched Aleksei in his trance and waited for him to return.

'You have noticed that your surges have been non-existent during this last exchange between us even though you have had to take in so much that it has distressed and angered you?'

Aleksei nodded his head.

'So this must be a sign that you are being advised to assist in our experiments, yes?'

Again Aleksei nodded his head but still remained silent.

The professor beamed as he witnessed this apparent acceptance.

'Then your grandson will be safe. I promise this as your grandfather was promised safety before you, and look – you are still safe!'

'How safe, Professor Strekalovsky? Do I feel safe? We

103

are all in a maze that is governed by a party system that wants it all its own way. They have taught us not to trust in anything else but that system. Even you with all your party allegiance, you are not safe. If you make a mistake what will happen to you? Look what has happened to so many of our comrades in the past. Look what they did to the army leaders just before the war. They disposed of them at Stalin's whim. Was he completely mad? What sane man would order such a thing and leave the entire defence of our nation in the hands of a few idiots, Surnyaev amongst them. How we missed our army leaders when Hitler turned his sights on us. If Stalin can think of ordering that to be done professor, then he is capable of anything. Anything! The Bolsheviks are atheists and God help them with that mistake. I believe there are enough who quietly fear people like me. They fear what I might reveal, is that not so professor?'

Professor Strekalovsky's smile disappeared as he realised what Aleksei was hinting at. He realised immediately that all the ground he had thought he had gained was now crumbling before him.

'So Aleksei, I think I know to what you are referring: if I put my trust in you on all of this and you renege on the deal, I will be facing a firing squad? But I, of course, already know this. But your attitude and very unwise choice of words directed towards our leader and the party faithful ... I should make a report of them and then it would be you who would be facing a firing squad. Why should I not do that? It would clearly be expected of me. But that is pressure I do not want ... so please do not use such expressions again.'

Aleksei remained silent. The professor glared back at him.

'Comrade Aleksei Vasiliy Rudikov, I will make this completely clear to you and I hope your grandfather will send you a similar message. Yes, we are all caught up in the party system, but those of us who are a little more adventurous and wise, as your grandfather was, wish only to survive and perhaps help some others to live also. It was always your grandfather's deepest wish that the Soviet people would, sometime in the future, be led out of the terror into a peaceful existence.'

For a moment Aleksei actually thought he saw some humanity in Strekalovsky's countenance, but this notion was negated by his next statement.

'Your grandfather tried his best but his powers were limited. It is evident that you appear to have a lot more paranormal capabilities than he had. Your grandson is likely to inherit more than both of you. That is why we will be keeping a close watch on him. If his identity were to become known and he fell into the hands of the enemy we would be severely at a disadvantage. That must not be allowed to happen. We will do all that is necessary to keep the boy away from them.'

'You would capture him and bring him back here? But he is a British citizen...'

Professor Strekalovsky shrugged his shoulders. 'You yourself have just described how our leadership behaves in certain matters. Let us hope it does not come to that.'

Aleksei's anger intensified. Pictures on the walls in the room and the chairs began to shake and rattle.

'Professor, you will have noticed by the signs about us that the power has not left me. Maybe this is to do with your views on my grandson's safety in the West? If it is that, as he grows, he will gain more power of sight than I, then he will have protection entirely beyond your capabilities of understanding. I would certainly advise you to make this fact known to whoever is pulling the strings, especially those who are the most superstitious.'

Professor Strekalovsky felt his resources draining as he

105

listened to Aleksei's words. What was he to report to the party committee? Stalin himself had taken a personal interest in proceedings, but Aleksei had directed his warning towards the superstitious amongst the party faithful. He was obviously referring to the leader himself. The professor stood looking at Aleksei for a moment and then nodded to him.

'I understand what you are saying, comrade. I will put something less provocative in my report to the Politburo. I really do not wish either of us to be the subject of a firing squad just yet.'

Aleksei remained silent as the professor left the room. Secretly, he had been slowly warming towards Professor Strekalovsky. Even though he had been angered at some of his remarks, he had to admit that the professor had been fair and honest in his approach and he could see why his grandfather had apparently got on with this scientist. But then he considered how long he would be entrapped in a laboratory, aware his kin would grow up without ever knowing him. Escape at this time was out of the question – but in the future? Aleksei had every intention of making that important break for freedom and being reunited with a family that were, at this moment, unaware of his existence. The thought overwhelmed him and he wept.

11

Luis Alvarez Suarez, 'El Matador', nursed a large cognac as he sat in a comfortable chair awaiting a return call. His fingers continued to trace the scars on his forehead. They felt damp, he thought. I am sweating. *I do not sweat!* Am I not the one who fought and killed one hundred bulls? Am I not the proud descendant of a noble conquistador? I am a killer. *I do not sweat!* Suarez, although Mexican by birth, could trace his lineage back several centuries and could point to Spanish nobility in his bloodline. His pride in this helped to make him the fearsome man he had become, carrying out many contract killings. He also possessed a formidable sixth sense that had been heightened through experimentation. In his younger years he had often made trips back to Spain to visit his distant relatives and during this time he had shown great promise as a bullfighter. After his first kill and the grand acknowledgment from the crowd he took great delight in returning to the bull-ring again and again thereafter, relishing the slaughter of many bulls with great zeal, but perhaps his boast of a hundred killings was not quite accurate!

The telephone rang, but Luis did not react at once. He was still smarting from the loss of face earlier. A mere child ... and he had backed off, but... Suarez finally reached across to the telephone.

'I was about to ring off. Where were you?' a rasping voice asked him.

'In ze alley, still.'

Luis Suarez was in no mood to listen to such words, especially from someone he considered unworthy.

The voice on the other end of the line softened. 'His Excellency requires a full report please, Luis.'

Suarez took another slug of his drink and put the glass on the table beside him. 'So ... *he* would like my report, yes? My report is ze boy is definitely one of those you seek ... but...'

The voice on the other end of the line became harsher again. 'But what? What have you to say? His Excellency has not all day to wait for your report.'

'His Excellency had better cross himself for the boy has tremendous support and power. He had one beside him – the one he will wish was not here. Ze girl ... she was with him on his shoulder. Only a brief glimpse, but it was she. I swear it is so. Father, if I can offer any advice to the monsignor it is to stay well clear. My friend, this should be left well alone. The boy has protection beyond anything I have ever come across before.'

There was complete silence on the other end of the line now. Then the connection was severed.

Suarez nodded to himself. 'Beeg mistake, Monsignor Venditti. Much and plenty beeg mistake, your Excellency.'

But as he muttered to himself Luis Alvarez knew the mistake involved him too, critically. Even though he was a flamboyant individual he always managed to keep his work separate from play and in that way maintained tight secrecy. But that afternoon all had been blown wide open by his chasing the boy, manhandling his way through crowds, alerting everyone of his pursuit. Why did he do that? His description would be circulated and it would not take long for him to be identified. Why had he behaved in such a rash manner? It was most unlike him. He sensed it could be for only one reason. Whatever power the girl possessed was in excess of his and she had broken through his defences, and his mind had been controlled from that moment on. That was why he had been drawn into chasing the boy. He was convinced of it. He got up and wandered into the bedroom where his suitcase lay on the bed. Suarez had packed this earlier in expectation of being picked up, but as no-one had arrived he felt certain he was now alone, a liability. Suarez had also spent time disguising himself: he had shaved off his moustache and sideburns and selected the largest pair of sunglasses he could find. He had gone through this process once before to pose for the photograph for his 'alternative' passport, now in his jacket. He picked up the phone and called a taxi. It was time for him to return to Spain. He knew his family would not desert him in his hour of need, but he realised this journey might not be as easy for him now that so many were alerted to his activities. He would soon be listed at Interpol as a fugitive, armed and dangerous; he cursed his stupidity. He had sensed something wrong with this assignment and had been going to refuse participation, but his pride had got in the way, as usual, and now he might pay the ultimate price for his failure.

Deep inside a fortified monastery in a region on the Italian-Swiss border an old man sat muttering oaths at the wall in front of him. His aide had just given him the news that his Mexican collaborator had failed to kidnap the boy, Rudy Metthewson.

Gustaf, an implacable Swedish aide, waited patiently for the monsignor to digest the news, knowling that it was a severe blow to his plans, and thus to his esteem, built up through many years of covert activity. Monsignor Venditti sighed heavily and slumped forward resting his hands on his knees. Gustaf immediately moved forward, thinking the monsignor was about to pass out, but the old man held a hand up to him.

'Thank you, Gustaf, but I am all right now. I know what has to be done. Tell me, did Luis Suarez say anything more about the matter?'

Gustaf thought for a moment as the old man began to rise from his stooped position and stood facing his aide.

'Your Excellency, there is one thing I sensed during my brief exchange with the Mexican. Suarez sounded irritated but I also detected a slight tremor in his voice. Fear? Could it be that the formidable Luis Suarez has been frightened by his experience with one so young? He also warned that you should stay clear and leave well alone. Apparently, the boy has much power around him. He also mentioned something about a girl on his shoulder. Does this make sense to you?'

Monsignor Venditti eyed Gustaf warily as he considered whether to divulge something he had kept from him for the whole time he had been employed as his aide. He decided the time was right to speak of it.

'Gustaf, you have been the most loyal and devoted servant of this old soul and I thank you for it. You are like a son to me. There is something I must tell you about this situation. And, yes, Luis has reason to be afraid. Very afraid.'

Gustaf's smile faded. He had always known that the monsignor dabbled in the dark arts and partook of secret rites and rituals designed to alter situations, for himself and for others. So much conflicted with Monsignor Venditti's venerated position within the Catholic Church. Monsignor Venditti noticed the change in Gustaf's demeanour.

'Gustaf, I will tell you this now as I do not wish to take you further along a road that may lead to ultimate sacrifice. From now on my soul will be tested by the powers of whomever I have linked with and those that have just shown their face. I wish things were different, I really do, but they are as they are and so I must ask you to seek another path, different from mine.'

Gustaf began to protest and fell to his knees. The old man walked slowly to him and placed a hand on the head of his distraught aide.

'Bless you my son, but it is for the best. Please believe me.'

After Gustaf had left the room Monsignor Venditti sat staring at the fire, considering all that had occurred. Then, he reached for the telephone and dialled a secret number which gave him direct access to the Vatican. This call, he considered, would, without doubt, set off a chain of events which would precipitate a showdown of magnificent proportions.

12

As the winter of 1953 drew to a close, Aleksei Rudikov felt a peculiar sensation that became stronger as time wore on. Late in the evening of the first day of March Professor Strekalovsky was suddenly called away from his laboratory. He had asked Aleksei to remain there, as they were mid-way through a session that would take them into the early hours of the next morning. This had become a regular event, as both Aleksei and the professor preferred the later hours for the conducting of such experiments.

Professor Strekalovsky returned sometime later and sat down at his desk. He appeared slightly shaken and remained silent as he shuffled papers around.

Aleksei eyed him curiously. He had been working with this man for over five years and could tell when something extraordinary had occurred simply by observing the professor's demeanour. To his own surprise, Aleksei had grown to trust Professor Strekalovsky, although not sufficiently to share many of his secrets.

'Is there something the matter, professor?'

The professor's reply was incoherent. Aleksei could not catch the words but he thought Strekalovsky was saying something about a family. At the same time the sensations were upon Aleksei again, but much stronger this time. He had experienced the same feelings earlier that day. He had sensed then that something was terribly wrong and feared it might be connected with his own family.

'What is it, Professor, what has happened to my family?'

Strekalovsky looked confused for a moment as he heard

Aleksei's words. Then he seemed to relax and a smile appeared on his face.

Now it was Aleksei's turn to feel confused but this soon gave way to anger. Objects around the laboratory began rising into the air.

The professor raised his hands. 'My sincere apologies, Aleksei Vasiliy. It was a shock to me but I am now back here and with you. No, it is nothing to do with your family. If I mentioned anything about "family" whilst my mind was wandering, it was my own.'

'Your own family?'

'Aleksei Vasiliy, are you so naïve as to believe that my position within the party system is not without a price?'

Aleksei remained silent, appreciating just what the professor was hinting at.

Professor Strekalovsky smiled again as he saw in Aleksei, at last, recognition of something they both shared.

'Yes, Aleksei, my family too...'

'But why have you never mentioned this before? In all of this time I never consciously thought of you having any family.'

'Perhaps it has become easier for me at this particular moment to speak of such things. I myself had nearly forgotten they existed.'

Professor Strekalovsky wrung his hands and looked down.

'What has happened?'

The professor looked Aleksei straight in the eyes. 'I think you have been waiting for this news. This evening Josef Stalin was found by guards in a collapsed state. It is feared it may be a stroke.'

Aleksei's eyes widened. 'Then these sensations were about him, not me or you?'

'What sensations, Aleksei? When did you experience them?'

'I felt something of it when I first met him and I think he must have experienced something too. That is what I sensed at the time. Josef Stalin was fighting with himself over certain matters. His superstition affected the way he lived and made decisions. I think that is why he shut himself away at times and read books or edited and watched his films. He was used to giving orders that meant the annihilation of many people and I think he hid from the reality of most of this.'

'Be careful, comrade. The walls have ears – especially big ears in this establishment.'

'Be it so, professor. It is something I would say to his face now anyway. He asked me then what I saw, but I said I would have to consider it and give him an answer later. He did not return for it.'

The professor shook his head slowly. 'From what I gather it is unlikely he would appreciate what you have to say.'

'You mean ... it is his end?'

Professor Strekalovsky looked down for a moment. When he looked up again he said, 'This is not a question you should be asking me. It is one that should be directed at those around you, surely.'

It was Aleksei's turn to smile.

'No, professor, I have told you this before. I cannot ask questions about subjects like this. If I am meant to know anything then it comes to me in dreams and thoughts. Sometimes the message is so full of cryptic clues it is almost impossible for me to understand. Then I have to rely on sensations, as I did today. I knew something had occurred but it took you, another entity, to show me the answer. That is how it works sometimes. But I think the whole subject is much more complicated than anything else imaginable. You have spent a long time analysing this in me and I know why. The reason for all this

114

experimentation is in the mind of a man now lying gravely ill. His dream was to learn the psychology behind it all. How a nation could come together in support of his leadership and fight as one against the Nazis, despite all the terrible things they had experienced. I was brought here so that, through experimentation, it might be possible by mind control to create the perfect Soviet citizen: one who asked no questions of his leader and united readily with all other Soviets, as people did during the war; one who gave total allegiance to the State, no matter what he was asked to endure. An army of such people would conquer the world, would it not?'

Professor Strekalovsky closed his eyes and mopped his brow with a handkerchief.

'I did not hear a word of that, Aleksei Vasiliy Rudikov. May I please remind you that we are possibly being listened to? Please be careful.'

Aleksei's sense of relief that what he felt had been to do with to Stalin's health was tempered by the knowledge that he must have been forewarned for a reason yet to be explained. If Stalin were to die, would it be for the worse or the better?

Professor Strekalovsky watched as Aleksei appeared to go into one of his trances. He still had not been able to penetrate the forces surrounding Aleksei Rudikov. One after another, time after time, the results were always the same. Negative! But now, with the probable demise of Stalin, perhaps the experimental programme that Aleksei had just described would be temporarily suspended or even abandoned altogether. The pressure on him to find a solution had been well nigh intolerable.

Aleksei gradually returned from his thoughts. 'Perhaps this is what we have all been waiting for really. Josef Stalin could not be expected to live for ever, but what will become of the Soviet State now if he dies?'

The professor sighed. 'Part of me is feeling strangely relieved, and I know I could be shot for voicing such a thought. But I am tired, very tired of pursing a goal which I think, deep down, is impossible of achievement. I was so confident at first but that confidence has long gone. At the same time I have received an education in spirituality I never thought possible.'

'I think we have both learned something in this time professor. I have had to learn more patience than I ever thought possible – and I have had worse companions.'

Professor Strekalovsky smiled back at him.

'If he does succumb it will throw everything open. It must surely be Nikita, as First Secretary of the party, who will follow. Krushchev, I believe, has not always seen eye to eye with Stalin. Perhaps...'

Aleksei left his next sentence unsaid but the professor had already read his mind and replied, 'I agree, Nikita Krushchev could be a breath of fresh air for us all. But he still has the rest of the party members to reckon with and some of them will need to die before *they* change!'

Joseph Stalin died four days later on 5th March 1953, aged seventy-four.

13

John Mackay received the news without emotion. Replacing the telephone he sat and thought for a short while, then picked the receiver up again and made a call to Bill Collins. Collins had just returned from a church service and was in good spirits.

'Yes, John. What can I do for you?'

'Mr Collins, I have had reports from three separate sources that something big is being planned. Apparently, our man in the Soviet Union believes that Aleksei Rudikov, our Stray Dog, has kin in the British Isles. A daughter and grandson, by all accounts.'

Collins whistled. 'How's it we have only just found this out, John?'

'Seems those Russkies have been keeping it tight from all their own people too.'

'But Stray Dog, he knows?'

'Sure he knows, but it doesn't do him any good. By all accounts they threatened him. Said they would round up and shoot his family – in Russia, or anywhere else – if he made an attempt to escape and find them. But there's something else. Our Mexican friend has been playing away methinks.'

'Luis, playing away? I don't understand, John.'

'I have had a whisper from the Vatican of all places. Seems our Mexican friend is in cahoots with a Monsignor Venditti, who had employed Suarez to track down the British end of Stray Dog – the daughter and grandson.'

Collins was quiet for a moment. He knew Venditti, who

was another member of the exclusive and highly secretive club. What was he doing employing Luis Suarez, and why was he particularly interested in the daughter and grandson?

Mackay had waited patiently for a reply as his boss absorbed this information. 'There's more. Apparently this kid has the same powers as Stray Dog, if not more developed. That's the long and short of it all. We and the Russians are not alone in discovering this phenomenon.'

Bill Collins straightened up, then nearly toppled over. His wife, who had fortunately been passing, held him up.

'Thank you, dear. I need a drink, please. Can you get me one?' Martha gave him a very old fashioned look but complied with his wish. Fortified with a few sips from the whisky glass, Collins returned his attention to the call.

'Jiminy crickets, John. Please tell me that's all now. Don't tell me the kid can perform superman stunts.'

Collins took another large sip from the glass.

'Even there, I can't offer you good news. Seems our late friend, Luis Suarez, had a real sweat on after his experience with the kid. Blew it completely and backed off. There is even talk of his being afraid. And if he *was* afraid then we have a mighty problem, knowing the Suarez track record. It would take something else to put that amount of fear into him.'

Bill Collins could not ignore how much Mackay was relishing conveying this information.

'Yes, I agree. But I think you said "our late friend". What does that mean, John?'

Mackay chuckled softly. 'Appears he was found dead a few hours ago, with his balls rammed down his throat. Someone was mighty upset, don't you think?'

Rudy felt a little guilty when he arrived home. His mother didn't appear to notice any change in his demeanour as

118

she served up his tea. But Rudy didn't feel hungry. The shock was wearing off and he shuddered as he felt a cold streak of fear course through him, remembering what could have transpired in the alleyway. He tried to eat but found it too difficult.

'Sorry, Mum. Not feeling too good – I need to have a nap. Nothing to worry about.'

Helen was about to say something as she got up to follow but Rudy turned and said again, 'It's all right, Mum. I just need a kip.'

As he disappeared out of the room Helen felt that same sense whenever Rudy had in the past been up to something he didn't want her to know about.

Later Rudy woke suddenly with a cold shiver, even though the night was warm. He looked at the clock which showed a minute past three o'clock. He lay back down on the bed, having kicked off most of the covers. He had begun the night covered with a single sheet but Helen must have been in and added a layer of bedclothes. Then, in the distance, a light shone. At first it was dim and ineffectual, but gradually it increased in intensity until it glowed with a multi-coloured brilliance. Then the room was filled with a congregation of voices quietly murmuring, speaking a foreign tongue similar to that used by Lorna. Then, from the shadows, Rudy could make out the forms he had seen on previous occasions emerging until he was surrounded by a sea of faces, eventually parting and leaving a pathway for Lorna to appear. She looked radiant in a white dress, with patterned designs. Rudy held his breath as he watched her, he being now of an age, and disposed, to appreciate such beauty. Lorna smiled at him.

'*Dorogaya* Rudy!'

'*Dorogaya* Liliya! *Vy ochen' krasivy!* Dear Liliya! You are very beautiful!'

'Rudy, *spasibo*. Thank you.'

119

As this short exchange took place the rest of the congregation closed in on the couple. Rudy felt light headed for a moment and thought he was going to faint. Then he felt another surge that took him with the congregation off into the white light of brilliance. As if in a dream he encountered images of snowbound scenes, strange animals he had seen only on television, people in animal skins fishing by icebound lakes, townships full of people in fur hats and heavy coats trudging through the snow, then on to a multitude of other places.

But as quickly as he had been gathered up he returned to his room and the congregation vanished, leaving only Rudy and Lorna together.

'What do you remember, Rudy?' Her eyes shone.

Rudy didn't expect a question, only an explanation. 'Many places ... I saw many places. And many people in a very cold place. But the sun shone elsewhere and it was so different.'

'And before that, when I arrived. Do you remember any of that?'

Rudy thought for a moment. 'Lights ... brilliant lights and faces, lots of faces. Then they moved aside and you were there.'

'And what did I say?'

Lorna's eyes penetrated Rudy's senses.

'*Dorogaya* Rudy!'

Rudy realised what he had said and looked even more confused.

'And you replied?' Lorna prompted.

For a moment Rudy was stuck for an answer but then he felt that same surge again. '*Dorogaya* Liliya! *Vy ochen' krasivy!*'

'*Spasibo*, Rudy! But are you afraid now?' she enquired.

Rudy thought for a moment, then said, 'No, not scared.

I just don't understand what is happening to me. What is that language you are using? *I* am using?'

'This is the mother tongue of your lost family – Russian. You are of Russian descent and those who come to you today are your ancestors and their many friends. All of them banded together through one common purpose and putting trust in you to comply with a wish for you to use the magic they provide wisely for the benefit of your homelands and the people who occupy it. The same people who throughout history have had to endure the terrible times without any hope of care and understanding and, because of this, have come together on this side, promising to support everyone in the pursuit of a better day for mother Russia. The magic performed from that emotional unification of all that have suffered is immense, Rudy. You have felt the surges; now understand what is given you. Given you because our trust is in you to appreciate what it means, what it involves, the sacredness of it and that it is not to be treated lightly. What you experienced earlier with that man who chased you is only a fraction of it all. You must learn to be wiser and not be tricked into revealing so much.'

Rudy was looking questioningly at her.

'Yes, the louts that attacked the lady, they were all infected by that man who chased you. He instigated it to trap you. Can you see that now?'

Rudy nodded slowly.

'Good, because you will need to be much more aware, but we will be here to assist. And assist we will, be assured of that.'

'Will you tell me about my family? Please. And why does Mum never speak of them?'

Tears were beginning to form in the corners of his eyes. Lorna noticed this and held out a hand. To Rudy's great surprise he felt a real hand, warm and very welcoming.

'From now on I am to you Liliya. Do you understand this, Aleksei Vasiliy Zvadsky-Rudikov? You are the grandson of Elena Zvadsky and Aleksei Vasiliy Rudikov, great-grandson of Svetlana Olga and Stanislav Aleksei Vostrikov. There is so much more for me to tell you. Lie down quietly and I will impart all which forms you from your past.'

14

John Mackay had organised a special meeting on the orders of Bill Collins. Collins was still reeling from the information he had been given and wanted some answers. It wasn't lost on him that all attending this meeting had been together now since the late 1940s. All were veterans of the Cold War campaign yet during all that time the Russians had managed to keep so much secret. He was considering whether this could be construed as a massive failure by all participants. But no-one outside the committee had a clue what they were up to so he could not be held personally accountable. That the Russians were still a threat was someone else's headache. When demands were being made and questions asked as to why they still presented such a threat it was not his department that had to face the music but other lesser organisations. The CIA in America and, in Britain, MI5 and MI6, together with other similar security services around the world would all have it straight in the eye. By some miraculous fortune the Soviets had held their ground, thwarting much of the West's ambitions and continuing to pose a threat to world peace.

Or was it fortune? The KGB had assisted in managing to keep everything so secret. No doubt the practised methods of terrorising the populace had a great deal to do with ensuring such obedient silence. But there had been times when the West had had double agents so closely connected to all departments it was extraordinary that no news of Stray Dog had leaked out. There had even been talk of this wall of silence being connected to a psychical barrier provided by the combined efforts of Soviet mediums, and particularly the involvement of Stray Dog in this experiment. Even further, it was being suggested that this practice had been long established in the Soviet Union. Had Rasputin, the mad monk, been involved only in second-rate psychic trickery or had he been the real thing and able to protect the Royal Family with a wall such as had been described to Collins, a wall apparently still there and presently surrounding the Soviet leadership? Was this why Rasputin had been murdered? As far as Collins could remember Rasputin was meant to have predicted that the demise of the Romanovs would swiftly follow his own. Collins was frustrated by their lack of success. And what was this about Suarez and Venditti? Surely the strict code of conduct observed by all in the top echelons of that secret society had been seriously breached by such conduct. Who else was involved in this conspiracy? Just how far along the web did this reach and who else knew about it? Was Venditti keeping it from his superiors at the Vatican or was the unthinkable a real possibility? If so, Collins could see a major conflict in the very place it could least afford to be at present.

If this were not enough, Bill Collins was also getting gip from Martha. His wife had protested on more than one occasion at his continued involvement in a project she did not believe could have successful outcome. He could no longer make decisions at the drop of a hat, increasingly worrying over each problem for days, if not weeks, at an end. This dilatoriness had been noted by Martha whose patience was wearing thin. Dismissing this unhelpful reverie, Collins got down to business.

'Well, John, we seem to have hit whatever wall we were meant to encounter, so now we have to repair the damage if we can. Losing Luis is a major shock. How long do we think he was in league with Venditti?'

124

'Can we trust the Catholics?' Mackay asked. 'Suarez was the only one amongst us who did the Pope deal. I never did like him that much but you have to trust at this level, huh?'

Mackay behaved and spoke as if he had been born and bred in New York, but it was well known that he had Jewish roots and his listeners expected this to colour his attitude towards Catholicism.

'Thank you, John. Has anyone anything to add to this? I mean we have been together for a very long time. How could this have escaped our notice?'

Doug James had sat and watched proceedings until Mackay had voiced his opinion. Doug, having undertaken some of the most dangerous assignments over the time, most of which required expert knowledge of espionage methods, viewed Mackay with disdain. For a split second he could see himself pouncing and slitting his throat with the carefully concealed miniature Bowie knife he always had about his person.

'If I may add something to this before Luis' reputation is besmirched any more... Luis and me, we did some joints. Shared some terrific broads. He was good at what he did and I got on with mine. He taught me a lot ... not just my Spanish. We are so encased in ourselves here in the US of A. He had folk back in his native Spain and took me amongst them. Good people. People I trusted. What do I tell them now? What do I tell them about their kin being found with his cojones down his throat? These are people I admire.'

Doug James angrily scanned the room for reactions, but no-one met his eyes. He looked back at John Mackay.

'So, John, you see now why I haven't a lot of time for you. Bigots don't belong in my company, huh?'

'Doug, I take your point about my bad feelings on all of this and, yes, I have a particular point of view, but are

125

you not just opening up some debate about whom you can trust? Do you trust any of the rest of us?'

Doug James looked hard at Mackay. 'What are you getting at?'

'I mean, do you think any of us were involved in taking out Luis Suarez?'

Doug James sat for a moment staring at the back of his hands. Hands that had seen rough work on the oil-rigs and, since then, had been used to kill various 'enemies of the West'.

Without looking up he said, 'This whole business stinks of something I no longer want to be involved in. I have had my fill of double-talk, double-crosses, double-dealing and double agents. Where the hell has it all got us? I'm too old for all of this. The whole thing is no longer worth jack shit. Gonna go back to down to Alberquerque. There's a good woman waiting for me there and this man is gonna settle down for however long I got left in this world.'

Bill Collins was about to say something but John Mackay interjected quickly.

'So now the going is getting tough you want to dip outta sight, huh? But haven't you some explaining to do anyway?'

Doug looked up. 'What's this then? Explain what?'

Bill Collins was uneasy at the way the conversation was turning and wanted to change the subject.

'Now let's leave it at that, John. No need to uncover old wounds. Let's...'

But Doug James wasn't having any of it. 'Spit it out, John. What the hell are you insinuating here?'

Mackay was looking at Bill Collins for support but his boss refused to meet his gaze.

'OK. Why am I making a question out of all of this? Whatever your operatives did when they were involved in your many schemes, and however noble your intentions, we never found our way to Stray Dog. How was this?'

Doug James looked both Bill Collins and John Mackay in the eye. 'What is all this? You know why I was there and so did they. It was cat and mouse the entire time, endless back alleys leading into mazes where no-one could find each other, let alone Stray Dog. If something made sense I would report back but even before you received it the classification would have changed and the information no longer made any sense at all. Something went seriously wrong. I can't describe it other than believing it to be the ultimate use of psychological warfare. We knew there would be attacks on us bordering on brainwashing but how do you compute something when you don't even know if your thoughts are your own? It's pretty scary when someone you have been having a very intelligent conversation with turns up again an hour later, looks straight through you and doesn't remember a damned thing. I thought at first it was simply stand-offishness, but when it happened again and again I knew I was in deep shit. You simply had to be there to understand what that meant. I'm lucky. My mind wasn't affected that much, thanks to Hans and his team of ghouls who always made sure I drank that special coffee, or whatever it was, before each trip, but some of those other poor suckers ended up in really bad ways. But there again, John, maybe you can't grasp something like that from behind your desk.'

Mackay finally took the bait offered him. 'You think just because I sit here at a desk my worth is less than your own, Doug? I think you would be found wanting trying to change places with me.'

Doug James scratched his chin. 'You know, you might be right there, John. I've never been much for pen pushing and my legs wouldn't fit under your dinky desk anyway.

127

Maybe I should put you in my pocket and take you out there on a field trip and see how you go, huh?'

John Mackay turned purple with rage but he was prevented hurling any further insults at Doug by Hans Muller's intervention.

'Gentlemen, this is not getting us anywhere. Please may I speak now?'

Bill Collins acknowledged the intervention with a nod of thanks.

'Yes, Hans, by all means. Please have your say.'

James and Mackay were still looking daggers at each other but both turned their attention to Muller as he cleared his throat.

'Gentlemen, I too feel saddened by the loss of Luis Suarez. He was a larger than life individual and a very good operative. A born killer but with a huge heart to go with it, which, I think can be said, is a little unusual in his trade. I have been listening to what Doug has said about the psychological warfare and must agree entirely with him. America has, of course, the upper hand in all other considerations – manpower, weaponry and technology – but we lag behind in our ability to access the voids necessary to compete with the Soviets. The German scientists, many of whom I know from working with them during the war, before they were taken to Russia, are all very adept, as are we, in exploring on all possibilities when dealing with phenomena. Unfortunately, we do not possess anything like their Stray Dog. If we did we would, without doubt, be the masters at last. Now the news of Stray Dog's having a grandson, who has similar ability, has raised the stakes. How I would like to have this boy for experimentation.'

'It appears others want him too,' observed Collins, 'apart from the Soviets, ourselves and probably Great Britain. Now this business with Luis suggests even the Vatican has designs on the boy. Could there be any others? I am looking specifically at the Russian Orthodox Church. They have needed something to prop them up for years, especially since the revolution forced them to deal with a State run by atheists.'

'I do not think anything can be ruled out. Wherever there are scientists, and that is the world over, there will be some form of experimentation on similar lines. For example, let us not forget China and Korea.' Hans Muller delivered this in an icy tone.

'Our remit is to find this boy and try to ensnare him before the others do. Luis had difficulty in doing this by himself so maybe we should send two operatives?' Bill Collins received a nod from both Mackay and Muller, who were very pleased that such action was being urgently considered.

Doug James, however, did not share their enthusiasm for such a venture.

'I have a little warning for you all. I needn't have revealed this, as the only other person who knows of it is now dead.' He paused waiting for that point to sink in, then continued. 'I had a telephone conversation with Luis shortly after his encounter with the boy. He made no mention of Venditti, so his loyalty to him was obviously above my own. But he was not his usual self – far from it. He had been drinking heavily and a lot of what he told me was slurred and unintelligible. But I realised straight away he was scared of something. Something to do with his meeting with the boy, and for Luis to be that scared there had to be a heck of a good reason. He refused to elaborate when I asked him what the matter was. All he kept saying was, "She was with him." It spooked Luis enough to back off and that's the hardest part of it to understand. Luis always stood his ground, even if a hundred bulls were charging down on him. No, sirs, my feeling is you have no comprehension of how powerful this boy could be. I for one ain't interested and am outta here today.'

No-one spoke as Doug James lifted his frame from his seat and sauntered out of the meeting. John Mackay was itching to call him back but one look from Bill Collins dissuaded him.

As Doug passed Hans Muller he gave him a sly wink; as he approached the other four operatives he held out his hand, which was met with a firm handshake by each of them. Bill Collins took this opportunity to scrutinise them all whilst they were saying their goodbyes to their long time partner.

Dave Little, now a forty-five-year-old, a fellow American who had basically kept himself to himself, was, like the rest, divorced. The relationship had foundered as a result of the strict régime demanded by a secretive occupation. He had always backed up Bill Turner from Montreal, a really dominant figure assisted by his six-foot-two muscular frame that belied his fifty-two years of age. He kept much of his past from those who enquired, but Bill Collins had befriended him at a special Congress meeting a long time ago and knew this son of a Frenchman had changed his name from Tournier and had distant relatives in Louisiana whom he visited regularly. This was cajun country and Bill Collins sensed he was proud of the people and his roots. Ordinarily, they were the perfect pair to consider for this assignment.

Harry Swenson was another matter altogether. Bill had never got to the bottom of this man's wish to be completely alone on his assignments. This condition had been respected most of the time and Harry had performed wonders, but whenever he was paired up tensions caused a real problem and on more than one occasion it had resulted in a mission being aborted. Harry had folks back in Sweden, but the tracking team always reported that he made no contact.

Klaus Zimmermann was the ultimate enigma. He had never divulged where he came from, but had balanced this reticence with complete obedience. All anyone could establish was that he had been in an orphanage from about five years of age, before his demeanour caught the attention of one of the representatives, who passed on the relevant details. The only information available was that he was an evacuee from a European country – possibly Switzerland or, more likely, Austria.

In the pit of his stomach Bill Collins felt a pain, but ignored it. He had thought before this meeting that he had all the answers, but now he had no clear idea of what situation he was presiding over. Doug James had really shown up as a renegade, deserting when he was needed the most. Collins considered his own position. He was aware of the financing of this whole deal and what the main players required for their input of hard cash. But he sensed that not all of them were pulling in the same direction any more. He thought he had known Doug, at least, and that he could trust Monsignor Venditti, but the situation was changing and Bill Collins's faith in those around him was diminishing. He suddenly felt a seizure approaching and reached into his pocket for a flip top pillbox, which he opened and dropped a pill into his mouth, swallowing with some difficulty as his throat had constricted. He reached forward, grabbed a glass of water and gulped it down. He coughed and spluttered, which brought him out of his reverie and, as he regained his composure, he found himself facing Hans Muller who, like the others, had moved forward in case he required assistance.

'You've gone deathly white. Are you all right Bill?'

Then Collins realised that John Mackay was beside him holding his arm.

'Thought you were about to keel over, Bill.'

131

'It's OK. The medication will kick in soon. It's my own fault. I should have taken it a while ago. I keep forgetting, now the dosage has been increased, I have to take them more regularly. Please, not a whisper of this to Martha. She wants me to pack it all in. Retirement. Gee! Sounds like a good idea but not just yet, huh?'

Relieved smiles broke out on one or two faces at this retort. Even though he had a debilitating condition he countered this most of the time with a steely determination and his views and decision making sometimes clashed with his strict religious beliefs, making him hard to figure out. John Mackay was about the closest to seeing the true Bill Collins and wasn't convinced by his boss making light of his condition. Martha had got to him far more than he was letting on, Mackay considered, and he could foresee this special squad being broken up and his own position becoming untenable. As long as Bill Collins remained at the head of things John Mackay was assured of his lofty position, but he wasn't deluded; he was able to see he had detractors, who were waiting for him to fall from a great height, especially those who knew what he got up to in his private life, something which Bill Collins had managed to hush up over and over again. Everyone knew John Mackay was a target for a set up, and thus a severe security risk. But this is where Bill Collins was as ruthless as the next psychopath, ordering anyone involved in the private affairs of John Mackay to be assassinated if there were the slightest hint of a security leak. Mackay was well aware of this and had curbed his appetite a great deal. That was until he had drunk enough – then anything in front of him was fair game.

Mackay came out of his thoughts to find Bill Collins eyeing him curiously. Not for a long time had John Mackay felt this uncomfortable. There was a look in Collins' eye that he couldn't make out.

Bill smiled at Mackay but his eyes betrayed him; his usual warmth had evaporated, to be replaced by something more sinister.

Collins addressed the gathering. 'I think that will conclude our affairs for today. Hans, if you would stay for a moment longer I have a few more questions for you.'

The rest made their way out of the room, except John Mackay who was used to the privilege of being in on such conversations. But not this time. Collins asked him to leave. Mackay could not conceal his dismay at such treatment as he slunk out after the others.

Hans Muller watched him leave, then looked inquiringly back at Bill.

'I know, Hans. I know what you are thinking. Has he done something to make me believe he is no longer trusted at this level? The simple answer is, I no longer know after that little outburst just now. And there have been some other misgivings of late to add to the long line already. He's been a good servant to me and I owe him much. But I think the tally is pretty even. Just something ... call it instinct or whatever ... I really do hope I'm wrong.'

Bill Collins did not need to elaborate any further as Hans was already nodding his understanding.

'So what is it you require of me, Bill?'

Collins thought for a moment. 'I still can't believe how this has gone wrong. We are going to miss Luis more than the others can appreciate. He seemed to be the one operative who might be able to cope with this phenomenon, but we have definitely been proved wrong on that score. What are we dealing with here, Hans?'

Hans Muller scratched the back of his balding head. Now well into his seventies, his advancing years had caused him to be less active physically, but his mind was as sharp as ever.

'It is still an unknown phenomenon. From all my past experience I have a good idea of the strength of the Russian we call Stray Dog. But this other entity, the boy, is yet to show us his total strength. As you know well from my experiments I have the notion we are practically at the same stage of discovery as the Soviets and that the tying in of psyche with other phenomena can produce a wall surrounding us that is virtually impenetrable. The Russians have managed to include the natural strength of Stray Dog in their experimentation, which is the reason we have so much difficulty penetrating their defences. But if we were able somehow to persuade this boy to help in our experiments I am certain this would assist us sufficiently to be at least a match for the Soviets, and my instinct tells me it would be a near certainty that the United States would end up the stronger in this field.'

'Now that would be good news. We ought to be the main superpower with all our wealth and resources. Capitalism should always be able to defeat Communism.'

Muller nodded. 'If Hitler had not gone to war with the Soviets what a different kind of world we might have had, don't you think?'

Collins winced. 'Now that doesn't bear thinking about, but I suppose it would have meant you and your buddies would still be in your homes with your families around you. Do you miss your homeland after all this time?'

Hans Muller shook his head sadly. 'It is not the country I grew up in. It has been despoiled by invasion and by all the terrible things attributed to Hitler, Goebels and the rest. No, I do not think I would ever wish to go back there again.'

There was another pause as Bill Collins again thought about the situation.

'What can we do then that might give us a chance of approaching this kid without setting off the alarm? We will obviously need to kidnap him, do you think, to bring him back?

'I agree, I do not think this boy will come willingly.'

Bill Collins sat back in his chair. 'Hans, who would you send to get this boy?'

'Let me have a couple of days more to experiment on each of the four left. We have developed something, which is only in its infancy at the moment, but could be the answer to blocking the mental waves spread by the surges in the boy. The disadvantages we have discovered though are that this blocking provokes imbalances in the phenomena, which can lead to uncertain reactions and unfavourable results.'

Bill Collins looked questioningly at the professor.

'Already three of our patients have ended up with severe mental conditions as a result of the experiments. A fourth under examination withstood what I would consider to be the strength of the boy, but this only lasted for four hours; then his head began to swell to enormous proportions. We tried everything but could not stop the swelling. His head exploded.'

'Sweet Jesus!' Bill Collins's face had gone grey. 'So what are our chances?'

Hans Muller shrugged. 'I wish I knew for certain. I really do.'

15

Monsignor Luigi Venditti sat calmly in his seat facing the Papal Commission in all its episcopal pomp and ceremony. Everyone attached to this delegation was supposed to be a model of piety, a necessary qualification, as the recommendations made by this able body were taken very seriously and acted upon.

Cardinal Medi had been having muttered conversations with the other members and looked across at Venditti. 'All we are concerned with at the moment is that His Holiness is not dragged into this situation of your making. Is that clear?'

The expression on Venditti's face did not alter and he remained in a calm state. He nodded slowly but remained silent.

Medi appeared a little irritated and repeated, 'Monsignor, you have a duty to answer this commission as to the dangers presented to all here, and especially the head of the church, His Holiness. We have managed to keep secrets for hundreds of years, but because of this situation we are facing the possibility of having to answer some very awkward questions, especially in political circles. Our whole system of faith will be questioned if anything else leaks out. What were you thinking of, employing that rough-necked barbarian on such a delicate mission?'

Venditti clasped his hands together but remained silent. Then, just as the cardinal was about to speak again, he put up his hand to stop him. There was steeliness in his eyes and the tone of his voice was icy.

'Cardinal Medi and my other esteemed brothers, you must understand one thing: our faith was always going to be challenged at some point but we knew not when. That time is now upon us, unfortunately. The power structure I always imagined as possible has arrived and manifested itself in the boy. Contrary to your opinion of him, Luis Alvarez Suarez was a highly capable and highly tuned individual in all the arts, especially as a psychic medium. He actually saw what the boy had around him and that was the reason I alerted you all.'

Medi threw up his hands in a gesture of despair. 'God help us all. I do not understand fully what you are describing here. Is the boy from the devil?'

A slight smile broke out on Venditti's face.

'I am sorry, brother. I forgot for a moment that not all here believe in such phenomena. But be assured they are there and this talk of the devil might have been pertinent five hundred years ago but not in this present day and age. We may pretend that all is well as long as we continue down the path we are taught to tread and hide away from anything that opposes our beliefs. But what if we are wrong? What would we face if the path we have trodden and taken so many other souls upon is not, in fact, the true way?'

This statement caused exactly the reaction expected and Venditti sat perfectly still as the Papal gathering vented its spleen. They might declare him an heretic but the monsignor was unrepentant.

'You asked me here to give my account. That I have given and I pray to God for forgiveness if any of it has been considered blasphemous, but I speak as I find in this matter and my final word is a warning to you all, even His Holiness. The boy has something about him that I believe is pure. What emanates is a truth. For many years I have personally been interested in such phenomena and quietly have experimented in my own fashion.'

This again brought great gasps from the members of the commission.

Venditti continued, 'Yes, I knew you would be greatly angered and upset by such revelations, but I am called here to speak as before God, and, therefore, my confessions are for him alone to judge. I realise that my sins are great and you as a commission have the right to do with me as you please. What will be will be – and I have no more to add.'

16

1953 was a long year in the life of Aleksei Vasiliy Rudikov. The demise of Stalin had left the Soviet Union unsure as to what the future held for it. But Aleksei was not particularly interested in the politics of such a change, only of how it changed his own position. His mind began to wander further and further away from the pressures of the daily grind and Professor Strekalovsky, in whom he noticed increasing signs of fatigue. Aleksei was now in his mid-forties but he still cherished his youthful longing for his sweetheart, Elena. He tried not to dwell on the fact that it was now over twenty-five years since he had last set eyes on her. The thought that if she were still alive they might no longer recognise each other made his heart sink. But Aleksei Rudikov promised himself one thing: One day he would find his dear Elena.

Aleksei's reverie was disturbed by a commotion in an adjoining room – what sounded like the scraping of chairs. Then the door to the laboratory burst open and a stout gentleman stood facing a shocked Professor Strekalovsky. The professor began to mumble but his words were halted by the appearance of Colonel Guznischev, looking slightly bewildered. Aleksei remained imperturbable. When the stout gentleman saw him his face broke into a smile.

'Tovaritch … Lyosha, my good friend. It has been so long, but I am here now!'

Aleksei stood up as the figure moved forward and hugged him tightly. Then he stepped back, appraising Aleksei.

'You have put a little weight on, my friend, since I saw you last, but that is peacetime for you!'

The figure then spun around to face Colonel Guznischev.

'Colonel, you must realise I am not your former master. I move slightly faster than he, so you must keep up, yes?'

He laughed but Colonel Guznischev did not share his mirth. He looked increasingly bewildered and at a loss for words.

Professor Strekalovsky then found his voice. 'It is a great honour for me to meet you at last. I hope to be able to continue to assist the Soviet Republic with research into all possibilities.'

Nikita Khrushchev merely nodded; then turned his attention back to Aleksei.

'I hope he has been treating you well, Lyosha!' Khrushchev then looked back at the colonel who stood to attention. 'Colonel, I hope you have been looking after my friend, comrade Aleksei. But you seem puzzled by all of this? Aleksei Vasiliy Rudikov might just be a name to you, someone you were instructed to befriend to protect Soviet interests, yes? But I know him from The Great Patriotic War. As you will both know, I moved about – or was moved about, should I say?' Khrushchev let out a short chortle and continued. 'I had to give up Kiev. Then they sent me to Stalingrad as a political commissar. What a hell-hole! Then Kursk and Kiev again – liberation and a wonderful feeling. But all of this would not have been so if this man here had decided not to do his duty. Myself, I was always aware that he had reasons to disappear and never be seen again. But he came back each time and, for me, in the nick of time. He would never have told you because that is his way, but I will tell you anyway. A German sniper had me in his sights at the same time as Aleksei Rudikov had him in his. Simultaneously, they both fired but my friend here must have been a fraction sooner

140

for the bullet meant for me merely grazed my shoulder. It took me a while to discover how I had escaped death and that was only because Oleg was with him. If he had not been I would never have known who saved my life. How many other lives he saved we will never know because he will certainly never divulge such information. Is that not so, Aleksei Vasiliy?'

In answer, Aleksei looked away, then back again, still with a smile of greeting on his face.

'And what of this woman you kept running off to find. Did you ever find her?'

At this Aleksei's expression changed and he looked down.

'I take it that is a "no" then, comrade. And my predecessor? He never helped you in that direction? Of course, I don't have to wait for an answer there. It would not have been in his nature to give such assistance, even to one such as you whose own grandfather saved his precious skin – but I am different. I will make enquiries, but I cannot promise anything. We still live in dark times, my friend, and every shadow still hides a lurking assassin. Her name?'

'Elena. Elena Zvadsky. She was last heard of at Stalingrad, then nothing. Some say she was killed there.'

Aleksei felt at last some hope looking into the eyes of Nikita Khrushchev, so different from the stark, unfeeling stare of Joseph Stalin. Khrushchev was another personality altogether. There was a definite light of change emanating from this man and his enthusiastic demeanour was contagious, although Aleksei could imagine how a lot of the other party members would find his manner offensive compared with Stalin's. They would not be used to such a display of positive thinking. The old guard would certainly be waiting for Khrushchev to fall by his mistakes.

Khrushchev gave Aleksei another bear hug and turned

141

to go, but Aleksei had another request. Colonel Guznischev had already prepared the way by opening the door and standing outside but he re-entered the room on hearing Aleksei speak, staring gravely at him and shaking his head.

'There is something else I have been told – that Elena gave birth to a daughter. Our daughter. But she gave her away to be taken to Britain where she was apparently adopted. She has since married and given birth to boy. My grandson.'

Khrushchev turned to Colonel Guznischev and asked, 'What further do we know of this? Has anyone been able to find them?'

The colonel looked embarrassed.

'I understand we have been watching them but your predecessor forbade any information to be passed on to us.'

Nikita Khrushchev eyed Colonel Guznischev with curiosity, then turned and slapped Aleksei on the back.

'I will make it my business to discover what we know and have this passed to the colonel here. I intend to travel abroad to such places in the West to broaden my horizons and, at the same time, give the world a better idea of how far forward we are moving. The Soviet Republic will never exist without at least some useful contact with the capitalist pigs. I am certain their views on a communist state are taken from a limited knowledge of how it all works. They know only one way to think. But I had better brush up on my manners, so I am told, or I will be accused of starting another Great Patriotic War!'

At that the First Secretary of the Soviet Republic chortled again and left the room, followed by the colonel who glanced ruefully back at Aleksei.

The professor had remained silent all through the exchanges, feeling ignored. In his capacity as the leading light in the affairs of the paranormal he was used to

142

more discussion about the results of his experiments, but he had been given the first taste of a different style of leadership, one that no longer saw Strekalovsky's work as a top priority. Aleksei was thinking along the same lines and praying that he would be relieved of the tedium of working with the professor and perhaps even allowed to pursue again life's one goal: to find the woman he loved.

He recalled when Colonel Guznischev had arrived one morning and interrupted yet another meaningless session in the laboratory. The colonel had looked uncomfortable as he began to speak and Aleksei had feared the worst.

'I have now been brought up to date with matters concerning your daughter and grandson. Apparently, the husband, James Metthewson, suddenly left the family home in 1950 and disappeared. He had been beating her before he left. Your daughter and grandson have since been looked after by her parents and appear to be in good health. As we have an interest in this we will continue to monitor them closely.'

Aleksei sighed deeply. 'So do we know why this son-of-a-whore was beating my daughter and where he went?'

'Someone told him that he had married a Russian refugee which angered him greatly. For some reason, he hated communists – probably something to do with the war.'

'And?'

'He will never strike your daughter again, comrade. This news should have been presented to you a long time ago, but Stalin gave orders you were not to be informed because he knew you would try to escape.'

Aleksei stared blankly at the colonel as he turned to go. Professor Strekalovsky knew it would have been pointless to pursue anything further that day and had left Aleksei to himself.

Despite his devotion to Elena, Aleksei was no monk.

He was permitted sexual gratification through carefully selected and briefed prostitutes. These meant nothing to him emotionally until Nataliya entered his life. She had captivated him as soon as she had arrived that day in 1954. With her bright green eyes, light brown hair and warm personality she had cheered Aleksei up immensely, so much so that he felt a new lease of life. He would look forward to her visits with such longing that he always had a present for her as a special surprise. For Professor Strekalovsky and Colonel Guznischev it was a relief to see him so preoccupied. At least Aleksei's thoughts would not stray whilst this lady presented herself to him. For some reason he could not explain he trusted her from their first meeting and, over time, she became a confidante. But one dark day in March 1955 he received the terrible news that Nataliya had been found stabbed to death. The official line was that she had been strangled and cut to pieces by a jealous boyfriend. Aleksei had not accepted this version of events, sensing that the truth was more sinister and involved someone who had already crossed him over Elena. Aleksei had found Nataliya to be fairly distant on the last couple of occasions she had been with him. He had asked her what troubled her but she refused to say. Now he sensed that she had paid the price for remaining faithful to him and refusing to reveal their conversations to a certain person. Aleksei believed that person to be Colonel Maksim Surnyaev.

17

Aleksei waited for further news of his daughter and grandson, but in vain.

He was, however, given other information concerning his immediate family. He learned that his mother had been taken ill and died in 1956 and that his father's death had followed during 1958. Shortly after this his elder brother, Yuriy, had disappeared, apparently with the widow of a best friend who had been tried and executed for some reason or other. Aleksei missed his mother but found it hard to feel any compassion for the passing of his father as the lack of any real contact for so many years had rendered them almost strangers. Also, lurking in the back of his mind was a suspicion that his father had known all along of the Zvadskys' decision to make a break for it but had failed to alert Aleksei. This was mainly why he had cut off all contact with his parents for years, only returning briefly for a month or two after the war. Aleksei had found relations so strained then he had left again, this time for good. Shortly afterwards, he found himself arrested for desertion. He knew his family and friends would be safe as long as he co-operated, and this he had done for many years. But of late he had noticed that his powers appeared to be diminishing. Professor Strekalovsky had also observed the phenomenon slowly reducing and had begun to worry.

The professor had also lost a tremendous amount of heart in the previous nine years since the demise of Stalin. He was now approaching his mid-seventies and his increased frailty was obvious to anyone who observed him closely enough. He was prone to the odd mistake which might not have been noticed by anyone outside the experiments but Aleksei had been with him long enough to note the downturn in the professor's ability. Aleksei had grown quite fond of the old man and they frequently shared confidences in whispers.

'I have something I must tell you, my good friend Aleksei, while I still have a mind active enough to remember what I am saying.' The professor grinned seeing the curious look on Aleksei's face. 'I have for a long time believed something I am unfortunately unable to prove, one way or the other, but my instinct tells me it is so. The reason you are here is not so much for experimentation – your mere presence is sufficient.'

'I do not understand. What are you saying?'

'Listen carefully, Aleksei. There is something around us that is impenetrable. Like a large wall built of psychic energy. We are behind that wall and that is why no-one outside knows anything about us.'

Aleksei looked stunned at first, then his expression slowly changed and a grin appeared on his face.

'I think I understand what you are saying. And the whole politburo is also behind it? Very crafty!'

'Yes, my friend, and I think this is the reason why they have wanted you simply to be here in this one place for so long, under the guise of experimentation. I think they have always known my experiments were for nothing and this is the reason they appeared so patient and gave us so much time. So you just went through the motions – and so did I.'

'You could tell that? That I was just playing along with you? Was I that obvious?'

'Of course, and at first I was seriously annoyed with you. I should have reported the fact to the politburo but something held me back ... maybe the memory of your dear grandfather, Stanislav. Whatever it was I am glad I went along with you. As I became tired I found our relationship a useful place to rest in. Do you understand that?'

Aleksei felt overwhelmed but kept his composure.

'Yes, I understand that fully. I was doing exactly the same. You are beginning to amaze me, and I am not easily amazed!'

'If I am not aware of that fact I am not aware of anything, but they have a problem, I think.'

'Problem?'

Professor Strekalovsky wandered over to the computer system, grabbed some papers and waved them at Aleksei.

'Here in this data is their problem, I think. For some time I have noticed your psychic energy fields deteriorating. You have felt that yourself, yes?'

Aleksei nodded. 'You are as wily as an old fox. I should always have kept my guard up when dealing with your experiments. But I can't deny that I feel less strong and, yes, it has been happening over a period of time. Perhaps more than a year.'

'There is something else. Some time ago someone told me something in all confidence and I swore to tell no-one else. Not even you, Aleksei. But I think I have to make you an exception to that oath. This friend, another professor, but in a different department, told me his experiments coincided in some way with our own. He believed that there was yet another department, separate from ours, who were conducting experiments on mind unification. Just as Siamese twins are attached, they were at that time attempting to join psyches together to construct an even more formidable weapon than any tank, bomb or missile built by man. My personal opinion is that what they were attempting was impossible and that this is why you are still here. I am convinced they would have disposed of us if they had been successful. You because you are still regarded as a dissident and me because I know too much about it!'

'I am still here because this other experiment has failed?' Aleksei was feeling agitated.

'Initially it was intended to be a back-up to your power but then the fools began to believe they had found a way of usurping your power and that the psychic wall could be formed without you. Fortunately for us it did not transpire and those who gave the impression they could succeed with this notion are now on a train to Siberia, or whatever outpost has been designated their final destination.'

Aleksei looked a little confused. 'So, if they realise I am losing power why have they not responded?'

'Because, Aleksei, I have not told them!'

'But why? They will find out eventually, and you will be in serious trouble.'

Professor Strekalovsky shook his head. 'I am not troubled by this any more, Aleksei. You spoke of Stalin being superstitious and I think the peasant in Khrushchev makes him also superstitious. It appears to be a fact of life that only the intellectuals of this world do not subscribe to such spiritual awakenings. Perhaps such higher education is not so important after all. I am only a poor scientist who believed in a system that derives from such thinking, but no more. I personally believe you have been chosen for a purpose, as have many in the past. Charisma is defined as having divinely conferred power or talent and a capacity to inspire followers with devotion and enthusiasm. You are a charismatic soul. Think back on Genghis Khan and his ability to unite the wild Mongol tribes into the most efficient and deadly army the world has ever witnessed, or the sultan Saladin who united the Arab world and won back Jerusalem from the Western knights; even our own Grigory Rasputin with his protection of the Romanov dynasty. Modern day premiers such as Khrushchev and Kennedy may be at opposite ends of the spectrum but are charismatic leaders all the same. I believe some are here to lead others, but something else is here to challenge that purpose. There are forces at odds with each other and things going on far beyond our knowledge and comprehension. I mean, how much of our own minds can we really call our own? With such forces in play who is ultimately controlling whom and where does it all end? I like to believe you and I have sufficient of our own minds to be able to reason soundly, but what of so many others who behave in an inhumane manner? Are they controlled by those forces without even knowing it? It is a frightening thought. You are blessed with something to counteract their power; that is my belief. We are of sound minds and can still imagine why, can we not? Something is around you, Aleksei, for the good of all in this mad world of ours. If it is the souls of the departed that give you the power you possess, I can understand why. Imagine the millions from our motherland uniting in such a manner, all with one single purpose. Anything might become possible, even dismantling this wall between East and West. That is definitely something to think on. It makes a great deal of sense to someone who has had to live night and day with it all.'

'But what does this mean in terms of my power diminishing?'

Professor Strekalovsky thought for a moment then said, 'Perhaps your time is coming to an end. I am not talking about your death, but whatever task you were meant to accomplish could be passing to someone else. As you inherited from Stanislav, your grandfather, so maybe your grandson will also inherit the gift. Could it be it is passing to him as we speak?'

Aleksei had never considered this seriously before. What the professor had said made sense to him, but he could not help feeling desolate at being unable to explain matters to his grandson, in the same way as Stanislav had done to himself.

The professor watched him closely. 'I am sorry to have brought that up so starkly, but it remains a possibility. I believe it to be the only answer and have already made plans for you, Aleksei Vasiliy.'

'What plans? I do not understand.'

'You have been a bird in a cage for too long, my friend. My intention has always been to find a way of opening the cage and releasing you.'

It took a few moments for this to sink in. 'How? And what about you? Will you be coming too?'

The professor slowly shook his head. 'I am too old and washed up for such heroism. But you have a world to discover and the possibility of joining your family at last.'

Aleksei began to protest but Professor Strekalovsky held up a hand to quieten him.

'You must remember where we are comrade. Sound travels and ears are wide open in this establishment. Please do not press me on this. It is my decision and I wish it to be so. My fate is my own concern. Please accept this.'

Aleksei's mind began to whirl with all that had been revealed and the actual possibility of freedom after so long made him feel excited. But his euphoria was mixed with concern for his friend and great sadness.

'Aleksei, my friend, never look back – only forward. It is very possible Nikita Khrushchev will lead us into another World War. He got away with invading Hungary by the skin of his teeth but the Cuban missile sites are another matter altogether. Provocation, provocation and more provocation. Insults thrown backwards and forwards. A wall now built in Berlin, keeping East from West. That is the physical wall that can be seen and reviled but what about the psychic walls we have talked of? Who actually has the expertise and knowledge apart from us? Has America discovered a way to protect its leadership? Has Mao Tse Tung developed it or have the Chinese had the ability all along for centuries? Who is really the strongest and would it make any difference if one decided to make a nuclear strike on another? I suppose we shall never know until some fool really does take it that far. God help us all!'

18

Rudy woke the following morning feeling absolutely drained. He remembered the words spoken by Liliya, still clear in his mind. 'I am a Russian,' he quietly said, still awed by the revelation. 'All my relatives come from there even my own mother.' Elena not Helen, Zvadsky not Fuller. Liliya said he would be known by his grandfather's Christian names, Aleksei Vasiliy, and have his surname and that of his grandmother, Elena. Aleksei Vasiliy Zvadsky-Rudikov. Liliya had told him that his grandmother, fearing capture, had passed her daughter, his mother, on to friends who had brought her to Britain; that his grandfather, Aleksei, had similar powers to those of his grandfather, Stanislav, before him. Rudy felt a distinct pride in his genetic line, and, even though he had no knowledge of Russia or what it really meant to be a Russian, he was elated, as if someone had opened a book of wonders and let him read all about the magic and mystery of places he had never known. He was reminded of something else though by the noises coming from downstairs. His mother was preparing his breakfast. Rudy had asked Liliya if he should tell his mother, but she had replied that some things were permitted for her to reveal and others not and she was not permitted to give an answer to that particular question.

'I am your guide, Rudy, but some decisions you will have to make for yourself, for that is how things are in the adult world you are entering. Your power is stable and I think you will make the right decisions as long as it remains so. But always remember your capacity and what can happen if you lose the stability – as you discovered yesterday in that encounter with the scarred one. He caught you off guard because you made the wrong decision. Please learn from that, for danger is lurking everywhere, but we are here and will assist if permitted to do so. I must say farewell, Aleksei Vasiliy. I will always be watching over you. *Da svi` daniya*.'

Helen knocked on his bedroom door and Rudy jumped, startled out of his recollections.

'OK, Mum. On my way down. Just need to splash my face and whatever.'

Helen sighed and descended the stairs. She had experienced a peculiar sense of foreboding when she had awoken that morning but put it down to mild depression.

A white-faced and dishevelled Rudy sauntered into the kitchen and sat down to his breakfast. His mother stared at his appearance but decided not to comment on it. She got up and started to clear away her own cup and plate, having already finished eating. Helen continued to clear the table and washed up in silence.

Rudy finished his last mouthful and sat looking over at his mother at the sink. She deserves to know at least something, he thought, but once I start where do I end? And what will she want to do about it? Will she want to visit Russia? Do *I* want to visit Russia?

'Mum, I had another visit last night.'

Rudy knew he had spoken the words but the utterance took him by surprise as he thought he had not decided yet whether to say anything. It seemed that somewhere the decision had been made for him!

Helen Metthewson continued to wash plates as if she had not heard Rudy, which further confused him.

'Did you hear what I said, Mum?'

Helen turned and wiped her hands on a towel. 'You haven't said anything yet. I thought you were in a mood so, as I am not feeling that great, I thought we could act like monks at prayer.'

Rudy stifled a laugh.

'But I did say...'

Then something about it made him hesitate. He was back to not knowing if he should say anything.

Helen, having wiped her hands, ventured over to the table and sat down.

'Rudy, you look awful. You had a very restless night and were moaning and jabbering. Is everything all right? Is it girl trouble? Have you broken up with your latest?'

Rudy shot his mother a look. 'Latest? Who says I have a girlfriend at the moment anyway?'

'Sorry, I didn't realise it was that sensitive a subject. So have you something to tell me or am I sitting here for nothing? I could be getting on with something else.' Helen had already made a fresh pot of tea and poured herself a cup, but Rudy shook his head when the pot was offered to him. Helen scrutinised her son as she sipped her tea.

Rudy looked down but could still feel her penetrating stare. He looked up and was about to speak when there was a sharp knock on the front door. It gave both mother and son a start – who could be calling so early? The paperboy had already delivered the newspaper and the postman had arrived soon after. The sharp rap was repeated, together with a ring on the doorbell. Helen got up and went out into the hall. Rudy could hear murmuring voices that got louder as the visitors were invited inside.

Helen entered the kitchen first and said, 'There is a policeman and another gentleman here wanting to ask you some questions about yesterday?' Rudy went deathly white.

The police constable and the other man had followed

154

Helen and she turned her attention to them as the man spoke.

'Well, Constable, is this the boy you saw yesterday?'

The gruff middle-aged constable had removed his helmet and was giving Rudy the once over.

'I can't be absolutely certain, but he very much resembles the lad I saw and spoke to.'

Helen intervened. 'What is this all about?'

The man had already identified himself to her as Graham Digby and the other as Police Constable Hardwick. 'There was a fight in the street. Walker Avenue, was it not Constable?'

Hardwick replied with a firm nod.

Helen Metthewson turned again to Rudy who looked down. She then addressed Digby.

'So what do you think this has to do with my son?'

'The fight involved several youths, some of whom were injured and have ended up in hospital. The constable here was about to take the name and address of one of the participants whom he believes to be your son, Rudy Metthewson. Is that correct Constable?'

Hardwick replied, 'Yes. I had reason to believe he was involved as he had injuries to the back of both his hands, which were heavily bruised and appeared to have been bleeding. But he made off when I was distracted by another outbreak of fighting.'

Digby looked across at Rudy sitting at the table. 'Well, son, is this correct? Were you the same lad who the constable approached at the scene?'

Helen intervened again. 'But the constable said he wasn't absolutely sure whether Rudy was the boy he spoke to there and I haven't noticed any injuries to his hands.' Then she turned back and said to her son. 'Show them your hands, Rudy.'

Rudy had put his hands under the table during the

questioning. He hesitated for a moment. 'Come on, son, show us your hands. Then we can sort all of this out.'

Rudy looked at his mother who was looking very disconcerted but her expression changed to one of relief as Rudy slowly revealed his hands from beneath the kitchen table. Neither had a mark on them, either on the front or back.

Constable Hardwick looked thoroughly confused. Digby examined Rudy's hands closely, only to confirm what he had seen from a distance – that they were both free of any injury.

'I don't understand, Constable. Are you absolutely certain the youth you saw had injuries to both hands?'

'I am. I asked him if he was all right and whether he needed treatment.'

Digby sighed. 'Then this can't be the boy you saw, can it?'

Helen asked, 'If you didn't manage to get my son's name and address, how is it that you found your way here in the first place?'

Graham Digby unbuttoned his overcoat and reached into his jacket pocket to produce a card bearing the title 'Security Services'. 'I was just about to come to that. The constable noticed a certain individual at the scene following the lad he had approached. He saw this individual chasing after the lad as he ran away. The pursuit took them through the shopping centre where the individual barged several members of the public out of his way. One of these members thought he recognised the lad being chased as your son, Rudy.'

'But this could not have been the case, as we have already established Rudy wasn't the boy running away from the constable.'

But Digby persisted. 'So, Rudy, where were you yesterday afternoon?'

Rudy looked at his mother as if waiting for her to speak for him but instead she asked the same question. 'Where were you? It can't do any harm saying where you were. Weren't you going to see Jimmy Anderson?'

'Yes, that's right. Jimmy will back me up on that. I was with him all afternoon.'

All Rudy had to do now was locate his friend and get their story right.

Helen nodded at him and then turned to Digby. 'Forgive me for asking, but why was it necessary for you to accompany the police? I mean, it seems to be a situation that they could handle by themselves without need of the security services, or is there something else you aren't telling us?'

Rudy's admiration for his mother grew.

Graham Digby seemed to diminish somewhat as he felt the awkwardness of answering Helen's question. He struggled to find an answer without revealing anything important.

'I mean, Mr Digby,' pursued Helen, 'the person who chased after the boy, whoever he was, is someone you must consider very suspicious, or even dangerous? Who actually is this person? Have we any need to be afraid? You realise if he is still trying to find this boy he might have managed to follow the scent you have left to our door.'

Rudy's innards began to churn again at the very thought. The statement was as pertinent as it was scary.

This rankled with Digby. 'I can assure you that that will never happen.'

'How can you be so sure?' Helen persisted.

He cleared his throat and looked at the constable, who was staring at the ceiling, thinking how much he would enjoy retirement.

'I am not at liberty to say any more but you can take

my word for it that this particular individual will never find his way to your doorstep or be any kind of threat to you or your son.'

'Have you arrested him then? Is that what you are saying?'

'No, Mrs Metthewson, I am not saying that. Look, I cannot answer any more questions. I think I have said enough already. I will say good day to you and thank you for your valuable time. Come on, Constable, let's go and compare notes.'

Constable Hardwick replaced his helmet firmly on his head and meekly followed the security agent out of the front door, which Helen closed quietly behind them.

'What was all that about, Rudy? Show me your hands again.'

Rudy slowly moved them from under the table again. Helen gasped at the sight of the bruised knuckles and the cuts on the back of his hands.

'How did you do that, Rudy? It was you there at that fight, wasn't it? And you who were chased by whoever that person was? Why? And how did you trick us all then with a show of perfectly clean uninjured hands?'

'Got another pair under the table, Mum!'

Rudy tried a grin to go with his boldness but his mother wasn't in the mood for joking.

'You have some explaining to do here. And you might have noticed I'm not in the mood for playing games. Out with it. I want to know exactly what this is all about.'

Rudy considered his position. He had to say something, but how much should he reveal?

'Mum, I'm sorry. I have wanted to share this with you for a long time but it never seemed the right time. I have been able to do such tricks for a while. And I got another visit from the girl last night. That's obviously what was happening when I was jabbering. In my dream she was telling me a lot.'

158

Helen Metthewson braced herself for what might be coming next. Did she really want to hear any of it? But before she could decide Rudy had begun to reveal his secrets.

19

Aleksei pondered much over what Professor Strekalovsky had said that day but nothing else was mentioned again for several weeks. Aleksei tried not to let his impatience show; he realised that to do so would be dangerous not only to him but, more importantly, to the professor. As the years had gone by it became not unusual for them to be seen together outside their closed quarters breathing the fresh air – or as much fresh air as Moscow would allow – and, as time went on, this extended to more social occasions involving all kinds of personalities. But always in their minds was the stark possibility that a slight mistake could bring the KGB breathing down their necks. At first both Aleksei and the professor were conspicuously followed but now there appeared to be real signs of relaxation and much of the time they enjoyed more freedom.

On the latest of these trips, to the shopping area in search of general items for the laboratory, the professor was strangely silent. His mood was sombre. Aleksei was about to say something when the professor turned to him.

'It is today, *tovaritch*. You move today.'

Aleksei stopped in his tracks. 'Today? But that is impossible. My belongings are not packed.'

'My friend, what would be the first sign of you no longer occupying your room? No, you must leave all behind and start afresh. I will be able to forestall them for a while. As you know well, their visits to us have been less frequent. I have also noticed the pattern of their visits and I believe we have a few days before they arrive again.'

'But what if you are wrong? What if they arrive tomorrow...?'

'Trust in my scientific acumen my friend. It might be tedious to some, the lengths I go to provide an answer to a question, but I am rarely found to be incorrect. So trust me on this one, Aleksei Vasiliy.' Professor Strekalovsky put a hand on Aleksei's shoulder and smiled. 'Be not fearful for me. You will need all your wits for yourself. Remember always: look forward, not back, and you will succeed.'

Suddenly a figure appeared out of the shadows and into the sunlight. The man was looking up and down the street. Aleksei observed the scene and noticed another person some distance behind them nodding towards them. The man who had joined them was casually dressed in a blue shirt and grey trousers with a thick brown jacket. His dark brown hair receded at the temple but was thick on top. He looked very fit, around thirty years of age.

'Quickly, in here!'

His arm shot out and he pointed to a doorway. All three entered the shop. The man closed the door behind them and bolted it.

'You were not followed this time. A very good omen to begin with. My name is Dmitriy and I will take you to the others who will be assisting you to the border. Time is of the essence and we must move quickly, do you understand?'

Aleksei was bewildered; he had not expected the departure to be so sudden. It meant a rapid farewell to the professor. He had things he wanted to say to him that he had bottled up for years but he was struck dumb at the enormity of the situation. The professor sensed his distress.

'I will be all right, Aleksei. You must go now. Everything has been arranged and you are with best people. Farewell, my good friend.'

161

Aleksei turned with tears streaming down his face. He put both his hands out and the professor came in to give him a bear hug and whispered into Aleksei's ear, 'May you find what you are looking for, my friend, and please ask your grandson to remember us all here. I truly believe he will be able to assist in breaking down the barriers which surround us all.'

Aleksei stood back and wiped his face with his sleeve, then turned away and followed Dmitriy. Once he was out of sight the professor crumpled and tears filled his own eyes.

Dmitriy moved swiftly through the maze of streets with Aleksei close behind. Aleksei had been keeping himself in good shape for a while now with a lot of exercise but his advancing years made it difficult to maintain the pace. He was about to call out for a breather when Dmitriy stopped by an old building that appeared to have been long disused. After a moment surveying all about him Dmitriy motioned Aleksei to follow him into the building. As they approached the door it opened and they rushed through as if being chased by a pack of wild dogs. The door then closed and Aleksei could make out the outline of a figure in the gloom. The place was damp and stank of the putrid water which lay in puddles on the floor. The figure moved closer and held out a hand.

'Welcome to our little group, Aleksei Vasiliy Rudikov!'

The voice was that of a female and as the figure approached he made out the pretty face and blue eyes of a diminutive and slightly built girl with straggly shoulder-length hair. She could only have been in her late teens.

'I am Irina.'

Dmitriy hissed, 'Introductions over. We must make haste. I am still not certain whether we are being followed.'

Irina looked at Aleksei and raised her eyebrows. He thought she resembled someone he had known. Then they were off, closely following Dmitriy. The building must have been a factory or at least a warehouse before dereliction had set in. Aleksei was amazed at the size of it. Their entrance must have been through an office block as the area they were running into now was as large as an aircraft hangar. At the far end he noticed a vehicle, which looked as if it had been converted from an army truck. Its engine was ticking over. As they approached the driver rolled his window down.

'What kept you? We must be gone immediately. Stepan will not wait for ever.'

Dmitriy cursed under his breath. Again Irina raised her eyebrows at Aleksei and whispered, 'Some men are born to and some are not.'

Aleksei looked back questioningly.

'To be heroes,' she explained.

Aleksei grinned.

Dmitriy opened the back of the truck and motioned for Aleksei to get in.

'If we are stopped make no sound whatever happens.'

Aleksei made himself as comfortable as possible in the dark space, most of which was taken up by various household effects. It looked to him as if the journey had a dual purpose: His escape and a house move! Aleksei crouched down among the furniture.

The vehicle eventually stopped to give Aleksei a chance to eat and stretch his legs. Dmitriy sensed that he might have offended Aleksei back at the warehouse earlier and was more polite. He explained they had to keep moving, for the distance to be covered was great. They were expected at the first safe house just the other side of Minsk.

'Minsk? Then where? Poland?' Aleksei thought he knew their final destination. 'Then Berlin?'

Dmitriy smiled grimly and nodded. 'Yes. It is a long

way but we have arranged for rest at safe places on the way. Everything has been meticulously planned. We are waiting for Stepan to arrive and he will guide us to the first stop-over.'

The journey seemed like a lifetime to Aleksei. Although the company of Dimitriy and Irina had been good and each time they found a place to stay he felt warm and in safe hands, Aleksei secretly wished they did not have to stop over so often as he was impatient to find freedom. But he realised that over such a distance there was a need to be cautious and not attract attention. As they passed through checkpoints Aleksei had his heart in his mouth, but they encountered no problems.

The last part of the journey was the longest stretch and Aleksei was relieved when the truck eventually stopped. He groaned quietly as he stretched, familiarising himself with the surroundings. Suddenly a light was shone in his eyes.

'*Kak de 'la, tovaritch*, Aleksei my friend.'

Aleksei recognised the voice but as the light was being shone in his face initially he could not see the features of the man who had spoken. He raised himself, climbed out of the confined space and stood a little unsteadily. The journey had taken its toll on his body. Facing the man who had spoken, Aleksei let out a gasp.

'My friend, you are white as a ghost!'

Aleksei spluttered, 'No, it is you who are the ghost, surely.'

The man laughed. 'No, Aleksei Vasiliy, I am no ghost. It is I. Still flesh and bone. Well, maybe too much flesh for the bone. Welcome, comrade, for we have waited so long to give you what you have always deserved. I am so pleased to see you again.'

'But, Oleg, they all told me you had died at Stalingrad.'

It was his old sniping partner.

164

'Aleksei, my dear friend, much is not what it seems. A lot of people died then and a lot since, but I have discovered that I am not the only one who survived when official records had put me in the ground.'

'Why? It makes no sense.'

'It makes every sense, Aleksei, my good friend. These morons are now trying to make some kind of political deal with the former enemy. We, and many more, are an embarrassment to them. Snipers from that time are seen as the lowest of the low in some political circles.'

'Are you saying we were always going to be the losers, no matter how successful we were. It was always political?'

'It would appear so. I left my papers on a comrade and disappeared quickly as I felt the icy wind of the Bolshevik machine slowly creeping up on us. Incarceration was not my idea of reward for our efforts. I came to warn you, but you had disappeared again. Pity, as you have suffered what I deserved, for I was a real deserter.'

'No, Oleg, that is not the way of it. You were doing what you needed to do for survival. I disappeared at times to try and locate Elena, which was technically a desertion each time. But that swine, Surnyaev – he had it in for me and managed to convince others I wasn't coming back, so they found and arrested me.'

'Yes, I know. I heard this from others. It has taken me a while to arrange things for your escape but you are here at last.'

Oleg moved forward and both men hugged each other.

'And what of Elena? Did you hear anything more about her?' Alexei asked.

'I wish I could tell you a different story, my friend. All I have is what the gossipmongers relayed. But, Aleksei, it is so unlikely that any of the stories are true. I for one do not believe them. That she was taken off by the bosh, then raped and killed. I have never given any credence to. I think that was made up by Surnyaev to get at you. He was trying to break your resolve, my friend.'

'I hope you are right about that one. But what of the other tales – that she ran off with a German officer or married a Red Army colonel?'

'Surnyaev again. That bastard deserves to boil in his own juices.'

Oleg lit a cigarette and offered the packet to Aleksei.

Aleksei lit one and passed the packet back to Oleg.

'No, my friend, keep it to remind you of me.' Oleg laughed heartily. 'Anyway, my friend, there is another possibility that makes much more sense.'

'What is that?'

Oleg took a long drag on his cigarette then lifted his head and puffed smoke out above him.

'I believe Elena was told you were dead and she became convinced it was the truth. That person who convinced her, I believe again, was Maksim Surnyaev.'

Aleksei looked as if he had been hit by a thunderbolt. 'My God! I never thought of that. Yes, it makes sense. That cunning swine had every chance to locate her with all his contacts and, being a non-combatant attached to the secret police, he was in the best position to know everything. And to think I had the chance to kill him on my arrival in the capital. If I had suspected him of that then I would not have hesitated.'

'It would have been the wrong time, Aleksei. Maybe you will be given another chance.'

'I hope so, Oleg. I really do hope so.'

In his laboratory in Moscow, Professor Grigoriy Strekalovsky sat at his desk pouring over recent notes of the last experiment. He was required to make a report of this and send it to the politburo. Three days had passed since

166

Aleksei had left and it had been a trying time so far for the professor, as he waited for Rudikov's disappearance to be discovered and considered the explanation he would offer. He had calculated that he had five more days at the most before a visit so was surprised to hear the outer doors opening. He looked up just as the internal door to the laboratory burst open. Through it rushed persons he immediately recognised as KGB personnel with Colonel Maksim Surnyaev at their head.

Surnyaev looked around the room. 'Well professor, where is your charge and protégé?'

Professor Strekalovsky, although taken completely by surprise, remained calm and collected. He looked at Surnyaev but remained silent.

'We know he is not here so where is he, professor? I warn you, if you refuse to assist us it will mean a firing squad.'

Colonel Surnyaev appeared to relish the thought of another execution. The professor remained silent, stacking the papers in front of him into a neat pile. Surnyaev sneered but showed just the slightest hint of annoyance at the professor's calm demeanour.

'It will do you no good remaining silent. Of course, we already know his ambitions if he were ever able to escape. He will not get far. We will capture him with, or without, your help. Do you wish that much for your life to end, comrade?'

The professor did not reply. He just glared back at his detractor.

'Of course it will be much easier to capture him now he has lost his powers, do you not think, professor?'

Strekalovsky continued to glare at the colonel. 'If you believe that you will believe anything, Colonel Surnyaev.

'Remember who you are addressing here, Professor Strekalovsky. I do not take kindly to insolence, even from such a highly respected member of our party as you are apparently considered to be. Is it not true that you had already discovered Aleksei Rudikov was losing his powers but decided to keep this secret from the politburo? It was in vain as we were listening to your every word, even the talk of an escape. What have you to say to this, professor?'

'All I have to say is to warn you not to believe for one minute that Aleksei Vasiliy Rudikov has lost his powers.'

Colonel Surnyaev began to doubt his assertion but thrust the doubt aside.

'What are you telling me, professor? That you lied in your reports? For how long?'

Professor Strekalovsky no longer cared. 'For as long as I deemed it to be necessary.'

'Deemed necessary? Necessary for what purpose?'

The professor made no reply.

'You are not making it easy for yourself, professor. Where is he now? Who arranged his escape?'

The professor looked up at the colonel. 'Are you telling me you don't know? I don't believe that for a minute, Colonel Surnyaev. Anyway, if I were to divulge anything of the whereabouts of Aleksei Rudikov, you are the very last man on this earth I would confide in – even as to which door he left this laboratory by.'

Colonel Surnyaev always wore a coat two sizes too big for him. He thought it gave him a more commanding look. Little did he appreciate that many others laughed quietly to themselves as it only managed to emphasise his scrawny frame and made him look ridiculous – but no-one was going to tell him this. The cheekbones on his chiselled face appeared to vibrate and his features became contorted as the anger rose.

'Comrade professor, I think you would do better to understand what I can order to happen to you here and now if you persist in this manner.'

The professor looked away. 'I have heard you rarely ask so many questions before disposing of someone. So I must be sufficiently important for you to show me some respect.'

'Respect?' The colonel spat as he unbuttoned his coat and took out a revolver. 'This is how much you are respected, professor.' Three shots rang out, but only one ended the life of Professor Strekalovsky. The colonel was a terrible shot. The first bullet grazed the professor's head taking off his ear, the second missed completely and the third, fired at close range, burst through his temple, scattering blood and bone fragments on the wall behind him.

The other members of the squad froze in alarm. They felt sure Surnyaev had over reached himself this time.

More personnel came bursting through the doors at the sound of gunfire, including General Guznischev who had just that minute arrived. His promotion had been a reward for loyal service to both Stalin and Nikita Khrushchev. He stood shocked and motionless, taking in the scene before him, then addressed Colonel Surnyaev.

'What has happened here? Why did you not wait for me, Colonel?'

Surnyaev was still looking at his latest kill. He shook slightly, as he always did after an execution. In the few seconds before the general had arrived he had managed to wedge the revolver in the professor's right hand. He stepped back and turned to face Guznischev.

'As you can see, comrade General, the professor has ended his own life rather than face the questions that would have confirmed his treachery.'

The general looked disdainfully at the colonel then walked over to the desk and, after briefly examining the body, turned back to face Colonel Surnyaev.

'It would appear he was not a very good shot either. But is this not your own weapon, Colonel?'

Colonel Surnyaev had obviously been thinking fast on his feet and answered, 'Yes, comrade General, it is my weapon. The professor asked me for it so he could do the only decent thing under the circumstances.'

Guznischev shook his head slowly and addressed the other members of Surnyaev's squad.

'I take it what your commanding officer says is true?'

All replied to the affirmative.

'As I would have expected, thank you.'

The general dismissed Surnyaev's squad and his own, leaving himself alone with Colonel Surnyaev.

'Whatever the truth is, Colonel, Professor Strekalovsky was a highly respected member of this institution and revered by both Josef Stalin and Nikita Khrushchev as a model Soviet scientist. His untimely departure from this world will be mourned by many, I have no doubt, but one especially will mourn him more than anyone else. I refer to the subject of this enquiry, Aleksei Rudikov. If I have any advice for you now, Colonel, it is never under any circumstances put yourself in the proximity of this man.'

Surnyaev grabbed the revolver from out of the hand of the dead professor, replaced it in his coat and sneered.

'Thank you for your advice, comrade General, but I will not be dissuaded under any circumstances from tracking down this traitor of the Soviet state.'

'As you wish, Colonel. But realise this: he will by now suspect that it was you who convinced Elena Zvadsky that he had died.'

The colonel looked curious. 'This is a new one to me.'

The general continued. 'Have you never wondered about this? I know the last thing that was on Rudikov's mind was any reason to believe she would think him dead.'

Surnyaev replied, 'She was taken away, raped and murdered by a group of hungry soldiers. I can't remember if they were ours or theirs.'

'This is what he was told, but he could not believe it and, I must admit, neither do I.'

General Guznischev looked hard at the colonel.

'You have your right to believe or disbelieve but he believed it all right. I saw the expression on his face when he was told. The rooster finally realised what happened to his hen.'

Surnyaev looked as if he was beginning to enjoy the conversation.

'But he has another version now. Someone has awakened him to the possibility that Elena was told Rudikov had died. Are you not going to ask me how I know this, Colonel?'

Surnyaev looked puzzled. 'I am trying to follow this. What is your point?'

'The point I am making is that the one who has organised Rudikov's escape is Oleg Nikolai Chehovsky.'

'It cannot be,' Surnyaev whispered. His face was ashen. 'It cannot possibly be.'

'The one man in this world you would not want to be alive, eh, comrade Colonel?'

General Guznischev was relishing the situation.

'But he was officially recorded as a casualty at Stalingrad. I do not understand. Surely we are talking about an impostor passing himself off as Oleg Chehovsky?'

'Word has it that Chehovsky left his papers on a dead body and then disappeared. Many have been loyal to him and protected him since then. And, under the circumstances, for good reason. As you know well, comrade, this particular individual had an enormous and thriving network before the war, which was most useful and which you used for your own purposes during the time you knew him. "A favour for a favour", was that not your usual saying?'

Surnyaev wanted the ground to open, but fought to keep his composure.

'I hear what you are saying, General. So there are now at least two common criminals on the loose. I think you have always underestimated the ability of the KGB.'

With that the colonel excused himself and departed, leaving General Guznischev shaking his head over the body of Professor Strekalovsky.

'Aleksei Vasiliy, God speed!' he muttered.

'We have a problem, Aleksei. I have information. They know you have gone. Sooner than we expected.'

Aleksei had been enjoying another night of festivities at the Chehovsky residence, but Oleg's news froze his high spirits.

'The professor?' he asked.

Oleg looked away, but Aleksei could see the anguish on his face.

'Who Oleg? Who?'

Oleg did not want to answer and looked away again.

'Who Oleg? Please give me an answer.'

Silence.

'It was that bastard. Oleg, tell me it was not him.'

Oleg looked back. 'No, Aleksei, you must not. Remember his words: not backwards, go forwards.'

Aleksei felt a surge inside him. At the same time all the light bulbs in the residence burst, plunging them all into darkness. It took a few moments for Aleksei to realise what he had done but he made no apology.

Candles were lit whilst replacement bulbs were found. Oleg turned to Aleksei.

'It is all right, I understand what has happened, even if no-one else here does. I told you that day we took out that German sniper you were a spooky man. Now it's a reality. You are the spookiest individual I have ever known and you saved me from a firing squad.'

Aleksei looked sideways at them all, still digesting the information.

Oleg continued. 'I had already crossed the top men. I was always used to creating my own world before that shit came to our door. As soon as they realised who I was and knew about my "empire"...'

'What are you going to tell me?'

Oleg spat it out. 'Double deals. And every day I signed up to them I vowed I would gladly kill every one of them, given half a chance.'

'Shut up!' Out of the flickering candlelight emerged the slight figure of Irina. 'You are talking of something that can never be resolved. This brave man is going through to the West. Leave him with his hope and fond memories of us.'

Aleksei wanted to ask Oleg more questions but Irina's entreaty was made the more potent by being spoken by one so young. He sensed that the answers Oleg might give would make their friendship untenable and, in light of all that was happening, this would make no sense. Aleksei nodded to Irina, who sighed with relief.

Oleg was also relieved that he hadn't needed to open up old wounds. He put an arm around Irina and hugged her tight.

'She worries me sometimes, Aleksei. She is the image of my lovely wife, Marina. God rest her soul.'

Oleg had already told Aleksei of his wife's sudden death three years previously. She had been fit and well practically all her life. Then suddenly she suffered a heart attack. His then fifteen-year-old grand-daughter, Irina, had come to look after things, at first on a temporary basis but had eventually decided to stay permanently. Aleksei remembered his first sight of the now eighteen-year-old girl whose face had looked so familiar. He could see Oleg in her now and her fire and passion also reminded him of his Elena.

'Everything is ready, Aleksei. We would have preferred another couple of days but it is no problem. Irina will lead you to the fence. I will be upstairs in an apartment I have rented for the past year to observe the activities by the wall. I will have my rifle and will distract the watchtower sentries by giving them a taste of sniper fire. Just like old times, my friend!'

Aleksei tensed. 'Berlin? Tonight?'

'Yes, tonight. We must make the move now. We cannot be sure of what is around us.'

Aleksei felt a jerk on his arm. The girl, Irina, had taken a hold.

'We go now. You and I.'

She looked into his eyes and he obeyed instantly.

Oleg drove the truck through the streets of East Berlin using the route he knew would be the safest. Irina sat beside him, her eyes darting backwards and forwards looking for any signs of danger.

Oleg murmured softly, 'It will be all right, I promise you.'

Irina smiled faintly but remained watchful.

Aleksei felt increasingly aware of the situation he faced as he tried to get comfortable in the back of the truck. No matter how many journeys he had made in the past few days he always felt cramped and uncomfortable. There was also something else he would not let on to any of the others about. In his days as a sniper, he had always felt slightly claustrophobic in confined areas. This had not hampered his success rate during the war but he had always been glad to complete each assignment and be able to breathe fresh air again.

The truck came to a halt outside a block of apartments. Oleg waited for a few seconds watching for any movements. Then a large door opened further down the street and from the shadows a figure appeared gesturing towards

174

the truck. Oleg immediately drove forward and turned into the opening, passing the person, who immediately shut the door behind them.

Oleg and Irina got out of the car and were greeted by Dmitriy, the figure at the door.

'I thought you had got lost!' he whispered.

Aleksei peered out of the back of the truck at them, getting used to the little light there was in the space of the garage workshop.

Irina assisted Aleksei out the truck whilst Oleg and Dmitriy climbed the stairs to the first floor and peered through a heavily curtained window that had a very small hole in it, used for observation.

Oleg whispered, 'It looks like they are all on a tea break, eh, Dmitriy?'

Dmitriy looked tense. 'They are most probably playing cards. If we are lucky we might not have to use the guns.'

Oleg shook his head. 'No comrade, I don't think that is possible. Too much ground to cover not to be noticed. We must take out the searchlights and keep their heads down for as long as possible. When they get to the other side Irina will take him to the safe house.'

'They? Irina is going too? I had no notion of this.' Secretly, Dmitriy had designs on Oleg's grand-daughter so this news was a bitter blow to his ambitions. 'When will she be coming back?'

Oleg sensed the dismay in Dmitriy but could not offer him solace. 'My friend, perhaps never. To cross once successfully is God's wish, but to attempt it twice is beyond any divine intervention. She is going back to her family there.'

Oleg descended the stairs, followed by Dmitriy who looked about to burst into tears. Oleg hugged Irina.

'Safe journey, my little angel. May I see you again when the wall comes down.'

Aleksei also looked surprised. 'Irina is coming with me? That is far too dangerous, Oleg. I forbid it.'

Oleg laughed quietly. 'My friend, Aleksei, you know nothing of this slight girl in front of us. She is a Chehovsky. If she desires something she usually gets it. And tonight she desires to be in West Berlin.'

Irina smiled at her grandfather and went to shake Dmitriy by the hand. He looked down as he took her hand, not wanting her to see the tears in his eyes. Irina sensed his pain and turned away, unable to provide comfort.

Oleg and Aleksei made their farewell with a hug. 'One day, Aleksei, my friend, we will drink together at the same bar as we used to. That is a promise.'

Aleksei grinned. 'That is a promise for both of us then.'

Irina sighed softly. 'How romantic! But now we go.'

Oleg chuckled as he saw them both to the side door on the opposite side of the building. Opening it he whispered another 'Good luck, comrades.' Irina took Aleksei by the hand and both made their way from the side yard into the street.

Dodging into shadows they crept closer to the fence. It was some distance to it over open ground. Irina took the wire cutters from inside her jacket and handed them to Aleksei. 'We run as fast as we can to the fence and then wait. Grandfather will take out the searchlights if they beam anywhere near our position. Then we have to move very fast indeed.'

Aleksei understood and nodded.

Irina crossed the open ground like a gazelle in flight from a predator whilst Aleksei puffed a distance behind her. They both made it to the fence and waited tensely as they recovered their breath. Aleksei began to cut through the wire whilst Irina looked about them for any signs of guard activity. Aleksei pulled the cut wire apart so that Irina could slip through. Then she took hold from the other side, pulling it wide apart for Aleksei to join her. There was still no beam anywhere near them. They waited a few seconds longer to get some idea of their bearings.

Just as they were about to run again to the other side and safety, a beam of light from the watchtower lit up their position and an order was shouted: 'Halt, or you will be shot!'

They both froze.

Irina groaned. 'They have seen us. Have they been watching us all along and just playing a game with us?'

'The lights, why does he not shoot at the lights?' Aleksei whispered hoarsely, looking back through the murk at the buildings in the distance.

Irina looked in the same direction.

'I do not understand. What is grandfather waiting for?'

Then a thought suddenly hit Aleksei.

'I sense something very wrong. If they were playing with us all along then maybe they have already arrested Oleg and Dmitriy.'

The blood drained from her face. She shook her head slowly.

'No God, please do not let that be.'

But Aleksei had held back from saying anything more of what he suspected. He did not want to believe his suspicions to be true and certainly did not want to alarm Irina any further by divulging his thoughts. Oleg had been about to admit his shady dealings before Irina stepped in and Aleksei had a nasty feeling that this was all a set-up. But, if so, would Oleg sacrifice Irina? Surely not. Before he could mull the situation over any further they both heard sharp words being exchanged in the distance, orders being barked. Aleksei thought he recognised the voice.

From out of the gloom marched four soldiers and a thin bespectacled figure in a uniform coat too large for him. Aleksei grunted an oath as he recognised Colonel Maksim Surnyaev.

The four soldiers had their rifles aimed at the pair.

'So we meet again at last, comrade Aleksei Vasiliy Rudikov. Did you believe it would be that easy to escape my clutches?' Surnyaev chuckled, his thin face a picture of contentment.

Aleksei spat on the ground. 'So it was all a set-up. Just how many comrades have you got feeding out of your trough of shit?'

The colonel kept smiling. 'Enough, comrade, more than enough to satisfy my desires, and when I tire of them I simply dispose of them to keep the security tight. Dead men don't talk much, eh?'

'That's a matter of opinion. I asked you before if you believe in life after death and you have certainly answered that one. Is it really your habit to get everything that wrong?'

The smile began to fade. 'I think we will be terminating this conversation very soon, but before we do I will tell you what we are going to do to this pretty girl beside you. All these fine fit men here have a real need to satisfy their lust and I may even join them.'

'You will have to kill me first.' Irina had folded her arms as she spat this back at the colonel.

'That might not be a bad idea. No chance of being scratched or bitten, eh?'

Surnyaev appeared to be in his element.

'I have one question to ask you.'

Aleksei was beginning to feel a slight surge as his emotions stirred inside him.

'I think I have a good idea what your question is about,' Surnyaev sneered. 'Elena Zvadsky. You want to know what really happened to her, yes?'

Aleksei was trying his utmost not to lose his composure

but he felt himself begin to shake. The colonel noticed this and continued.

'I have waited a long time to see fear in your eyes, Aleksei Vasiliy Rudikov. It gives me so much pleasure.'

'The only fear I have is that you will be lying again. Do you remember ever telling a truth?'

Surnyaev's expression changed and he glared angrily at Aleksei as he opened his coat, pulled out his revolver and pointed it at the girl.

'This is truth sitting here in my hand. One twitch of my finger and your little friend here will meet her maker.'

Irina retorted, 'What a big brave man you are, picking on a defenceless woman.'

The colonel reacted angrily. 'Silence, or I will order these men to start stripping you here and now. I am sure you will enjoy that once you have overcome your inhibitions and it will be fun for those up in the watchtower to see you being ravaged under a beam of light.'

Colonel Surnyaev turned his attention back to Aleksei. 'The truth you seek is that Elena Zvadsky was informed of your death at Stalingrad and this was backed up by official documents.'

The surge inside Aleksei rose a notch.

'So it was you all along spreading the disinformation to keep us apart. Why? What perverted instinct drives you, Colonel?'

'From the very moment I set eyes on you at your village all that time ago I immediately took a dislike to you, Aleksei Rudikov. You were always too big for your boots, showing off your prowess with a rifle. Much good it did you in the end. I made sure of that.'

'I am well aware of your dislike of me and the feeling is mutual. I suppose you are going to tell me more of what happened to Elena so as to torture me before execution. That is your usual way, is it not?'

The colonel laughed grimly. 'You flatter me with your assessment. But no, I have nothing to add to what I have told you. As far as I know Elena Zvadsky went off and married another soldier.'

Aleksei's heart skipped a beat. He felt like weeping, as he had done all those years ago when reading the letter left by Elena. He put his hand up to his neck and touched the silver cross he always wore in her memory.

Seeing the hurt and anguish he had managed to cause in his prisoner gave Colonel Surnyaev much satisfaction. His eyes gleamed as he watched Aleksei's demeanour deteriorate.

'There is one other truth I must tell you. It is about your great friend and mentor, Professor Strekalovsky. This great man was a revered scientist but one who did not report to us that you had lost your powers.'

Aleksei felt the surge again. He tensed himself, waiting for the news he dreaded. 'What has happened to the professor? Has he been arrested?'

The colonel grinned. 'Oh no, not arrested, not this man – a traitor of the Soviet people, guilty of assisting a renegade, a so-called war hero, to escape imprisonment.'

'What are you saying? What has happened to the professor?' The surge inside him was reaching epic proportions.

'He took his own life rather than face the music. Shot himself through the head in his laboratory.' Surnyaev said this with another of his sneers.

'He did not own a gun. He had never fired a gun. You are lying again. I can smell it all over you. It was your gun, wasn't it? And the professor didn't shoot himself – it was you, wasn't it.' The anger welling inside Aleksei tipped over the limit. 'And Nataliya, my sweet "Natasha"?'

'Ah, of course, I had forgotten about your desire for that whore. Nataliya, yes, I remember her well and how

180

satisfying it was to see her naked and taken by my men, one after another, whilst under my interrogation. She would not reveal what you had confided in her – a faithful bitch to the end.'

Surnyaev was still enjoying his triumph when he felt his right arm rising. He tried to lower it but it continued to rise and then turned so that the pistol he was holding pointed directly at him. He lifted his left arm and clamped hold of his right wrist, struggling to lower it. He tried to shake the revolver out of his hand but it stuck fast, still pointing at his head.

The soldiers watched the movement with puzzled expressions. Then they began to notice that they no longer had control of their own weapons as they all lifted to vertical position and then spun backwards out of their hands. All four froze to the spot as they watched the colonel struggling.

Irina too stood motionless, not able to believe her eyes. She looked at Aleksei whose eyes were blazing like red-hot coals. She began to feel afraid.

Colonel Surnyaev's right hand slowly moved forward towards his mouth, which began to open. His eyes were bulging in their sockets as the pistol came closer. He continued to struggle, as the gun entered his mouth. The terrified colonel looked at Aleksei whose face was expressionless.

'Lost my power, eh, Colonel Surnyaev?'

The colonel tried desperately to reply but all that came out of his mouth was a high-pitched squeal as he shook his head violently in an attempt to dislodge the pistol.

'Good-bye, Colonel Maksim Surnyaev,' Aleksei whispered as the colonel's finger twitched and the revolver fired, bursting a hole in the back of his skull and spreading blood and bone fragments over the terrified soldiers. The body seemed to be held up for a few more seconds then,

181

as if having been released, it crumpled into a heap on the ground.

Irina looked at Aleksei with terror but he put his arms around her and held her close.

'Do not worry, Irina. What I have is reserved only for such people as him. You are totally safe.'

The soldiers on the watchtower were shouting down to the four on the ground who were still transfixed. Then a shot rang out and the beam was extinguished.

Aleksei grabbed Irina's hand and pulled open the wire again. He pushed her through and told her to run for cover, then turned back to face the four stricken soldiers who dared not make eye contact with him.

'Which one of you brave comrades is going to assist by holding the wire back for me?'

All four were terrified but one managed to call out, 'I will help you if you promise not to hurt any of us.'

'Well said and thank you. I have no quarrel with you at the moment but if I don't make it to the other side it might be a different matter.'

The soldier walked forward and held the wire high as Aleksei crouched and slipped through.

Those on the watchtower were still calling, questioning the others on the ground. The soldier who had assisted Aleksei shouted back, telling none of them to move a muscle until he said it was safe to do so.

Aleksei reached the other fence, which had already been cut by their welcoming party, Irina's two older brothers, twenty-year-old Lev, and Leonid, nineteen. Irina was still getting her breath back, not just from the sprint to the other side but from the shock of what she had witnessed. Her brothers looked very curiously at Aleksei, as he approached them. He noticed their looks and smiled.

'Good to see friendly faces again.'

After a moment's hesitation both young men laughed

and shook Aleksei's hand. But Irina was still looking at him strangely. Her fear had been replaced by something else. It reminded him of the look Elena had given him on occasions, which he had never been able to fathom properly. He shrugged this memory off and said, 'Was that Oleg, d'you think, who put out the light?'

Irina shook her head. 'No, it was Lev here.' As she said this, her brother produced the rifle he had used. 'His grandfather taught him how to use it.'

'A very good shot, if I may say so. He taught you well,' Aleksei said. At the same time he was thinking of what went wrong earlier. Had Oleg been mixed up in it or was he dead now?

Irina watched Aleksei as he put his head down in thought.

'I know what you are thinking, Aleksei, but I would never believe our grandfather would betray us. There must be a good reason. I hope they are all right but something inside tells me to fear the worst.' Irina shivered and Leonid put his arm around her but she shrugged it off. 'I am all right, thanks. We should be going before we are picked up by the police.'

All four stole off into the night, seeking the safety of the family home.

20

Helen sat perfectly still throughout Rudy's rendition of the facts he had been given by Liliya. She did not interrupt him during the entire disclosure, which took a good twenty minutes. He now sat watching her closely, waiting for her to digest it all, knowing it would have come as a massive shock to her as much as it had been a wonder to him.

Helen suddenly came out of her thoughts and said, 'So many years, so many untruths and no-one gave us any clue about this. I asked many times where I came from and I can see now why I wasn't told.'

Rudy looked puzzled. 'Why would they not have wanted to tell you about this?'

'It might have been because it was impossible in those days for them to admit to others I was a Russian refugee.'

Rudy was still confused. 'Why should that be? What is so unacceptable about being a Russian.'

Helen sighed, still feeling the shock and sadness of having all this withheld from her.

'We live in a very bigoted world where people are branded by others. Each time a war is fought it causes more bigotry and suffering and all the decent people in the world have to worry about the views of others. Look at the strife caused by religion, Catholics and Protestants, Muslims and Christians, all with a few hotheads causing the trouble and stirring up bigotry. Take the example from any of the wars that have ever been fought because politicians and leaders can't agree. Then there is Fascism, Communism, different kinds of ideologies antagonistic to one another. So much of it is taught by parents who pass it on to their children who, in turn, pass it on to theirs – a never ending line of bigotry.'

Rudy had never heard his mother speaking like this before.

'I never thought you had such views, Mum. You've kept them to yourself all this time.'

Helen forced a faint smile. 'A lot of it is to do with the fact that women are supposed to be dumb and not have an opinion on anything so grand – only good for the ironing and washing up and the cooking, of course. I have always wanted to be able to voice my ideas on things but have never had the opportunity. When your father walked out it stung me and my confidence hit rock bottom. I never seem to be able to find anyone I can talk to like this and here I am talking to my own son as a last resort.' Helen saw the hurt look on Rudy's face. 'No, I don't mean it like that, so don't feel upset. It's just that I would like a proper adult relationship with someone who valued my opinion for a change. Does that make sense now?'

The grin returned to Rudy's face as he nodded.

'Learning we have Russian roots is one thing but I am very worried over this business of the man chasing you. You could have ended up badly injured or even dead. Or maybe he wanted to kidnap you and take you away for experiments.'

Helen could see that Rudy was at least taking this is in and also showing a look of concern.

'Experiments? What kind of experiments?'

'Probably to see how your mind works and try and find out how you are able to do these things. I want to call that man from the security services, Graham Digby, and ask him for protection.'

Rudy became alarmed. 'No, Mum! That's just what they

would want us to do. I don't trust any of them, especially if what you are saying is true and they want to experiment on me.'

'But we live in Britain. They wouldn't do experiments like that in this country.'

'No, Mum, I don't agree with you. I was warned to be very careful and to keep a watch out because there is danger everywhere. We must not go anywhere near them.'

Helen sighed heavily. 'So what do we do then? What are we supposed to do to protect ourselves?'

Rudy sat thinking for a moment as his mother filled the kettle.

'I think we should try and find any of our Russian family that are still alive. They might be able to give us advice. How would we find out anything about them?'

Helen turned around with a curious look on her face. 'I never thought I would want to try and trace anything from my past as it might have turned out to be a mess. But that was before I learned what you have been told. It's all such a long time ago. But if there is still someone alive somewhere that we belong to, then I think it is a duty to find them, don't you think?'

Rudy felt excitement brewing inside. 'But how would we find out? Russia is a long way away.'

'Not just a long way but also a very hard place to seek information as Russia has cut itself off from the West. Trying to get information is not going to be easy, but they have the Russian Embassy in this country so I think that is the first place to go. Write down the details of everything you can remember and we will begin there.'

Nikita Khrushchev took the news very badly. He had been aware for some time of a possible conspiracy against him because of his radical and liberal ideas. He had sensed

186

that the party was split and that the old conservative ideology was becoming more popular again. With criticism mounting of the premier's inconsistency and inability to move the Soviets any further forward in the power struggle, most considered another war was inevitable.

'But how? How could this have happened, General Guznischev?'

'With respect, comrade President, I tried to warn you of this. Colonel Surnyaev was always going to cause such a situation. I just wish that he were here now to face us both. I had warned him not to approach Rudikov, but he would never listen to me.'

Khrushchev remained silent for a while, during which time General Guznishev stood to attention waiting for another outburst. The premier came out of his thoughts and noticed the strain on Guznischev's face.

He measured his words, 'General, you have been here in the middle of all that has taken place over such a long time. You were loyal to Comrade Stalin and now to me and I trust your word. I do not say that lightly as I know every step I take could now be my last.'

Nikita Khrushchev held the general's stare long enough for there to be no question over the sincerity of his words. He continued.

'My time is almost up, General.'

General Guznischev had always felt that Khrushchev might be out of his depth in the world of politics. He considered his leader a good and honest man who lacked the proper backing of the party system when he needed it the most.

'I am at a loss for words.'

The general looked down as he struggled to form a constructive reply.

Nikita Khrushchev chuckled quietly. 'We are in the wrong jobs. The Soviets do not deserve us. They deserve

187

the old style leadership and I for one will not be surprised if I am replaced sooner rather than later. Do you know something I do not, General?'

The general looked curious. 'Why would you think that, comrade President? I, of course, hear the usual rumours but I am not one who has ever been invited into that cell that operates with skulking efficiency.'

Khrushchev looked serious for a moment; then his expression changed as he laughed at the general's acute observations. 'Oh yes, General Guznischev, we are definitely on the same wavelength there. Surnyaev and his KGB chums conspired with whoever had the future plans in their grasp. All those smiling faces surrounding us are masks concealing contempt and disunity. If only I could tell one from the other.'

General Guznischev felt sure President Khrushchev knew, or suspected, a lot more than he was letting on. Russia was on the brink of a major world crisis. The Cuban missile sites and the aborted Bay of Pigs operation had left diplomatic terms with America at an all time low.

The general looked worriedly at his premier who noticed and chuckled. 'Fear not, General, nothing will stick to you – I will make certain of that – and you will serve the next leader as you have us.'

Khrushchev then stared for a while out of a window at a bleak Russian sky full of snow clouds. He muttered quietly to himself then turned to face General Guznischev again.

'Professor Strekalovsky was like a father to me, as I know you felt also. He was a wise man and I valued his words. And I saw something in Aleksei Vasiliy Rudikov that warmed my heart. I will miss them both.'

With that the leader of the Soviets sauntered out of the room leaving General Guznischev wondering just what his own position would be in the near future.

* * *

Several days had passed during which Luigi Venditti had sat in a small room that was meant to be his prison. However, all amenities were at his disposal and he was able to roam through the corridors to other parts of the Vatican, though always accompanied by a priest or another member of the brotherhood. Now he was heading for the hall housing the Papal Commission. They had summoned him again. The priest who accompanied him appeared nervous.

The Monsignor, noticing, asked, 'What troubles you, brother? It should be I who am nervous, don't you think?'

The priest tried to offer a smile and whispered in hushed tones, 'I am sorry, Monsignor Venditti, I just feel it is a great shame that someone of your eminent and revered position is being put through such a shameful exercise. There are many who feel as I do – that you have offered a true account of what is possibly a major threat to our faith and that you should be listened to and your advice acted upon.'

'Thank you, Brother Anthony. That is reassuring at least but, as we all know well, the decisions are made by those who are too exalted to listen to such idle gossip!'

Before the priest could offer anything further in the way of reply the pair were approached by Swiss Guard officers, one of whom waved Brother Anthony away. The soldiers continued the escort of Monsignor Venditti into the hallway.

Cardinal Medi was already seated, surrounded by ten other prelates who made up the Papal Commission. All wore their sumptuous robes of office.

Monsignor Venditti nodded to those surrounding the cardinal before turning his eyes on Medi. The cardinal spoke in a soft but commanding voice.

'May I again offer my sincere wishes for you, Brother Luigi. We have all prayed for you night and day and hope that our prayers will be listened to and finally answered so as to find a solution to this problem.'

Luigi Venditti was not intimidated. 'I thank you one and all for your prayers and the sincerity of your wishes but, in all humility, your prayers would be of more consequence if directed at what I consider to be the main problem: blindness.'

Cardinal Medi glared down at the monsignor. 'I would remind you, brother, that we have the power to excommunicate anyone whom we find to be no longer a trustworthy agent of Christ.'

Monsignor Venditti smiled in return. 'Your Eminence, please accept my apologies if my words are offensive to the agents of Christ, but I feel absolutely certain that even He would listen to what I have to say on this matter.'

There were gasps and angry mutterings. Cardinal Medi waited for these to die down.

'You are close to being accused of blasphemy, Brother Luigi. I would advise you to adopt more conciliatory language.'

Venditti waited a moment before continuing.

'I have a suggestion to make regarding this boy's power, if you are willing to hear me. It might provide the solution for all concerned.'

As he waited patiently for a reply, whispered conversations took place between the eminent members of the commission. Finally Cardinal Medi spoke.

'We are of the opinion that no power this boy may possess is of any direct threat to our Church and thus to His Holiness.'

Venditti shook his head slowly. 'Why are the Russians and Americans so keen to find him? There is a lot more to this situation. I sense a lot of things are going on behind the scenes and I fear we will be left behind in the rush.'

Medi remained calm and aloof but one or two of the other members of the commission were whispering feverishly into his ear. Medi spoke again.

'Please go on, Brother Luigi.'

'As we are all aware, there is a major power struggle going on between the Russians and the Americans, which appears to be nearing boiling point. Both have developed in the past highly sophisticated psychic walls that act as shields protecting one from the other. I believe these walls are crumbling as we speak, so both are seeking a replacement, and what better than a natural power structure emanating from this boy? Of course, he would have to act willingly to provide such protection and both countries might struggle in convincing him to comply with their wishes. But what if there were a third party, a party willing to offer him sanctuary?'

'You mean the Church?' Medi asked, now looking curious.

'Yes, your Eminence. Why, even as we speak other religious brethren may also be aware by now of the power surrounding this entity and would wish to incorporate it into their own structures for purposes that would not bode well for ourselves. That is the threat to our Church that I speak of and if you did not understand the implications before I beg you, in all humility, please reappraise the situation now. Others would covet this power for themselves and, if successful in containing it, would without doubt then have the means to develop a power structure that could eventually attack and destroy all that our faith has built up over nearly two thousand years.'

The cardinal looked pensive. His eyes had lost much of their previous glare as he spoke.

'I hear what you are saying, Brother Luigi, and what you present to us cannot be taken lightly. What more have you in mind?'

'We could offer him the protection of sanctuary within our Church. He could be inducted into a seminary and from there gain rapid promotion to the safety of these walls. Such a solution would guarantee the unity of our Church and the protection of His Holiness for years to come.'

Venditti was pleased at last to have reached this crucial point in the debate.

Again Cardinal Medi appeared to lose himself in thought for a few moments, as did those around him.

'But even if we were to consent to this, why would the boy wish for sanctuary with us?'

Venditti looked up slowly as the cardinal asked this question.

'My plan was to ensure that the boy and his mother became sufficiently frightened to seek a safe haven. I am certain that they will have been sufficiently disturbed by the antics of our dear late friend, Luis Alvarez Suarez, to be persuaded that seeking such sanctuary as we would offer would be to their advantage, especially with others breathing down their necks.'

'But, what if you are wrong, Brother Luigi? What if, in fact, his power is of the devil? If so, would we not be in danger of allowing ourselves to be hoodwinked by this entity, offering up our very souls?' The other prelates appeared to agree with Cardinal Medi's assessment. 'How can we be sure that he would not destroy us?'

Luigi Venditti had waited so long for this moment. All his prayers were about to be answered if he could just convince this commission to agree with him and he sensed he was close to achieving this result.

'I admit I lured Luis Suarez into a situation which would enable me to gauge the possible power of the boy. I have studied such phenomena for many years but only with the intention of assisting in the protection of His Holiness and our Mother Church. If I appeared hostile earlier I beg forgiveness. My wish is to continue to discover ways of harnessing this phenomenon for the good of us all.'

Those around Medi again began to murmur and whisper to each other as the cardinal weighed up what had been said.

'How do you propose to approach the boy and his mother?'

'By chance, some time ago, a priest of my acquaintance heard the confession of an elderly lady, a former school nurse. Of course he could not break the secrecy of the confessional but something was bothering him enough to contact me. In his own way, without breaking that secrecy, he put me on the road to finding something myself. I discovered that the nurse had been at the same school as the boy and it would appear he saved her from a terrible beating by a gang of louts. This occurred on the very same day Luis Suarez had contact with the boy. The boy and this former school nurse have become friends and he has since visited her to make sure she is well. I believe this lady can be of assistance to us in these circumstances by convincing this boy to become of the faith.' Monsignor Venditti had reached the very pinnacle of his argument and was ready to deliver. 'In all humility, I would offer myself up as a guarantor and be involved in the training and assessment of this boy. If for any reason I considered him to be less than one-hundred-per-cent committed to protecting our faith I would immediately offer him up, body and soul, to those we might still consider as the Inquisitors.'

Cardinal Medi sat perfectly still as those around him again muttered quiet whispers into his ears. After all had had their say Medi clasped his hands together and bowed his head in prayer. All others, including Venditti, followed suit. After this the cardinal gazed for a short time up at the rafters, then looked down on Monsignor Venditti.

'I have listened to your wise words, Brother Luigi. It will take a while longer for us to make a sound judgement on this situation. Please bear with us whilst we make this consideration. My own view is that we should adopt your proposal but if we were to take this direction there would be no turning back. We must be certain in what we do.'

Luigi Venditti bowed his head to the members of the commission as it rose and quietly filed out in an orderly line behind the eminent Cardinal Medi. Venditti felt a great pleasure growing inside him. His face, however, remained inscrutable.

21

The telephone rang as Bill Collins relaxed in his favourite armchair, having just eaten a grand meal cooked by Martha. She picked up the receiver and looked disapprovingly at her husband.

'It's your work for you, dear.'

Martha sighed heavily and walked back into the kitchen to finish the washing-up.

'Hello. This better be important.'

Bill felt the icy air of Martha's sigh surrounding him as he spoke into the receiver.

There was a short chuckle on the other end of the line. 'Is it still the same there, Bill? Martha not letting up on wanting you to retire, huh?'

Bill Collins recognised the soft tones of Doug James.

'No Doug, no change there unfortunately. What can I do for you? Not changed your mind and coming back to us?'

Doug chuckled quietly again. 'No chance on that one Bill. Sorry, but I've a real taste of freedom here. Retirement I can wholly recommend, so I'm afraid I am falling heavily down on Martha's side. I hope that doesn't make me too much of a traitor!'

Collins let out a short chuckle in return. 'No, Doug, that could never happen. We all miss your wit. So what can I do for you?'

'It's more what I can do for you, Bill. The word's out Stray Dog escaped and is through the wall. One of my buddies there contacted me thinking I was still a live un

195

and I didn't let him think otherwise. Seems SD killed that KGB snake in the grass, Colonel Maksim Surnyaev, on the way out.'

Bill Collins felt a cold sweat pour over him and was left breathless.

Doug James noticed the change in Bill Collins' breathing. 'Jesus, are you OK, Bill? I shouldn't have given you the news all at once.'

Martha had by this time re-entered the living room and seeing Bill's condition rushed for his medication.

In the meantime Bill managed to utter breathlessly. 'Just need to take my pills, Doug. Please bear with me.'

'Sure, Bill, take it nice and easy. Don't want you croaking on account of me. Martha would never forgive me.'

Bill Collins managed a very brief chuckle and was met by the steely glare of Martha offering him his medication and a glass of water. He popped the pills in his mouth, then reached for the glass and gulped them down. He passed the glass back to his wife, who grunted her further disapproval.

'That's better, Doug. Shocks, even minor ones, seem to affect me a lot these days. And I don't think I have earned any remission from Martha after this one. Just gonna make it that much harder. So what's this all about, d'you think? He can't have just walked out of the country. There must have been some pretty damned good planning behind it. Who else do you think is involved?'

'Can't be sure. The buddy there gets very cagey when talking about names in case anything is traced back, and I can't blame him for that. I've seen too many having a knock on the door after providing information. All he can tell me is that it was organised by an old friend of SD.'

'Ok, Doug. I appreciate very much you contacting me about this.'

'For old times, Bill. We had good and bad and talking of bad – please don't offer my good wishes to that punk, Mackay, but please say "hi" to the rest from me.'

'Doug, I think you caught John on a bad day that's all.'

Bill sensed he had trodden on a nerve as Doug went quiet for a moment.

'We all have bad days, Bill, and I'm not one who usually bears that much of a grudge, but there is something not quite right about that man. Can't put my finger on it because, if I could, I'd tell you what it is, Bill. All I can repeat is get the hell outta there and let someone else spill the gravy. Take great care, Bill. Be seeing ya, and give my apologies to Martha.'

The line went dead and Bill Collins stood for a short moment looking at the receiver. Then he made another call.

22

Helen Metthewson spent a restless night thinking over the whole situation. When she did manage to sleep she had recurring dreams that she just could not recall each time she woke again. In her frustration she finally decided to get up and make herself a hot drink. As she descended the stairs she noticed a smell that was strangely familiar, but she couldn't quite remember what it reminded her of. At the same time she felt a slight breeze. Entering the kitchen she found the source of the wind and immediately froze. The back door was slightly ajar. Helen wanted to put the light on but at the same time did not want to illuminate the room and discover who, or what, had made an entrance. All kinds of thoughts rushed through her mind. The back door began to creak, the wind blowing it further, until it was fully open and a figure appeared on the threshold. Helen caught her breath just as the smell she had identified earlier became that much stronger. Something was thrust close to her face and a cloth pressed over her mouth. As her senses left her she recognised the smell as a mixture of disinfectant, chlorine and chloroform.

Rudy awoke with a start. The light shone through the curtains and his eyes hurt but he couldn't understand why. He also noticed a pungent smell he normally associated with the bathroom or kitchen after his mother had decided on a major clean up. He looked at the clock on the bedside table but his vision was blurred and he could not read the dial. He tried to stand then fell back on to the bed, feeling nauseous. He lay for a while trying to make sense of his condition but all he could think of was that he was going to puke. Then the sensation became reality and he rolled off the bed and began crawling on all fours towards the bathroom. His mouth began to fill with what he was bringing up and his throat burned as he struggled to get to the bathroom before he burst. Rudy made it to the bedroom door, but no further, before he vomited. He lay down for a few seconds, trying to gather his thoughts, then he felt another bout closing in and made it to the toilet just in time. He lay back down again feeling absolutely drained. Rudy regained consciousness with his head still spinning. In the distance he thought he could hear the faint sound of knocking on an internal door. He tried to call out but his throat felt as if it had been recently sandpapered. Instead, he got unsteadily to his feet and began to stagger into the hallway, where he came face to face with the figure on whom he could not focus properly. Then the effort became too much for him and he fell to his knees. The last thing he remembered was being lifted up, followed by the sense of a cool soft landing, then sleep.

Aleksei sat at the table listening to the brisk chatter around him. It was a typical Russian family moment at mealtime, but he did not feel part of it. The many years of solitude had worn away his memory of how to engage in such moments. He simply did not feel it anymore. Aleksei had been looking down at his plate but suddenly felt that someone was watching him. He raised his eyes. Irina looked back at him the same way she had done at the wire and with her look came a vivid memory of his dear Elena at that same age.

Oleg and Marina Chehovsky were married in 1922,

when he was twenty years of age and she eighteen. Nina had been born the following year. Nikolai Dmitriev was a childhood friend of Nina and they married when she was just seventeen years of age and Nikolai nineteen. Three children were born in quick succession: Lev in 1942, Leonid in 1943 and Irina in 1944. Oleg had many contacts through his business connections, mainly to do with the thriving black market, and subsequently arranged for the Dmitriev family to move to West Berlin before the wall was built. The family prospered in the West but not without a helping hand from Oleg Chehovsky and his black market chums. Sadly, Marina had contracted an illness in 1959 and died at the young age of fifty-five. Oleg, still a fit man of fifty-seven, fell to pieces for a while and took to drinking heavily. Young Irina had volunteered to return to their village just outside Minsk and help with the family chores. Nikolai and Nina had not wished her to go but since so much of their prosperity had been due to the sacrifices made by Oleg and Marina they acknowledged it was a way of returning their generosity. Gradually, with Irina's help, Oleg began to recover his zest for life. Now she was back amongst her family and her brothers, who had missed their sister, and were excitedly asking her all kinds of questions about her experiences in their former homeland.

Irina returned her attention back to her brothers. Nikolai had also been watching Aleksei with some concern.

'Are you feeling all right, Aleksei? Please tuck into the meal. Do you want more wine?'

Aleksei smiled in return. 'No, thank you, Nikolai. You have all done me proud and I am filled to the brim. But may I ask when I will be moving again? Not that I do not enjoy your hospitality, but as long as I am here you are in danger.'

The family stopped talking. Irina broke the silence first.

200

'I will be sad to see you go, Aleksei Vasiliy. I have grown fond of you.'

'Ira, you are too forward for your own good,' said her mother. 'It is a good job Aleksei here understands that or he might have taken it as a marriage proposal!'

Laughter broke out around the table but Irina did not look as if she appreciated the joke.

'I do not think I would ever find another as suitable as Aleksei, even though he is old enough to be my grandfather. Age is not always relevant in matters of the heart, mother. Anyway, Aleksei is already spoken for, are you not? Somewhere out there Elena is waiting, probably without realising that her man is searching for her. How much more of a romantic story could be told than that?'

Nina shook her head. 'Sometimes I wonder if you might be wiser than I with the things you say, Ira. You have grown up so fast in the three years you have been away.'

'I'm sorry Mother, I have been too long in a different environment. I must learn to adjust again.'

'We understand Ira. Do not worry. We have also to adjust to having a worldly-wise daughter amongst us.'

This brought laughter from Leonid and Lev who received digs and playful punches from their sister.

'See, some things do not change, eh, Ira?'

Irina heard this and reacted by running around the table and raining pretended blows on her father.

Aleksei grinned as he watched the playacting and waited patiently for his answer.

Nina said, 'Aleksei we are not afraid of the danger. I am my father's daughter and proud of my blood. I miss them all, all my relatives, but most of all I miss visiting my mother's grave. I hope you find Elena alive and well.'

'It is the only thing that has kept me going all these years but, I have to admit, up until recently I had been giving up hope. As each year goes by another line appears and I wonder, if we passed each other on the street, whether we might recognise each other after all these years.'

'I think you would know her, even if your eyes were shut. Remember, Aleksei Vasiliy, you still have that power.'

Irina broke away from the assault on Nikolai. 'Yes, and did I not witness that power? You frightened me so much.'

'I know and I regret you had to witness such a thing. Sometimes I have had reason to curse everything it stands for, but then I remember that my grandfather, Stanislav, had this power and now, apparently, I am a grandfather, and this power is shared with my grandson. It is not just Elena I am searching for, but my daughter and grandson too. I am eager to get started, but do not want to appear ungrateful for all you have done for me.'

'No, you are not ungrateful. We all understand your needs and wish you well in your search. We have papers for you – a passport and travel documents. They are excellent forgeries and should see you safely to America.'

Nikolai produced these from a wall safe and handed them to Aleksei.

'America? But my daughter and grandson are in Britain.'

'I know, Aleksei, but the route of your escape has to go as planned. Our contacts are able to smuggle you in and out of America, but not Britain yet. That is a much more difficult task. Please remember there are others who know about your daughter and grandson and they will be expecting you to go there, so all ports will be on alert. As soon as we feel confident enough to get you into Britain, we will do so. We just cannot afford any mistakes. For all our sakes.'

Aleksei suddenly felt drained. He had escaped from prison, but was not yet totally free!

Irina poured a shot of vodka and handed it to Aleksei. He thanked her and immediately drank it down. She took the glass from him and repeated the exercise. Aleksei began to smile. Irina smiled back.

'That's better. I like it when you smile. Vodka can sometimes cure a broken heart – well, maybe for a while.'

Aleksei looked at the passport he had been given. It was in the name of a Jacques Poupard.

'French Canadian?' he asked.

Nikolai nodded. 'It was Oleg's idea. He managed to obtain it through his usual connections. This man was reported missing in action during the last days of the war. His identity was taken and used by someone else for some years, but that person no longer requires it. You are now he. He would have been around the same age as you and, best of all, he has no known family. That is why it was chosen. All we have to do now is get you safely into Canada. Then you will be taken to a safe house in America. I am told you speak a little French.'

'Yes, I was fortunate in that respect to have been with Professor Strekalovsky for so long. He was quite a linguist and taught me French, Spanish and German. Even a bit of Chinese too!'

Everyone around the table laughed.

'We move tomorrow, Aleksei. As we have no way of knowing yet of what happened back there, we have to move fast.'

'Still no news of Oleg or Dmitriy?' Aleksei asked.

All at the table lost their smiles.

Nikolai said gravely, 'It is not like Oleg to leave it so long before giving us instructions, so we are going ahead anyway. There might be a simple explanation, but each day that passes makes us less confident about his welfare.'

Aleksei was restless and did not sleep much that night. He sensed something was not quite right about the whole business, but he had no option but to go along with the plan devised for his escape. If it meant a period in America before he could begin the search for his family, then that is what he would have to accept. He did not want to return to the life he had been forced into for nearly seventeen years since his arrest in 1945. He got out of bed and wandered over to the window, looking out into the dark night illuminated in the distance by the streetlights of West Berlin. Everywhere appeared to be at peace. Aleksei heard the bedroom door opening softly and someone slipped in. He was about to speak when the figure moved towards him and put her finger to his lips.

'I have come to say goodbye, Aleksei Vasiliy. I will have a broken heart but I know this must be and that your future lies somewhere else.'

Aleksei could see the tears in her eyes. He hugged her close and whispered, 'When I find them I will bring them back to meet you all. Irina, please promise me you won't go back to find Oleg.'

Irina shrugged him off and stood back.

'How did you know? I have told no-one.'

Aleksei smiled grimly. 'It is in your eyes, Irina. Remember, I have a certain power and can sometimes read the minds of people.' Irina had that same look which Aleksei had found so puzzling before. But he could guess what it meant from the words she had spoken at the dinner table that previous evening.

He continued, 'Some things are better left unsaid. A certain look can win any argument. I wish it were different too.'

Irina moved forward, hugged him again and said, 'When you find Aleksei Vasiliy Zvadsky-Rudikov, your grandson, please remind him of Liliya.'

It was Aleksei's turn to be surprised. 'I don't understand. How do you know he is called these names after me? And who is Liliya?'

Irina smiled. 'You will have to wait and ask him that.'

She kissed him lightly on each cheek, then turned and left the room.

Aleksei sat down on the bed, his mind whirling. 'Liliya'. He whispered the name as if she might be in the room and could tell him what he was eager to learn.

There was no sign of Irina that morning as Aleksei said his goodbyes to the Dmitriev family. Nikolai and Nina apologised for her absence but Aleksei told them not to worry. He understood. Both boys had returned after searching high and low for her, but with grins on their faces. Nikolai shook his head.

'They have always been the same, the three of them. Keeping secrets. Why should it be any different now?'

Nikolai was to drive Aleksei to a meeting place where they would rendezvous with another contact who would then take Aleksei to a port in Holland, where he would embark on a merchant ship bound for Canada. From there he would be met and taken to a safe house, then on to the United States. The movements would coincide with the Christmas period, when everything and everyone would be more relaxed, including security.

23

When Rudy regained consciousness his head felt as if it were in a vice, with a hammer playing a tune on it. He looked about him. The room was empty but he could hear someone moving around downstairs. It took him a few moments to gather his senses and remember what had happened. He recalled waking and being sick and passing out afterwards. Someone had lifted him up and he remembered enjoying the soft cool feeling of being let down again on to what he now realised was his bed. But who had lifted him and who was the person downstairs? He decided to investigate and stood up but was not fully in control of his faculties and sat down on the bed again. He tried to get up again but only succeeded in bumping into his bedside table and knocking the alarm clock onto the floor. Rudy froze as he heard the footsteps on the stairs; this was not his mother. The footsteps reached the top of the stairs and came to a halt. Rudy felt a cold sweat on his brow. The doorknob began to turn and the door opened slowly.

'Well, there you are awake, Rudy. How are you feeling now? You gave me quite a scare.'

Rudy felt an overwhelming sense of relief as he came face to face with Bernadette Cullen, the former nurse at his school and now a friend.

'Oh, Miss Cullen, am I glad it's you. I just did not know what was happening to me.'

'Poor boy. Did you eat something perhaps that didn't agree with you?'

'I don't think so. Whatever it was it doesn't taste nice now.'

Rudy then noticed the glass in her hand.

'Here, drink this down,' she said.

'What's in it?'

'It's an old Irish recipe, guaranteed to cure the worst hangovers...'

She chuckled.

Taking the glass, Rudy sniffed the concoction first and pulled a face but he drank it down. His eyes widened as he felt the mixture seeping into his system and then a smile broke out on his face.

'Wow! That's a lot better. What did you say was in it?'

'Now don't be asking me because it's a secret recipe.'

Rudy looked at the stern but kind face of Bernadette Cullen. Her hair was fixed in a bun at the back. He had been terrified of her at school but here she was now, doting on him like a favourite aunt. Then he looked past her at the empty doorway. She turned to follow his gaze. She felt goose pimples as she remembered Rudy's strange gifts and looked back at him.

'What is it, Rudy? What can you see that I can't?'

'I can't see anything. I was just wondering where my mum was.'

'Your mother isn't here. The door was open and all was quiet so I took the liberty and came in, hoping to find you. That is why I knocked on each door before entering.'

Rudy rose to his feet and wobbled as he made for the doorway. Bernadette Cullen took his arm and assisted him.

'Be sure, Rudy. You are still weak. You need to rest more.'

He ignored her.

'Where's Mum? I need to find her. Are you sure she isn't down there? Has she left a note?'

He stopped at the top of the stairs breathing heavily, feeling the effort taking its toll on his body.

'Rudy, please go steady. I will help you down the stairs but be careful. What if your mother comes back and finds you at the bottom with a broken neck and me standing over you?'

Rudy managed a wry grin that ended in a grimace.

'I promise not to fall down the stairs.'

Then he lurched forward, taking her with him. It took all her strength to hold him from falling and she breathed a huge sigh of relief as they reached the bottom safely.

'To be sure, I'm too old for this kind of thing. There's a time I could have carried you down, but not now. My bones are good for nothing.'

'I don't think that's quite true,' Rudy gasped getting his breath back. 'Who lifted me from the hall onto my bed?'

'Oh, that was different. I really thought you were at death's door. At times like that you find some miraculous strength. And I'm telling you this, with what *you* can do.'

She laughed.

'I don't feel I could perform miracles at the moment. My mind seems to be submerged in water.'

As they staggered into the kitchen Rudy noticed an envelope taped to the wall. He reached out and grabbed it, then sat down in a chair by the table.

'What is it, Rudy? I didn't notice that before.'

The envelope had no writing on it so Rudy ripped it open. A sheet of paper dropped out onto the floor. Bernadette picked it up and read it.

'O, my God! Tell me I am not reading this. *This is a message for Rudy Metthewson, concerning his mother Helen. Firstly, do not on any account contact the police or anyone else about this or it will be for the worst. We have taken your mother and she will be locked away until you agree to help*

208

us. We know all about your amazing ability. If you agree to assist us then your mother goes free. If you don't help us then you will never see her again.'

Rudy sat perfectly still his face white with shock. Then it slowly crumpled as he began to weep. Bernadette put her arm around him but she found herself sniffing back tears.

'We must go to the police. I know that letter says we must not but I think we should.'

Shaking his head and wiping his face, Rudy replied earnestly, 'No, Miss Cullen, I don't trust them either. In fact, I don't trust anyone at the moment.'

She frowned. 'You mean you don't even trust me?'

'No, no, I don't mean that. Of course I do. It's just that I was warned not to trust anyone, and to be careful because of who I am and what I can do. But I never thought they would take my mum. I would never have let her out of my sight if I had thought that.'

'That would have been noble of you but quite impossible. You would have had to sleep sometime.' Bernadette's face showed him that she meant this kindly and he accepted it with a nod. 'So don't feel badly about that. Anyway, I have a confession to make.'

'Confession?'

'Yes. You haven't asked me what brought me around to visit you. I can't believe how this might look to you, but a priest visited me yesterday and asked me questions about my friendship with your mother and yourself.'

Rudy sat up looking alarmed.

'I know and I am truly sorry. You know about the confessional box in a church, Rudy?'

'Yes, I do but what has this to do with my mum being kidnapped?'

'Let me finish. When I saw you do that in the playground at school that day it spooked me enough to want to confess, in case it was a sin. I know it might seem foolish to be so scared and superstitious, but you have to remember our faith is very strict and as a child the fear of God was put into me over certain matters. You don't lose that easily, even at my age now. Anyway, I was absolved of any sins and left it at that until we had that problem with the infamous five, as you called them. I tried not to let it affect me but my faith is too deep for it to be ignored so I went to confession again. This time though I was asked all kinds of questions and yesterday the same priest who had heard my confession came to see me and to propose something.'

'Propose something?'

'Yes, and I feel awful now that we are facing this terrible truth. He proposed that you and your mother be given sanctuary by the Church. He wanted to talk to you about entering the priesthood as a way of hiding from those who are after you.'

'Why would I want to do that? I am not afraid of them that much. I would hate to be a priest.'

'But I believe he was only trying to find a solution to your troubles, although I fear he is too late now. I still think we should go to the police.'

'No, Miss Cullen. Please believe me. They are all in it together, helping each other with information. I would end up being locked up one way or another by whoever was called in to investigate. No, we have to do this ourselves. I am going to have another lie down and hope I can relax enough to be given something to help us. Will you stay here with me, please?'

Bernadette Cullen had tears in her eyes. 'Of course, Rudy. I have nowhere else to go.'

24

Aleksei had so many days to reflect on it all. He was now a fugitive again, not just from those who would gladly have welcomed him back into a Soviet prison but also from those who had brought him this far and left him to the mercy of the West. That he believed implicitly. He was sickened by the knowledge that he had been set up. Who in the line could he ever trust again? Every telephone number he had been given had been unobtainable since that day. He shivered as he sat in his makeshift dwelling, an old sheet tied between two trees and camouflaged with twigs, branches and leaves. A thick winter overcoat, hat and gloves were still not enough protection from the cold nights. Aleksei felt as miserable as he had ever remembered being in all his life – and afraid, very afraid.

For months he had been shifted from one safe house to another across state boundaries from town to town and city to city. Now he was in Dallas, Texas.

After nearly a year in the West, on 22nd November, 1963, he had been shocked to see the television pictures of the assassination of United States President, John F. Kennedy. But later a much greater shock was to come. A news report had identified the person arrested on suspicion of the killing of JFK as Lee Harvey Oswald. The report went on to say that there was a strong rumour of another one or more gunmen also being involved in the shooting and that one of the suspects was alleged to be a Russian defector who had escaped from the Soviet Union the previous year. The report identified the man as one Aleksei

Vasiliy Rudikov also known as Jacques Poupard, possessing a passport in this name and posing as a French Canadian citizen. Aleksei sat stunned for minutes not knowing what to do. Then he had grabbed the telephone and started dialling the numbers he had been given. All were discontinued or unobtainable. Before this event someone had visited him every day to see if all was well, but no-one came that day. Aleksei bundled up some belongings and fled the apartment and the city. He had managed to hitch a lift to a small town just over the border, hoping the truck driver wouldn't be up with the latest news, which appeared to be the case. Once there he risked visiting local stores and stocked up on supplies. Deep down, though, Aleksei knew he was fighting a losing battle. He would eventually have to give himself up.

One thousand five hundred miles away in a smart suburban district of California, a fifty-four-year-old lady was tending her flower garden and waving at any neighbour passing by. Her sun-tanned complexion and slender body made her look at least ten years younger. Her dark hair was tied back in a tight ponytail revealing a face with fine bone structure. But this lady was not delicate in any way as her movements and the fire in her eyes betrayed. Her husband called from inside the house and she turned with a smile and a wave. She stopped what she was doing and skipped inside. Jim, her husband, handed her a cup of coffee and she sat down for a breather. He was watching the latest news on the presidential assassination. Then she saw Aleksei's picture and heard his name. She dropped her coffee cup, and tried to speak, but all that came out was a strangled cry of anguish.

'You look as if you have seen a ghost dear,' exclaimed her husband. 'What is the matter? Do you know this man?'

His wife still could not speak. She stared at the television without blinking.

Jim approached and tried to comfort her but she shrugged him off and she began to pace up and down wringing her hands. At last she found her voice but when she began to speak it was in Russian, fast and angry. Elena had not spoken in Russian for many years.

Jim was dumbfounded.

Gradually, Elena calmed down. Her diatribe in Russian was punctuated with the odd word in English, until she finally sat down and ceased speaking all together. Her face suddenly crumpled and she began to weep uncontrollably. Jim went to the drinks cabinet and poured her favourite tipple. A large one! Then handed it to her and she stopped crying and nodded her gratitude and drank it down in one. Then she took a deep breath. 'Another, please!'

Jim looked questioningly at her but the glare he received in return had him scuttling back to the drinks cabinet. When he returned she was muttering quietly.

'They lied to me, the whole lot of them lied to me. And Surnyaev – may his bones rot in hell! – he was the one who convinced me Aleksei was dead.' Elena looked at her husband who was looking very confused. 'This is such a shock. I cannot believe what I am seeing. I am sorry, Jim. I should have told you this long ago but it was too personal for me, much too painful, but it is relevant now and I must tell you it all. It will not be easy.'

He took her hand. 'It's OK, dear. You don't live with someone this long without detecting that something has been nagging at them.'

'Has it been that obvious? All I can do is explain why and you will see then, I hope. Aleksei was my childhood sweetheart and we were to be married. But times were dangerous and my family thought we might be the next

213

in line to be picked up for the camps, so we decided to flee. I did not have time to warn Aleksei; all I could do was leave him a letter. We wrote to each other and we arranged to meet but the opportunity never came about. We always seemed to be moving in opposite directions. Then, at Stalingrad, I was officially informed of Aleksei's death. Colonel Maksim Surnyaev showed me the official documentation. After that I gave up completely. My heart was broken. I became reckless, not caring really what happened to me, only wishing to kill as many Germans as I could to avenge his death. But now I can see it was all a ruse by Maksim Surnyaev to get back at Aleksei, as the two of them never saw eye to eye. I think Surnyaev secretly wanted me for himself. Fat chance! The rest you know.'

Lieutenant Jim Earnshaw of the United States marine corps had met Elena Zvadsky during the 1945 post-war celebrations in Berlin, and he pulled many strings to arrange for her to return with him to America, where they were married the following year. Jim left the army and set up his own engineering business, which thrived over the years giving them a healthy living. Their only child, Ben, was born a year later in 1947 and had reached high academic standards and hoped to be a lawyer.

Jim Earnshaw listened patiently to Elena's account but he was secretly wishing that this situation hadn't presented itself and that he didn't have to face the problem. He had always suspected that she was holding something back from her past but as time went on it became less of an issue in his mind. He was contemplating this when Elena hit him with a further bombshell.

'There's something else, Jim. I hardly dare mention it because it is going to change our whole existence now I know Aleksei is alive. He will never forgive me.' She put her head down not wishing to see the shock and pain in her husband's eyes. 'I am sorry to say this but I gave our daughter away. The daughter Aleksei has no knowledge of, as far as I know, as I never told him.'

Jim looked aghast. 'But I don't understand. How did he not know and what happened to her? You gave her away to whom?'

'I was pregnant when I left with my family and did not mention this in my letters. We were constantly close to being captured so I decided the best option was to hand my daughter to a friend for her to be smuggled out through Finland and then on to Britain. As far as I know she was adopted but I never discovered by whom or where she is now. I suppose I could have made more enquiries, but my family, as you know, are all dead or missing, so I decided long ago just to get on with my life here and forget the past. But the past has come back to haunt me, Jim.'

Jim sat looking into the distance his mind full of mixed thoughts. Then he said quietly, 'Why did you think you could not tell me? I would have understood, really.'

Elena shook her head slowly. 'Too painful to share with anyone, even you Jim. You are a good man but something like this is not easy for anyone to take. I did not want us to break up so kept it to myself. It is only an issue now because of this revelation on the TV.'

'And do you think he could be capable of killing our president?' Jim asked.'

'The Aleksei I know and have kept in my heart was noble and above such things. He killed in wartime, but I do not believe he would be capable of such an act as this. There must be so much more to it than meets the eye and for one who knows that much about Soviet scheming I would not put it past them to have arranged for Aleksei to be set up. That is the feeling deep inside of me.' Elena looked grimly at her husband. 'I know this will upset you, but I must try and find Aleksei. At the moment he will not have friend in the world and all of America will want to lynch him.'

'That's a fact. Kennedy was much loved and respected. But, hell, your man has at least two friends here. If you trust in him as much as that, then so do I and I will help you all I can.'

Tears fell from Elena as she hugged him. 'Thank you from the bottom of my heart. You are a good man. But what about Ben. Should we tell him anything about this?'

Jim shook his head. 'No, not yet anyway. It's got to be kept tight and, as much as I trust Ben, he's young and young people sometimes don't see the full picture. I'd hate for him to suffer.'

'Where do we start, Jim?'

He thought for a moment then replied. 'I have kept pretty close ties with one or two people in the know. I will give them a call and see what can be arranged. But under the circumstances I am going to have to tread carefully.'

25

General Guznischev stood to attention as Nikita Khrushchev stormed into the room. He walked to a desk and leant on it with both hands and sighed heavily. He then walked to a window, staring out on the view below. He stood for a long moment, after which he turned to the general.

'I am angry General Guznischev, very angry indeed. What little space we have for manoeuvre with the United States has been seriously jeopardised by all of this. It is only an allegation, and a flimsy one at that, yet they have it on their prime time news bulletins and without even a hint of consultation with us. I know it must have been a shock for them to lose such a good president. Despite our differences, I liked and respected him. But to accuse so distinguished a former Soviet soldier without any evidence is shameful. To broadcast it is unforgivable. Who do you think set this all up, General?'

Guznischev shook his head slowly. 'I wish I knew. I am totally at a loss over it all. There are some who must know though.'

Khrushchev grunted and sat down in a chair. 'I am being asked how it is possible that Aleksei Vasiliy Rudikov shot the President of the United States and my reply each time is "*impossible*". This is the man whose grandfather saved Stalin. Aleksei Vasiliy himself saved my life. Why should such noble acts be sullied by the blood of a Western leader? It is inconceivable. This whole matter smells as rotten as the corpses still rotting in unknown graves. I do not think I will have much longer to wait until I am assassinated as well. Not with a bullet but with some other way to organise my removal from this office.'

He eyed the general as he said this and saw the reaction he expected. General Guznischev was about to protest but Khrushchev held up his hand.

'General, I am not blind – neither am I deaf. I see the discontent, even though I believe I can still give prosperity to the Russian people through peaceful coexistence with the West. But my terms are unacceptable to some who appear to be growing more powerful within our party system. If it is to be so it will be so. But while I am still here I will do what I think is best.

'Are we going to ask for him to be returned to us?'

'Return? What! To face a firing squad? He may not be in a very healthy position there but his treatment would certainly be worse if he were to be sent back here.'

'Who gave that damned order to allow this to be released to the press? That could have been used as a way to pressurise him into coming over to us, but not now. No-one else was supposed to know about it except us.' Bill Collins spat this out after charging into John Mackay's office. Collins, as usual of late, had been at home when Martha had given him the news of the assassination of his president and had sat speechless in shock looking at the news for a long time before he had responded.

'What release? I don't know what you are on about, Bill.' John Mackay got up from his seat and switched on the television set in his office, just as the report was repeated. He stood rigid as he took it in.

'Well, John, do you know anything about this? Jesus! This has messed up years of planning.' Bill Collins fumed.

John Mackay still thought he had the measure of his boss.

'Bill, I am surprised you would think that of me. I have been with you a long, long time. Do you really think I would release this without your authorisation?'

Mackay's eyes narrowed as Bill Collins looked suspiciously at him. 'There is something going seriously wrong here. That is our president lying there in the morgue. Some son of a bitch is responsible for it but we know for a fact it wasn't a hit by Stray Dog. Who the hell set him up for this, I ask – and, more importantly, why? It's blown everything out of the water and how the hell can we repair the damage? The Russkies are hopping mad, as you would expect.'

John Mackay began to bluster. 'Look here, Bill, it's not anything to do with me or anyone else I know. I might have been a silly sod over my bed partners in the past but this is a bed I would never have soiled. You gotta believe that.'

Bill Collins looked hard at him. 'So?'

Mackay winced. 'Hell! I ain't been that bright with my personal life and I am indebted to you for all your restraint, but I ain't no traitor. I know it's infuriated and angered some of the others but I have tried to make up for it. That Doug James really laid me on the line and I just wonder now why that was. I mean, he walked out and he is down that way ... so?'

Bill Collins was shaking his head. 'Shut up John. While you might just be a fraction ahead in all this, shut up, now, do you hear?'

Bernadette Cullen had dozed off, so was startled by the knock on the door. It took her moment to remember where she was and why. Opening the front door she was met by a smart, suited individual who proffered a card and introduced himself as Graham Digby.

219

Upstairs Rudy was awake; he heard the quiet voices below. He first sauntered into the bathroom and splashed cold water over his head and face, then, feeling rejuvenated, made his way down the stairs to encounter those below.

One of these he was sure was Miss Cullen and as he entered the front room he breathed a sigh of relief to see that she was still there. But his face changed when he saw Graham Digby.

'We were just talking about you, Rudy. How are you feeling?' Digby appeared to be trying just a little bit too hard to sound concerned.

Bernadette Cullen immediately noticed the look on his face and replied for him.

'For sure he is looking a lot better, aren't you, Rudy?' She threw a look at him.

Rudy nodded slightly. 'Why are you here?'

Bernadette again intervened. 'Rudy, we have been talking and it seems your mum is OK. Mister Digby here has been keeping an eye on things. They have followed them and kept them under surveillance, isn't that right?'

Digby was still looking closely at the boy as he answered. 'Yes, we have been watching this lot for a long time. Your mother is completely safe, believe me.'

'Then how did they capture my mum if you were watching them?'

Graham Digby coughed as he began to lose his composure. 'We have been watching these for a long time now. I can guarantee your mother will be safe.'

Rudy saw the change in Digby's demeanour. 'You watched her being taken off?'

Digby nodded, now feeling embarrassed as Bernadette Cullen trained her eyes on him.

'It is not in our interests to intervene just yet as we want them to lead us to their paymasters. And it isn't quite as bad as it seems. We have an under-cover operative

220

with them who has been given orders to protect your mother no matter what it takes.'

Rudy was about to speak but Bernadette Cullen spoke for him.

'I can't believe what I am hearing here. You are saying you allowed her to be kidnapped. And for, the love of God, how do you expect us to believe you can save her? You must stop all this cloak and dagger stuff and rescue her now.'

Rudy glared at Digby. 'You will rescue her, won't you? Because if you don't, I will. That I promise.'

Before Digby could reply Bernadette Cullen had a warning for him.

'If you think this young lad is not capable of doing that then think again. He is stronger than you imagine.'

Digby cleared his throat. 'I am well aware of that and it is the reason why Mrs Metthewson has been kidnapped, isn't that a fact? We know, Rudy has special powers. A lot of people are very interested in him and what he can do. I feel quite sure they are looking for a way of capturing him. I have every reason to believe they have something else up their sleeve and may now have the ability to negate his powers, so it would be advisable for him not to go anywhere near them. Just leave it to us.'

'Why should we believe that?' Rudy was beginning to bristle.

'All right, but I didn't really intend to tell you any of this as it is very hush-hush. These secrets are highly classified. I am telling you to prevent Rudy making a grave mistake and finding himself captured by this gang. They want to experiment on him – that is a certainty – and you wouldn't want that, eh, son?'

Rudy still glared defiantly but the message was understood and he shook his head.

'Good, I am pleased you understand that much. There

is something else we can do for you and that is to offer you our protection, which will mean moving you to a secure place.'

Bernadette shook her head. 'No, that will not be necessary. We already have an idea where we can go to find safety, haven't we, Rudy?'

Rudy looked confused for a moment, then realised what she was hinting at and nodded his head.

Digby watched the exchange, looking disappointed. He shrugged and handed his card to Bernadette.

'Well, the offer is there. So if you change your mind my number is on my card.'

He got up and Bernadette saw him out. They chatted briefly on the doorstep, but Rudy did not hear what was being said as he was concentrating on the televised news report. On the screen was the image of a man he thought he recognised. Then the name was mentioned and Rudy stood up in surprise. 'Aleksei Vasiliy Rudikov!' Rudy stood transfixed as Bernadette came back into the room.

'What is it Rudy? You look as if you have seen a ghost.'

He pointed at the television set and exclaimed in a strangled voice, 'My grandfather! I think that's my grandfather – and they are saying he shot President Kennedy!'

Back in his office Graham Digby made certain he was alone then used a secure telephone line.

'Good day to you. I have good news. I think the fish is about to take your bait.'

Sitting in a quiet room in the heart of the Vatican, Monsignor Luigi Venditti thanked the caller and replaced the receiver, smiling with great satisfaction.

26

Louisiana

Aleksei shivered as he rose from his seated position. He had to get his circulation going. As he walked out of his makeshift lodgings, he was reminded of all those years ago when he had to assemble similar camps, stalking game in the forests, a skill that became very useful later on during the war years for stake-outs. He looked at his watch but noticed it had stopped again. Shaking it to get it started didn't work this time. He guessed it must be mid-afternoon, but he had lost all track of the date. Aleksei moved away from the camp, walking down the slope towards the water's edge. Everything appeared calm and peaceful as he scanned the bayou and the horizon for any signs of life. He was about to turn back when he suddenly saw a shape moving in the distance, between the trees. He reached into his coat pocket but froze as he realised he had left one of his wartime spoils, a luger pistol, inside the camp. It was most unlike him to make such a mistake and he cursed himself under his breath. The tall figure emerged from the trees into the open, stopping a few yards away. Aleksei could not make out the man's features as the massive fur coat he was wearing had the collar upturned and the woollen hat he wore came down over his ears. All Aleksei could make out were the eyes, which were trained on him. But Aleksei's own eyes were on the shotgun the man was carrying. He wondered if he should make a run for it but reckoned

223

he wouldn't make cover. Then, to his amazement, the man lowered the gun and called out a greeting in a quiet but gruff voice.

'A good day to you, mister, thought I would find you here. You that fella that's causing all the commotion down these ways, ain't ya?'

'Have you come here to arrest me?'

'Hell, no mister, that would mean I'd be doing their job for them and I ain't one for giving no assistance like that, and that's fer sure.' The man lay the shotgun on the ground and then reached up, turning his collar down and removing his hat to reveal the bald head of an elderly black man. He noticed Aleksei's surprise and chuckled. 'Suppose you ain't used to seeing the colour of my kind, seeing how you come from Russkieland.'

Aleksei remained silent.

'Makes no difference to me if you're not keen on my colour because lots of others feel that way about us. One more ain't gonna make no difference.'

'I do not dislike your colour. I am not that sort of person.'

The black man whistled. 'Well, that's mighty nice to know. You shoot the president but you don't mind us coloured folks, huh?'

Aleksei felt tense on hearing this, reminding him of the danger. 'I did not shoot your president.'

The black man stared at Aleksei.

'You do not believe me?'

'Ain't quite sure. A lot of others think you did and they're mighty pissed off. Plenty of rednecks running around with guns and the like, that's why I came to warn you, mister. Best you get away from these parts because them are close, very close.'

'Why do you come to tell me this? You believe I shot your president.'

'Didn't say that mister, just said I wasn't sure, but anyway, it makes no difference to me.'

'No difference?'

'Hell no, mister. Suppose you don't know too much about American history, especially the history down here in the South. We blacks are not highly thought of by whites, especially in this state of Louisiana. So as the president was another white man I don't really see it as my problem, even though he was better than most.'

Aleksei nodded. 'That is what I thought and another reason why whoever killed him was guilty of murdering a good man. I would not dream of killing a good man.'

'Guess I am beginning to believe you, mister. So if they catch up with you they will be guilty of the same. Killing a good man. My name is Samuel, Samuel Johnson.'

Aleksei smiled. 'I am Aleksei Rudikov, but you would know that by now.'

'Sure do, mister. So do a lot of others so I think I best guide you out of this place back to somewhere they will find it harder to find you.'

'That would be kind of you but I do not understand why you are concerned for me.'

'Had me a dream last night. Used to having them and finding some of them coming true, just like this one. Someone somewhere wants you looked after, that's for sure.' Samuel chuckled quietly.

Samuel assisted Aleksei in dismantling his camp and guided him through dense forest to a track where his battered truck stood. 'Ain't much but it gets me around.'

Samuel drove for some miles over rough tracks chatting to Aleksei, asking a lot about Russia. Suddenly, he put his foot down hard on the accelerator causing Aleksei to grab hold of his seat.

'What's wrong?'

Samuel tugged the steering wheel as the old truck

squealed on its axles, forced to manoeuvre in and out of a line of trees. 'Rednecks.'

Aleksei looked over his shoulder and noticed another truck following behind, catching up fast. There were three men with rifles, two standing in the back taking aim and one inside accompanying the driver. Suddenly, shots rang out and bullets skimmed off the roof and sides of Samuel's truck. Ignoring the fire Aleksei leant out of the passenger side window, firing two shots from his luger and bursting the front nearside tyre on the chasing truck. It spun out of control and hit a tree, throwing off the two men in the back. But the third managed to get out and fire another volley of shots at the departing wagon, the bullets bursting through metal and putting a hole in the fuel tank. Gasoline poured out as the truck sped off into the distance.

'We have a problem, I think. I can smell petrol.' Aleksei opened his door and looked back at the trail of gasoline glistening on the ground. 'Yes, we have big trouble, the tank is punctured.'

Samuel tapped the fuel gauge, which was going down fast. 'Guess I ain't gonna get you to that place I was talking about, sorry.'

Aleksei grabbed his shoulder. 'Let me out here. I will be OK. Use what fuel you have left to get clear.'

Samuel protested. 'No, I will take you to my home and shelter you there. You can meet my family.'

'Samuel, you are a good man and I thank you for that invitation. And I promise one day I will come back and meet your family, but not today. I refuse to put you in any more danger.' Aleksei offered his hand and Samuel took it, sadly shaking his head.

As Aleksei took his bundle out of the back he ripped off a piece of cloth and rammed it in the hole, stemming the flow of gasoline. Then he waved him off. 'Go, please go, whilst you have time and I will visit you again one day my friend, Samuel Johnson.'

Aleksei watched the reluctant black man disappear back towards the road. He knew by now that any chances of remaining free were greatly reduced after this episode, but he had given up on the idea of surrendering, considering Americans to be as trigger-happy as many Russians he had known. He made his way to a river that appeared navigable and where, to his relief, he found an old canoe. It required some repair but Aleksei managed to make it float and headed out along the river. 'I am not caught yet!'

Over the following days Aleksei, more through luck than judgement, steered clear of search parties, some of them he heard speaking French with an odd dialect. The Cajuns had been set a task by Bill Turner, who had briefly visited his cousins, co-ordinating the search.

The sound of a tree branch snapping woke Aleksei with a start, but before he could move a flashlight shone in his face and he could feel the barrel of a gun pressed against his cheekbone. Other armed men stood in the background, an angry party spitting with vengeance.

'Com' on, you shit bastard.'

Aleksei made a move to stand up but was knocked down again by a uniformed policeman wielding a baseball bat. The blow caught him on the side of the head and he lost consciousness for a moment. When he came to again he was being kicked and punched. He tried to defend himself but he lost consciousness again as blows rained down on him.

Aleksei vaguely recollected being thrown into the back of a truck. He awoke to find himself on a filthy bunk bed inside a jail. His whole body was bruised and battered and his innards especially were protesting at the treatment meted out by the posse. Aleksei groaned.

'I need a doctor.'

The words alerted the police sergeant at the desk. 'What you asking for, boy?'

'I need a doctor.'

The sergeant spat on the floor. 'The only doctor you are getting is one who pronounces you fit enough to be executed, you son of a bitch.'

The police sergeant bit off a piece of tobacco and chewed on the lump, as he looked the prisoner over. 'Don't look as if you are that bad anyway.'

Aleksei glared through puffed up eyes, his face heavily distorted with the swellings and bruises. Dried blood lay on his ears, neck and nostrils. He coughed and rolled over depositing a gobbet of blood on the floor.

'Fetch me a doctor, I'm in a bad way.'

The sergeant spat the contents of his mouth through the cell bars.

'You got a mess to clear up there, boy. Ain't you just pretty pissed off you came into my county. Plenty of folks 'round here aways want a lynchin'. So I am doing you a big favour, boy. Just don't forget that, huh?'

Aleksei could feel some of the surge related to his power beginning to form but fought against it. He did not want to make matters any worse than they already were. He had to keep cool, calm and collected. He couldn't afford to lose it this time, as it would mean there would definitely be no way back.

'You would do me a bigger favour by fetching me a doctor. Your friends did not need a rope. They wanted to kick and punch me to death.'

He groaned with the effort of talking.

'Now see here, mister, don't you go making allegations about the fine men of this town. You clearly walked out in front of a truck. A very large truck at that!' He burst into laughter, which was echoed by the two deputies who had just walked in.

'Say, Sam, is that dude still breathin'? Thought he would have been a gonner by now. That truck sure did roll over him pretty good!'

More laughter followed. Then the telephone rang.

Sergeant Sam Holt looked at the phone for a moment waiting for it to stop, but it continued to ring.

'Damn. Who the hell can be calling at this time of the morning, unless it's Ivy bringing me my breakfast?' The deputies smirked as they watched Sam pick up the phone.

'Sergeant Holt here. What can I do for you early-bird folks?'

He grinned at the deputies who were enjoying his usual banter. But the smile disappeared from his face as he listened to the caller. He tried to interrupt a couple of times and his face began to lose its colour as the blood drained from it. The deputies looked at each other. The caller rang off and Sam stood looking at the receiver.

'What's wrong, Sam? Who was that?' Charlie Coombes, one of the deputies, asked.

Sam stood still for a few moments, then shook his head. 'Jesus! They are coming for him. Said we should have alerted them earlier. Asked if he's OK. They are coming to take him back.'

Coombes looked nervously at his buddy. 'They? Who are they?'

'FBI, CIA, or something like that – damned important whoever, by the sounds of it. Shit! Run and get the doctor quick. Don't let on to anyone else what's going on.'

Aleksei heard the commotion but could not comprehend it. He began to lose consciousness again.

229

27

John Mackay sat at his desk wondering what was going on inside the head of his boss. Increasingly, in his presence Bill Collins appeared edgy and suspicious. His general health was fast failing him, not helped by the present situation between Russia and America over this latest episode concerning Stray Dog.

Bill Collins had decided to take another day off to recuperate. Martha had insisted on it and he had agreed unwillingly as the whole situation was still in his mind wherever he sat. The telephone rang and Martha answered it. She told the caller that Bill was taking a nap, but he came out into the hall and took the receiver gently from her. She glared at him and sighed, then left him to it.

'Hello! Anyone still there?' the caller had been asking.

Bill recognised the voice.

'Doug, it's good to hear from you. Becoming a bit of a habit now, eh?' he chuckled.

'I hope I haven't put my foot in it again. Martha didn't sound too friendly.'

'Martha is being Martha as far that goes. She is only trying to protect my interests, I suppose, but it would be very hard to do that at the moment with all that's going on.'

'Yeah. I just can't get over it. Of all the presidents we've had, Jack Kennedy was one of the best, even though he was a Catholic!'

'Well, I never held that against him. Sometimes I think

we see too much of the religion and not enough of the
the man, don't you think?'

'With you all the way, Bill. Damn shame! There's been
a lot of activity in the background since. All kinds of
conspiracy theories and names coming up.'

'Yeah, I know what you mean. Lee Harvey has got to
be one of 'em. But nothing convinces me yet that he was
acting alone. I think there must be a lot more riding on
this one.'

Bill had wound the extension wire out and was now
sitting comfortably in the armchair again.

'I agree, and our Soviet friends are in agreement too.
They have come up with one interesting name – Oleg
Chehovsky. Heard of him?'

'Oleg Chehovsky? No, I don't recall the name.'

'Well, no surprise there as he has been officially missing
in action since 1942 at Stalingrad, but it appears it was
just a ruse and he went on the run under a different
name. He already had a very neat black market business
before the war and kept the contacts going. A really
reliable bunch of people by all accounts as there was
every possibility of a double-cross but, I think this Oleg
is in with some who pull the strings of the real Soviet
show.'

'So what's this Oleg been up to of late?'

Bill was clearly becoming very intrigued by the
conversation.

'The dog is out of the kennel,' Doug replied.

'I think I'm with you … code for our Stray Dog?'

'Yep, a code all right and it was for SD. Oleg was an
old sniper buddy of Aleksei Rudikov. It was Oleg who
planned his escape under that code.' Doug heard Bill suck
in his breath and continued. 'I know, Bill. Quite a shock
– especially as it has taken the assassination of our dear
president for all this to come out. I think a lot of people

231

are wetting themselves and don't want to be tied up in it at all. That's the impression I am getting. Many are saying that Kennedy's murder will result in a lot of nasty business being flushed out of a lot of messy holes.

'Are you thinking what I am thinking here, Doug? This Oleg Chehovsky, could he also have arranged the set up, even the assassination?'

Martha overheard the last few sentences and began to take an interest. She fetched him a drink, sat down in a chair opposite and listened intently.

'It's early days for that to be confirmed but, all things considered, it's a real possibility. A pretty neat set up, springing a wartime sniper and smuggling him into the States, then having him seen around Dallas just before the president is shot. I was surprised his name was in the news though, especially as *we* had designs on having him defect to us.'

'That's a sore subject at the moment, Doug. As you can imagine, I was pretty angry over that but no-one is owning up.'

'John Mackay?' Doug suggested.

'Here you are again with John. I told you, Doug, he can be a pain, but I have put it to him. He was most indignant.'

'Easy to show false indignation, Bill, but I won't mention it again. So this Aleksei is on the run now as all his channels have closed up on him?'

'Appears they have all deserted him, and if he's been watching the news he'll know now and believe he has to hide pretty damned good. I just hope he sees sense and gives himself up.'

Doug James hesitated for a moment and then said, 'Got a bad feeling on that one, Bill. What if he goes somewhere where they don't ask too many questions? Nigger meat and all that? If he's fled Texas I hope he doesn't go

Louisiana way because some there don't need an excuse for a lynching.'

Bill Collins suddenly shuddered.

'Are you OK, Bill? There I go again, making you to take more of those pills.' He laughed.

'Sorry, Doug. I had a premonition then. I got a feeling he may already be having his skin flayed. Perhaps we need to alert the authorities in those areas that he's no longer a suspect.'

Aleksei came around hearing the key turn in the lock as the cell was opened. In strode a man carrying a black bag. He took a quick look at the prisoner, then barked, 'Hell! Get an ambulance here right now.'

The doctor opened his bag, took out a syringe and injected Aleksei's arm. He felt a warm sensation and passed out again.

'How is he, Jack?' Sam asked as he stood by the cell gate mopping his brow with his hat.

The doctor half turned and said coldly. 'Jesus, Sam! What the hell did you do to this poor guy? He's in a really bad way.'

'Truck ran over him. Isn't that right, Sam?' Deputy Coombes said, laughing nervously.

'Shut up Charlie. That's not funny anymore,' Sam replied.

Jack Hart, the town physician, glared at the three officers. 'You better have a better story than that when someone asks you what happened to him.'

'Who do you think will care about that, Jack? The son-of-a-bitch shot our president,' Sam Holt said as he looked past the doctor at the crumpled body on the bed.

'I think you might be in for a shock there, Sam. The latest news reports are that it was a case of mistaken identity. This guy is no longer a suspect.'

Sergeant Sam Holt stood rigid with his mouth hanging open. Both deputies looked at each other, white as sheets.

'Charlie here was saying you have fellas on the way down here to fetch this man. Well, you better warn 'em that this fella ain't going anywhere – not for a while, I guess. It's hospital for him, if he makes it that far.'

The doctor turned back and checked on the patient.

Finding his voice again Sam Holt asked, 'Jack, it's not as bad as that, is it? I mean, the guy is going to be all right, ain't he?'

'Can't be sure, but he is showing signs of bleeding internally. Where's that ambulance? We need him in hospital right away.'

The ambulance arrived just as Aleksei went into convulsions and stopped breathing. The paramedics worked furiously on him, aided by the doctor. Suddenly, Aleksei began breathing again and was carefully removed to the ambulance. The three officers stood watching, their faces grey. Somehow they were going to have to find a lot better excuses this time around.

The telephone rang again at the Collins residence. Bill had been filling Martha in with more of the details provided by Doug James. It was John Mackay on the other end of the line.

'Sorry to bother you, Bill, on your day off but something has come up. You are not going to like it one bit.'

Bill Collins' face told Martha all she needed to know and she went to fetch his medication.

'What is it, John?'

'We were too late with that news report turn around. Perhaps we shouldn't have delayed it. Stray Dog strayed into badlands territory and got beaten up badly. He's in hospital with our best men there around him. It's touch and go for him. They have already lost him twice.'

Martha handed him his pills, which he swallowed before answering.

'Jesus! Can this get any worse? I am on my way in. Arrange a flight for us down to wherever he is hospitalised. I'm taking complete charge from this moment on.' He replaced the receiver and turned to his wife. 'I'm sorry, Martha, but this situation has gotten out of hand. I need to go down there and make sure nothing else goes wrong.'

'I know, dear. But please be careful and come back in one piece. Promise me you will not overstress yourself, and remember to take your pills.'

Bill kissed her forehead and said, 'After this is sorted out I am going to retire. That I will promise you, dear.'

'That is good news, but what if this man dies?'

'That doesn't bear thinking about at the moment. It could start the third world war if Khrushchev has anything to do with it.'

Elena and Jim had seen the news reports stating that there had been a case of mistaken identity and that Aleksei was no longer considered a suspect. Jim was waiting to hear back from one of his ex-army chums who had a way in to the higher echelons of the Pentagon.

Elena walked around the room mumbling something in Russian. Jim watched her, wondering how this would affect their relationship. He had been thinking this over since she had revealed her past involving a man she clearly still loved. Could he stand to lose her because of it? Would she want to be with him and trace her other family? And what of the effect on their fifteen-year-old son, Ben? He had already remarked on how different his mother had been acting these past couple of days. How do you tell a boy of that age his mother had another child long ago and gave her away?

Elena thought she could read her husband's thoughts.

'I am sorry Jim,' she said. 'I just can't stop thinking about all of this. There are so many twists and turns. I still do not know what to tell Aleksei, if I ever get the chance.'

'Get the chance? I don't understand. Surely you will be able to meet him now?'

Elena shook her head slowly. 'He is a Russian who has entered this country illegally so he faces deportation I would have thought … and once back there who knows what his fate will be?'

'But he could ask for political asylum. Surely, after all this trouble he would be granted it.'

'That's something you might discover from your friend. Maybe he could find a way to stop him being sent back to Russia?'

Elena had some hope at last in her eyes.

'I will give him another call and see what he thinks.'

Jim left the room to use the telephone and Elena took the opportunity to offer up a prayer for the safe keeping of her lost love. She had already made up her mind what she would do if Aleksei were free. A lost life would no longer be lost.

28

Irina Dmitriev sat sullenly at the dinner table. She had been depressed since learning that Aleksei was wanted in connection with the assassination of United States President, John F. Kennedy.

There was still no news of Oleg and Dmitriy and, after such a long time, everyone in the family was resigned to the fact that they had both been captured and silently disposed of... Irina had woken the previous night bathed in sweat and feeling terrible after a dream that obviously frightened her, but she could not recall the details. It was nagging at her mind as she sat there staring at her food. Leonid and their mother, Nina, were at the table but neither of them had much appetite either.

Then suddenly the door burst open and Lev appeared breathing heavily and gasped excitedly.

'I have run all the way home from the factory. There is talk there of Aleksei being in hospital. Apparently he was hit by a truck and is in a very bad way. But there is good news as well. He is no longer being accused of killing the American president. They say now it was a case of mistaken identity.'

Irina looked at her brother but said nothing. Her face was taut and she appeared to be somewhere else.

'Ira, did you hear that? Lev is saying Aleksei is safe now.'

Nina hoped the news would raise her daughter's spirits. Irina showed no emotion.

'I had a dream last night that disturbed me greatly. I

237

could not remember what it was, but now I know. I was being told of this. Aleksei nearly died. He could still die. What have they done to him?'

Nina asked Lev, 'Who are saying these things? How did they find this out?'

Lev replied, still excited, 'Someone had heard it on the radio.'

Nina shook her head sadly. 'I do not understand. What has happened? Aleksei was supposed to be free and looking for his family. Why did they send him to Canada and America anyway?'

'To set him up as stooge so that he would be blamed for the killing of the president.' Irina said coldly.

Her mother and brothers looked at her in amazement.

'You are shocked? Why are you shocked? Is it not obvious to you by now that all this was a set up? It was never about allowing Aleksei the freedom to find Elena, or their daughter and grandson. I just ask this – was my grandpapa responsible for all of this?'

Nina sucked in her breath and then gasped out loud.

'How could you say such a thing? Your grandfather was a great friend of Aleksei Rudikov. He would never have betrayed him like this.'

Irina remembered that night when Aleksei and she were making their escape through the wire. Oleg and Dmitriy were supposed to fire on the watchtower and extinguish the lights. But they did not fire a single shot and it took the good aim of her brother Lev to do what her grandfather had failed to do.

'Then explain to me what happened that night when he was supposed to put out the searchlights.'

Nina shook her head. 'I cannot explain it and do you not think I have thought about it too? But that is my father you are talking about. A Chehovsky, like me, like you and your brothers. I cannot but be proud of being a Chehovsky and, no matter how it looks, I cannot believe Oleg Chehovsky could betray a friend.'

Lev exclaimed, 'Mother is right. You have no right to cast aspertions. We have no way of knowing the truth until we find out what happened to grandpapa. Until then keep those dangerous thoughts to yourself, do you hear?'

He shook his fist at Irina but she was unmoved by any threats.

'I hear what you are saying brother but I know this much: you were thinking the same as me at one stage that night. I saw it your eyes when Aleksei asked what went wrong. You might have changed your mind since, but I haven't.'

Lev glared at his sister for a moment, then stormed out of the door.

'Are you happy now?' asked Leonid. He had the softer nature of the two brothers but he too glared angrily at his sister and followed his brother out of the room. Nina sat quietly fuming as her daughter got up from the table.

'I am sorry if I have upset you but my thoughts at the moment are for Aleksei and him alone.'

As she passed out of the room Nikolai entered. His daughter looked straight through him. He shrugged his shoulders. Then he saw the look on Nina's face.

'What has happened?'

'We no longer have a daughter,' Nina replied icily.

Bernadette Cullen sat thinking about the matter whilst Rudy packed a few things into a suitcase. They had agreed that he should make the move right away as there was no knowing if the gang might return at any time for an answer to the letter they had left. They reasoned that it might only be for a few days so Rudy did not bother to pack much. They then secured the house, after leaving a message in a place only Helen would know where to look if, by chance, she were to be released in the meantime. Catching a bus, Bernadette Cullen and Rudy made their way to the church frequented by her and spoke to the priest, Father O'Flaherty. He asked them to wait in the vestry while he made the necessary arrangements.

'I am doing the right thing, am I not, Miss Cullen? I feel a little frightened now and wonder if I shouldn't be looking for my mum rather than hiding away. What if it annoys those who have kidnapped her and they do something to her because they can't get me?'

'Bernadette. Call me Bernadette. Yes, I think it wiser for you to go into hiding. Remember what that Digby chap said about that gang. We just have to put our hope in his being true to his word. I liked him enough to trust him, or I wouldn't have agreed to this at all.'

A short while later Father O'Flaherty returned.

'I have made the arrangements. A car will be picking Rudy up in about half an hour. It will take him to a private airfield.'

Rudy and Bernadette looked at each other in surprise, then back at the priest.

'Airfield? But you didn't mention this before, Father.'

Bernadette was beginning to have second thoughts. Father O'Flaherty had also not realised their plans would involve a plane flight until he had contacted the Monsignor and advised him of the news. He had then been informed that the boy was to be flown to a residence in Europe. He knew he had to choose his words carefully.

'We no longer feel the boy will be safe in this country whilst that gang are at large. We hope also to fly your mother out to meet you as soon as we are able. We have much trust in the British secret service. We are sure they will save your mother.'

Bernadette looked at Rudy who was beginning to shake slightly.

240

'Rudy, you're a big brave boy. The same brave boy who rescued me from those yobs that day and we have been friends ever since, have we not? We trust each other and I think whatever Father O'Flaherty has arranged should be trusted too.'

Father O'Flaherty silently blessed Bernadette Cullen. 'Well that is settled then. Do you wish to accompany Rudy to the airfield?'

Rudy looked appealingly at Bernadette and she replied, 'Of course. You know I would.'

Aleksei Rudikov woke that morning with the sunshine breaking through the curtains of his room. He tried hard to focus. He looked first at the pipes and drips around him. Then at the elevation of his badly injured legs and he sensed he must be on some really heavy medication not to be able to feel what he was looking at. Then he began to remember some of what had happened to him. He especially remembered the fear of being accused of shooting the United States president. Then he remembered the beating – the reason he was here in this hospital. Then a kindly face in a nurse's uniform appeared as if in a dream.

'So you are awake at last. We thought you were never going to wake up. How are you feeling?' The nurse's American accent brought him back to the reality of it all. He felt a fear he had never felt before. The nurse noticed his expression and quietly reassured him. 'You obviously weren't told this. You are a case of mistaken identity. You didn't kill our president and I am so glad about that because you are one hell of a fighter to have got this far, mister. So no more of that in your eyes, just stay calm and get better, huh?'

Aleksei wanted to speak but realised his face was covered

by a cage of wire. The nurse also saw his eyes moving left and right as they took in this scene.

'It's OK. I take it as you agree with me. Don't worry about all of this. It will come off shortly. Like a lot of the other contraptions they are only there to ensure you mend properly, but you are doing fine. You have really surprised the doctors with your speed of recovery.'

Aleksei was warming to this nurse's attention already and he tried to nod his head, but the cage prevented this so he crossed his eyes instead.

'Now that is a novel way of communication. OK. So if you agree with anything we get the boss-eyed look?'

Aleksei crossed his eyes again.

29

Jim Earnshaw had known Bill Collins for a very long time. The connection went back to a meeting at a religious rally and the two had kept in touch. Jim wasn't as devout as Bill but there had been a general sharing of sufficient belief for the two to remain good friends.

Jim had tried Bill's office but had not been able to get through so he called his home number. Martha answered.

'Jim, nice to hear from you again. No, I am sorry, Bill isn't here. He was called away to take charge of something and I don't think he will be back for a few days. Is there anything I can help you with or shall I get Bill to call you back?'

'That would be good of you, Martha. There was just something I'd like to discuss with him over the Kennedy assassination.'

'Terrible, just too terrible for words, Jim. I am still feeling the shock of it. To think that could happen here in the United States. It just goes to show no-one is really safe, are they?'

'I wonder about that myself, Martha, I really do. You must worry about Bill being so involved.'

Martha had spent too many moments alone and because of it she just needed to talk sometimes, as lonely women do.

Martha sighed. 'You are right on that one Jim, I have been trying to get him to retire for ages now. But he has promised me he will get out after he has dealt with this last business. What was it exactly you wanted to ask him about? He has filled me in with one or two things, so maybe I can help.'

Jim wondered if he should say anything to her but then considered if Bill had confided in her he must have total trust in Martha.

'It's a difficult one, Martha, really difficult. The Russian guy who was first circulated as a suspect ... we have some more details about him.'

Martha began to feel the intrigue. 'What? The man who is in hospital now?'

'Hospital? I didn't know about that.'

'It will be on the news that he was hit by a truck. That's the official line.'

'Official line? So what really happened?' Jim was beginning to sense a major problem.

'That's why Bill has gone down there. To organise everything and to make sure no-one else messes up.'

'So what really happened to him, Martha?'

'This must not go anywhere, Jim. Bill's got a real headache to deal with. The Russian was found and beaten up. He was in a very bad way and nearly died.'

Jim suddenly felt cold. 'Nearly died? My God, what a mess!'

'You can say that again. Anyway, what do you want me to tell Bill?'

'This is going to shock Bill as much as it did me when Elena told me. The Russian, Aleksei Rudikov, was her lover when she was in her teens. She thought he had been killed during the war and, as you can imagine, everything is going haywire here now.'

Martha was left speechless.

'Are you all right, Martha? Sorry – it must be a shock to you as well.'

Martha shook herself and found her voice again. 'My God! I just don't know what to say. You must be in

244

turmoil, you poor man. If she is still unaware of his being hospitalised it makes matters even worse.'

A wail from the front room confirmed that was no longer the case. Elena had been watching the television news report of the incident. Martha clearly heard the cry.

'Oh my God! Was that Elena?'

'Sorry, Martha, must go. I will wait for Bill to call back. Thanks again for your help.'

He replaced the receiver and wandered slowly into the room where Elena was sitting with a handkerchief pressed to her face as she sobbed.

Jim glanced at the television set as the news report repeated the information he already knew. 'I am sorry, Elena dear. I wish I could do something for you, but it just seems to get worse every time I ask.'

Elena looked up at him. Through her sobs she cried, 'Take me down there, to where he is, please, before they end up killing him.'

General Guznischev had news for President Khrushchev. The premier was not in a good mood.

'What have you for me today, General? More bad news?'

'We have asked to be updated every hour on the condition of Aleksei Vasiliy. We have been assured he is over the worst and that the next few hours will be crucial in determining his recovery.'

'And what of this trumped up allegation that they so conveniently used, then withdrew? And when he is finally discovered, badly injured, do they expect us to believe he was hit by a truck? A truck with many arms and legs, no doubt. They cannot even lie well. There is pressure on me to require an official apology and demand repatriation of this Soviet citizen. As you well know, I have resisted this up to now but this latest assault has made it very difficult for me to argue my case any longer. All I can hope is that they offer him diplomatic immunity. Whether that will save him I don't know, but if he is returned to us it could mean a firing squad.'

'I understand fully. There is another matter that has come to our attention. Our Embassy in Britain have reported receiving a letter requesting a search for missing persons, a daughter and grandson, searching for their family.'

The general waited for a reaction from the Russian president. Khrushchev looked warily at him.

'Is this the good news, General?'

General Guznischev read from the report he had just been handed.

' "I would respectfully ask if it is at all possible please for a search to be made through your records for the possible whereabouts of members of my immediate family. My mother's name is Elena Zvadsky and my father Aleksei Vasiliy Rudikov." It goes on to give details of her adoption and marriage and then the birth of her son.'

'So they have discovered the missing link after all this time? Are we still keeping close tabs on them?'

'Yes, we have been keeping a close eye on them but there has been a further development. I am afraid it is not good news. According to one of our contacts in Britain, since sending the letter she has been kidnapped and the boy is heading for sanctuary at a monastery.'

Khrushchev shook his head slowly as he paced the room. 'Another farce. Why is it always a farce? I will leave it with you, General, to make every attempt to bring this boy here. Who kidnapped his mother?'

'We are not yet aware of the full details of how she was kidnapped and ultimately who is responsible, but it is being worked on by our agents and contacts there in Britain. According to the information we have received on the boy's present whereabouts it appears he is being given instruction as a possible introduction into the priesthood by a Monsignor Luigi Venditti.'

'So the Vatican is tied up in all of this, you think?'

'Without doubt, comrade President. It makes things very complicated.'

Bernadette Cullen watched as the small jet took off from the isolated airfield. Rudy had shown a reluctance to embark but she had reassured him again that he was in good hands, but secretly she had some serious doubts about it all. She had not expected him to be taken out of the country.

The flight took a couple of hours, finally descending between two mountaintops towards an airstrip. As the jet landed Rudy had felt sick. Not airsickness, but a bout of homesickness had struck him already. There had been no chatter from the pilot during the flight so Rudy had had much time to think about what he had been told by Liliya. At least this had been of some comfort – the knowledge that the guides were working their own miracles. She had explained how they had made their presence felt when the kidnappers arrived. That the kidnappers were intending to take him as well but he was told how they had fled when faced with the phenomena they had produced, though not before the perpetrators had managed to pour substances over Rudy that had caused him to lose consciousness. He was also assured that his mother would not come to harm. The last piece of advice had been to do with where he was destined to go. He was asked to go along with everything for the time being but to be extremely careful when dealing with Monsignor Luigi Venditti.

A Jesuit priest was standing on the tarmac as Rudy

alighted from the aircraft. He nodded to the pilot, then waved Rudy towards a waiting car. The priest sat in the front passenger seat but neither he nor the driver spoke a word during the forty-five-minute journey. A large, dark-walled building came into view as the car turned off the mountain pass. The car drove up a narrow dusty track and, as they got closer, Rudy could see that the building was a very old monastery, but areas of it had been modernised to provide offices and comfortable living quarters. A large iron gate opened and the car drove through into a courtyard. A figure in a black cloak stood by the entranceway to the building. He walked slowly forward nodding to the priest.

'Welcome, Rudy. We are delighted you have decided to join our happy band. Once you have tasted the fruits of our labours I am certain you will realise you are in the right place and your protection from the outside world will be guaranteed. I am Monsignor Venditti and I will be your guardian during the time of your inception.'

'Inception? I do not understand. I am only here waiting for my mother to be saved and for the bad men to be caught. I did not agree to any inception.'

Venditti smiled, showing the gold fillings in his teeth. His eyes turned to red-hot coals that burned uncomfortably into Rudy.

'I think you will change your mind when I show you the alternative you face if you do not comply.'

Rudy shuddered but remained silent, remembering Liliya's warning.

30

Graham Digby scratched his head as he read through the reports on his desk. Even though he was well versed in counter-espionage he was finding the present situation becoming more complicated by the day. Venditti had his prey at last. Digby knew that the Russians were also aware of this as he had been the source of the information and he tried not to ponder on just how complicated things were becoming for him as a double agent. The telephone on his desk rang and he picked up.

'Digby.' He listened to the caller who garbled a message and quickly rang off leaving him staring incredulously at the receiver. Then he exclaimed, 'Jesus Christ! What the hell do we do now?'

Aleksei opened his eyes. The usual nurse was tending him.

'You have a visitor who wants to talk to you.'

The cage had been removed and he was able to nod or shake his head. He was now shaking his head as furiously as his other restrictions would allow.

The nurse shook her head back at him. 'I am no longer your sole lady friend. This one speaks your language.'

Aleksei looked surprised but his gesture was a shrug of despondency fearing the worst.

'Don't you go backwards on me, mister, do you hear?'

Aleksei looked at her and crossed his eyes.

'That's better. So I can show this lady in now?'

Again, he crossed his eyes but at the same time the

woman entered impatiently. At first she caught the bossed-eyed look but then took in the extent of his injuries and gasped.

The nurse watched her closely and whispered, 'I told you it wasn't pretty.'

Elena nodded to her and waited for the nurse to leave.

Aleksei was trying with difficulty to focus on the woman who had entered but as he strained his vision became blurred. Maybe it was for the best as Elena, at first sight of Aleksei's broken body, had reached for her handkerchief. In her anguish she recoiled, wiping her tears at the same time.

Aleksei noticed that the figure had faded from view for a moment but then it slowly reappeared and came closer until she was close enough for him to see her face clearly.

He sucked in breath and whispered harshly, 'Elena? Is that you, Elena?'

The woman who had built a new life and been happy for so many years crumpled and the resurrected remnants of Elena Zvadsky fell to her knees weeping bitterly, kissing and holding the hand of the man that she had always loved. Aleksei also had tears flowing from his eyes, impairing his already blurred vision. He managed another harsh whisper.

'Elena, I love you. I am so happy at last.'

She got up from her knees and bent over him bringing her lips to his as their tears mingled together. Then she whispered to him things she had been longing to tell him for many years.

Standing just outside the room Bill Collins and Jim Earnshaw watched at the scene. Each had different reasons for being upset at such a sight. Jim could clearly see that he was going to have a hell of a fight on his hands to keep his wife. Bill Collins had been extremely shocked to learn from Martha that one of his best friends had been married all that time to *the* Elena Zvadsky whose connection with Stray Dog his secret department had been discussing for years. Feeling extremely frustrated, he just could not take in how close they had been all that time. He felt completely demoralised, especially now he realised they had lost the battle in securing the services of Aleksei Vasiliy Rudikov. Elena Zvadsky would protect his interests ferociously, and he would certainly be granted political asylum with no strings attached. On the other hand, at least the Russians would now have no hope of persuading anyone to agree to their request to extradite him.

Bill Collins shrugged off his pensive mood and noticed the defeated look in Jim Earnshaw.

'Hell of a problem for you, Jim. I am truly deeply sorry. It must have come as an awful shock.'

Jim nodded his head sadly. 'Sometimes situations in life can come up and kick the breath out of your body. I just feel totally lost. I can't blame Elena for feeling the way she does and I know there's a strong possibility that I will lose her, but her happiness comes before any other considerations. I have to remember she has had one hell of a shock too and, knowing her as I do, it won't be easy for her. She has already admitted she feels sick with guilt about everything now. But I won't stand in her way. What's the point?'

'That's very noble of you, Jim. I wish I could offer you some words of comfort but I don't think there are any.'

The nurse nodded to them both as she passed and went into the room, at the same time whispering to Elena that she should allow the patient to rest. She bent down and kissed Aleksei lightly on his forehead. He smiled and closed his eyes. Elena turned and walked out quietly. She noticed the grave looks on the faces of both men but was not in any mood to offer sympathy.

251

She ushered them out of sight and hearing of nurse and patient, and said, 'Aleksei has told me much. I am so angry about what has been allowed to happen to him. In Russia this is commonplace but here, in the West, where you are all supposed to be civilised ... but it is not so, is it? It is a gigantic myth. I hope you are going to deal harshly with those who caused his terrible injuries?'

Bill Collins assured her this would be the case.

'There is no excuse for it. Even if he *had* been the culprit in the shooting of our president he still has his rights. That mob had no right at all to inflict their own retribution – but human nature is such, I guess.'

'That was not human nature. It was animal behaviour. Dangerous animals that should be put down. Anyway how were things allowed to get that far in the first place? You knew he was not responsible, yet he appeared on your news reports as a suspect. How was that allowed to happen? Did you have some other devious plan up your sleeves?'

Her husband intervened. 'That's a bit much, Elena. That is a hell of an accusation.'

Elena ignored him and continued. 'We have known you a long time, Bill, and I have always trusted you, but at this moment I do not think I can trust anyone over all of this. Aleksei was held prisoner in my homeland for all these years and I know what that represents. But I also know that he has something special about him that would have made you here in the West want him to defect – even if it meant a bit of coercion, is that not right, Bill?'

Bill Collins felt every ounce of his resolve evaporating. He reached in his pocket for his pills and took a couple.

'I'm sorry, Elena, I just can't discuss this with you. You are asking me to discuss State secrets. I just can't do that. If you will excuse me I have to make some calls and I think I will also take a short nap. I am not feeling that great.'

252

With that he wandered off along the corridor towards the cafeteria. Jim Earnshaw looked hard at his wife.

'That wasn't a very good idea, Elena. We still need Bill's cooperation and I think you might just have somewhat damaged relations. I know you are angry but it's no use taking it out on those who want to help you and Aleksei.'

Elena shook her head slowly. 'You are wrong Jim. I sense there has been a lot of conniving and double talk. Well, I am not going to have the wool pulled over my eyes anymore. Aleksei has a lot more to tell me when he is able and then I will know exactly what I have to do.'

Jim looked questioningly back at her.

'I know you are thinking about Ben and yourself and I am sorry if it looks as if I am going to be neglecting you both for a while but you must understand this – I was lied to, Aleksei was lied to. We each thought the other had perished. If it had not been for that there would not have been you and me, or Ben. I am sorry. I am sounding unkind and extremely selfish. You must understand what this means to me. I need time to adjust to this situation. I just can't make any promises at the moment.'

Jim Earnshaw was trying very hard to maintain his composure but he felt he was slowly losing this and decided to follow the path set by Bill Collins and wandered away towards the cafeteria. Elena watched him go. Her emotions were in tatters. To her dismay she felt unable to share anything of her turmoil with anyone, least of all her husband. The fact of having been denied a life with the one she truly loved was now working against any considerations about her subsequent life with Jim and Ben. She felt enormous guilt, but her anger overrode that emotion. She stood in the doorway watching the nurse fussing around her man. To her he looked so peaceful.

Elena whispered to herself, 'Please do not die again, Aleksei. My heart cannot take any more pain.'

Helen Metthewson sat despondently in the chair with her right hand firmly manacled by handcuffs fixed to a rigid pipe that rose from floor to ceiling. Apart from this she had not been badly treated. She wondered why, and also why there had been no sign of Rudy. She had asked after him, but the two men had merely grunted back at her in unintelligible words. She had thought at first that they were talking in a foreign language but as time went on she began to realise the sound was more like those one hears in an asylum for seriously disturbed mental cases and she became increasingly alarmed by this thought.

The two involved in her kidnap were Klaus Zimmermann and Dave Little. An unusual pairing but considered the best option after experimentation. But this experimentation had left both operatives slightly at odds with themselves and showing signs of mental illness Hans Muller had decided to ignore these symptoms as he had been given a tight time schedule. The pair of them had first secured the capture of Helen Metthewson and placed her in the back of the van. Then they had returned for Rudy, only to be met with a ferocious assault. Klaus had managed to pour a substance over Rudy that had been given to them by Muller's team and which was strong enough to knock out a herd of elephants. Then Dave Little had suddenly felt himself being lifted and thrown against the wall. Stunned by this he had picked himself up off the floor only for this action to be repeated twice more as Klaus Zimmermann watched with increasing alarm. They had decided to abort the kidnapping of Rudy and fled the house. Both had been trying to make sense of it ever since, but because of their failing mental capacities, found themselves just jabbering at each other – these were the sounds Helen couldn't understand. And when the men had tried to report back to John Mackay all he had received were garbled messages making not much sense, which he then passed on to Bill Collins. Bill had asked Professor Hans Muller what this represented but Muller had either prevaricated or blinded him with science.

However, the news of Rudy escaping to the confines of a monastery under the guardianship of Luigi Venditti had Bill Collins wondering what the hell was going on. He decided to send the other two operatives over to Britain. Once there Harry Swenson and Bill Turner teamed up with Klaus Zimmermann and caught a flight to Switzerland, leaving Dave Little in charge of Helen Metthewson.

On the flight both Harry Swenson and Bill Turner watched the antics of Klaus Zimmermann with alarm. He began by jabbering and crying, then ended up sucking his thumb. Other people on the flight were beginning to notice and Bill made a decision to end the life of Klaus Zimmermann, which he did with one short jab to his neck. In the same movement he managed to pull the cap he was wearing down over his eyes to give the impression that Klaus had gone to sleep. The murder thus went unnoticed.

Back at the house where Helen Metthewson was being held captive, Dave Little was behaving in more bizarre ways by the minute. He approached her position several times, causing her to wince, not knowing what to expect. On the last occasion he reached into his pocket and brought out a set of keys. Selecting one, he proceeded to unlock the handcuffs used to chain Helen to the pipe. She looked questioningly at him but his eyes were blank and staring into the distance. His face was expressionless. She sat perfectly still as he wandered over to the telephone and proceeded to make several calls. Each time his conversation was virtually incomprehensible. During one she actually heard him say, 'I have had to release the woman,' before slamming the receiver down. His behaviour became more erratic. He mumbled and jabbered away to himself as he paced the room. Suddenly, after making another call, he stood up and now began to rush around the room moaning, apparently in pain. His head began to swell and he gripped it with both hands. Suddenly his head exploded, sending brains, blood and bone fragments in all directions. Helen screamed and passed out.

A while later she regained consciousness. She felt extremely nauseous and could not bear to look at the corpse. Then she moved her arms and remembered she had been freed from her manacles. She looked around and listened for any sounds of movement but there were none. Praying that this was not another trap she got up gingerly and stood for a moment, then she made for the door and fled. Once out on the street she felt safer, but still kept a watch about her as she made her way home. The house she had been imprisoned in was a surprisingly short distance from her own, so she decided to walk. On her mind the whole time was the fact that the man guarding her had admitted releasing her so she thought she should be alert to further possible danger. She did not want to be captured again. Then she remembered Rudy having mentioned the address of Miss Cullen and she tried desperately to recall where it was. By some miracle Helen saw Jimmy Anderson in the distance. She knew now why Jimmy had become one of Rudy's best friends after learning of his heroic rescue in the play-ground that day. Jimmy had also seen Helen and was waving.

As he approached he said, 'This is a surprise, Mrs Metthewson. I thought you were on holiday with Rudy. Miss Cullen has just told me.'

Helen felt a cold shudder. 'Is that what she said? Do you know where she lives? I would like to talk to her.'

'I know where she lives – at forty-eight Lancing Avenue. It's very near where I live. But she was at your house just now when I called around for Rudy. Is everything all right, Mrs Metthewson? You look worried. Has something happened to Rudy?'

Helen tried hard not to scream as she asked, 'Miss Cullen is actually at my house?'

'Yes, I thought you knew that already, because when I asked her she said she was looking after the place for you. Is everything all right?'

Helen began to nod her head slowly. 'Oh, of course. Thank you, Jimmy. I must be going now.'

Jimmy called after her, 'Please let Rudy know when he gets back I have some things for him.'

As Helen Metthewson arrived in the vicinity of her home she began to feel anxious again. Rudy had spoken well of Miss Bernadette Cullen, but Helen had only met her briefly in the street on one occasion. Now apparently she was inside her house. She really did not know what to make of this at all. The curtains in the front room twitched as Helen approached her house. Then the front door opened suddenly as she reached the step. Bernadette Cullen stood in the doorway with an agonised expression on her face.

'Thank the Lord you are safe, Mrs Metthewson. Jimmy has just telephoned here to me and said he had seen you. The poor boy is really confused about events and you must be too. Are you all right? Did they harm you? Do you want me to call the police?'

Helen felt bewildered by all of the questions but at the same time she was thinking of all of the questions she had for Miss Cullen.

'Please, no police. I am really tired and confused but

no, I was not harmed and they let me go. It is still all such a shock. I need to sit down with a cup of tea.'

Helen began to stumble into her house and Bernadette held her arm, guiding her into the front room and into an armchair.

'You poor dear. Just make yourself comfortable there and I will put the kettle on.'

She disappeared into the kitchen and Helen still had a feeling of the surreal, having entered her own house but being treated as if she were a visitor. Bernadette reappeared with a glass filled with her secret recipe.

'Rudy found that this revived him so I hope it will do the same for you.'

Helen took the glass and sniffed it. 'What is in it?'

Bernadette laughed. 'That is exactly what Rudy asked and I told him it was a secret Irish recipe that works wonders every time.'

Helen took a sip and remarked, 'Wow! That is strong. You said you gave it to Rudy to help him recover?'

Bernadette's expression changed. 'I wish I could give you more encouraging news. I came around to see you and Rudy, as my local priest, Father O'Flaherty, had suggested Rudy be offered protection by the church until the bad people had been apprehended. But when I arrived here I found your door open and Rudy lying upstairs being sick. The same people who took you had obviously tried to take Rudy too but he had fought them off somehow, but not before having some noxious liquid poured over him, the poor soul. I suppose they were trying to knock him out because of his power, but it didn't work.'

'You know about this power he has?'

Helen was feeling much more relaxed, having taken several more sips of the special concoction.

'Oh yes, I have seen some of it. Wonderful, but at the same time frightening, wouldn't you agree?'

258

'Yes, it has given me a lot of concern and, of course, is the reason these people are trying to kidnap him. For experimentation or something similar.'

Bernadette shuddered at the very thought, especially now that he had been whisked off to who knows where. She suddenly felt very guilty for making the arrangements but could not imagine that those of her faith would harm him in anyway.

'A man called Digby called around and said he was investigating your kidnap, but the strange thing was that he admitted his people knew where you were and were watching the situation. He said he even had one of his own men in the gang and that he would ensure your safety.'

Helen did not wish to remember the terrible scene she had just escaped from. 'He said that? Well, I didn't see the one who was supposed to be protecting me. There was something about that man Digby I did not trust. He tried to offer us protection.'

Bernadette nodded slowly. 'I am beginning to worry about that myself because he didn't put up much of a fight when I said we would be protected elsewhere. As if he knew something already.'

'What do you mean?' Helen asked.

Bernadette hesitated. 'Just something in his demeanour. I didn't trust him. That is why we went immediately to the church, and Father O'Flaherty arranged for Rudy to be hidden until you were freed.'

'Hidden? Where is he now? Can we go and fetch him?' Helen was already on her feet.

'I am sorry. It is my fault. I should have enquired more thoroughly before agreeing, but everything was done so quickly ... Rudy was taken abroad by jet plane.'

Helen looked aghast. 'Jet plane? Where is he now?'

'A monastery or seminary somewhere in Europe. I think

259

we need to visit Father O'Flaherty and get him to arrange for Rudy to be returned now you are free.'

Helen sat down again and put her head in her hands. 'Oh my God! This is all a nightmare.'

The kettle whistled in the kitchen and Bernadette disappeared to make the tea. Whilst it was brewing she returned and said, 'While I think about it, Rudy left you a note somewhere. He said he would put it in the usual place and you would know where to find it.'

Helen jumped to her feet and disappeared upstairs. She returned a moment later with a small envelope. She had already opened it and read the contents by the time Bernadette brought the tea.

Bernadette waited for Helen to speak but she was reading the letter again with tears in her eyes. Then she looked up.

'Rudy just says he hopes by the time I read this everything will be sorted out and that he can come home again. But he has written here something about his grandfather.'

'Of course – I am sorry – you will not know about this. It was on the news. Rudy was watching a report of the assassination of President Kennedy and one of the suspects named was this Russian whom Rudy claimed was his grandfather.'

'Aleksei Vasiliy Rudikov?' Helen said in a whisper.

Bernadette looked surprised. 'Yes, that was the name. It means something to you? Rudy was terribly upset about it all. Is he really his grandfather?'

'As far as we know. Has he been captured?'

Bernadette was reluctant to make any reply. She hesitated long enough for Helen to sense something else had happened.

'What is wrong? Is he dead?'

Bernadette shook her head slowly. 'Rudy wouldn't know

this as he left before the other news. They were saying that it had been a mistake. Mistaken identity or something like that. Then they were saying he had been hit by a truck and was in hospital.'

Helen Metthewson shook her head in bewilderment for the umpteenth time that day.

'Then I have a father in a hospital. A mother ... somewhere perhaps. And my son is where?'

31

Yegor Strashnikov had done well for himself under the guidance of his mentor, General Guznischev, and had reached the rank of captain. Since those early days, when he was just a mere foot soldier, he had become a trusted general's adjutant. He was being given an extremely important assignment.

'Yegor, we must not fail with this. It is probably the only chance we will have of securing the services of the boy, Rudy Metthewson. He is presently under the guardianship of a Monsignor Luigi Venditti who was granted dispensation by a Papal Commission for the spiritual education of the boy, with a view to his becoming a priest and enjoying the full protection of the Vatican. Of course, we have made overtures to the Vatican, pointing out that he is a descendant of a Russian family and insisted he was baptised into the Orthodox Church. At first we met a stony silence, so we reminded them of just how easy it would be for some mishap to befall the Pope. To our surprise they have become very co-operative.'

The new recruit into such matters responded, 'I am amazed, General Guznischev. The Pope himself?'

Guznischev chuckled dryly. 'So they have instructed his guardian and potential mentor to release the boy and hand him over to us, so he can be placed in the care of the Russian Orthodox Church. You have been selected to take your team and collect this boy, Rudy Metthewson, so that he may enjoy the privilege of Soviet citizenship. One other small problem is the fact that the British also lay claim to him and have been aided by the Americans who have sent their own team to the monastery where he is held. It is now a matter of extreme urgency and we wish you to depart today. Have you any questions, Yegor?'

Captain Strashnikov thought for a moment. 'Will we be armed? And whose soil will we be on?'

'Yes, you will be armed, and the country you will be entering is Switzerland. But the monastery lies outside their jurisdiction as it is privately owned and under the guardianship of the Vatican. It could even be considered an extension of their territory. Once on that soil I do not think you will be in danger of causing a diplomatic outrage if shots need to be fired. The Vatican has nearly wet itself over this already!'

Bill Collins sat nursing a now cold cup of coffee. Opposite him was Jim Earnshaw who had ordered a coke but not drunk a drop of it. In the pit of his stomach he felt tightness, a real raging discomfort caused by all the stress of the last few hours. John Mackay appeared and his expression did not bode well. He stopped at the entrance to the cafeteria and Bill sighed. Getting up from his seat he apologised to Jim and said he would be a few moments. Then he joined Mackay and they both walked out of the building. Jim watched them through the window as John Mackay gesticulated as he spoke to Bill Collins, who did not show any emotion. Bill looked completely defeated as Mackay finished speaking. He muttered a few words to Mackay who then rushed away. Obviously he had been given orders. Bill returned to the table and sat down. He was looking extremely old and frail.

'Are you OK, Bill? You don't look at all well. Have you taken your pills?'

Bill reached inside his pocket and took out a sachet of

medication, emptied it into his cold coffee and drank it down.

'You are getting as bad as Martha.' He managed a short chuckle. 'No, I am not feeling too great and I think the best idea is for me to go back to the hotel and rest. But before I go I have to admit something to you, Jim. My conscience won't allow me to do otherwise.' Bill sighed deeply. 'We've known each other nearly fifteen years? In all that time I have never lied to you and I am not going to start now. Elena was right to be angry. We had Aleksei Rudikov under observation the moment he arrived in the States. We watched him being led around on a sightseeing tour and thought no more of it when they hit Dallas. Jesus! How I felt when all that happened. Then someone suggested we pin it on the Russian, but say nothing to the media. It was meant simply to be a ruse to pressurise him into defecting. Then some son-of-a-bitch leaked it to the press and you know what happened then. I still haven't got to the bottom of that. I can't help but feel it was to throw us off the scent of who really was responsible for the shooting. One thing is for sure: someone in our team knows who really shot JFK, and why.'

Jim Earnshaw eyed Bill closely. 'Do you know who that person is, Bill?'

Bill Collins looked down. 'I can't say any more, Jim.'

'You don't have to, Bill.'

Bill began to say something. then hesitated.

Jim asked, 'Something else?'

Bill nodded slowly. 'Now here is the really hard bit. We have had information on the whereabouts of Elena and Aleksei's daughter and grandson...'

Jim was incredulous. 'Grandson? Her daughter gave birth to a boy?'

'Yes. I haven't had the courage to tell you. When Elena got angry I just recoiled. I could have stuck to saying it

264

was all classified and that I couldn't discuss it but what's the point? It would have come out anyway. The whole thing is turning into a nightmare.'

That nightmare turned on the news Bill had just been given, which had been imparted by John Mackay. Hans Muller had discovered someone had tampered with his experiments and that the operatives Dave Little and Klaus Zimmermann were in extreme danger, but this discovery had come too late. Little had been found dead at a really messy scene and Zimmermann had had to be negated by Bill Turner on the flight to Switzerland. On top of this Helen Metthewson was free and there was nothing anyone could do about what might happen next.

'I don't want to say too much more, Jim. But I will promise you this much: I will provide Elena with what help I can in repatriating her daughter and grandson as soon as it is possible.'

Jim heard the words but he was still considering what it might all mean to his own personal life. Yes, the situation was turning into a nightmare, but a completely different one for Jim Earnshaw. A second family to go with Elena's lost love meant any hope Jim had of saving his own marriage now looked forlorn.

Bill Collins lay on the bed after taking more medication. He was just dozing off when he heard something move behind the draped curtains. He sat up as a dark shadow emerged. It came closer until Bill recognised the figure.

'What the hell are you doing here? Why aren't you...?

Two shots were fired silently into Bill Collins' chest and he collapsed backwards on to his pillow, which was then dragged from behind his neck. He just managed to gasp, 'Martha! Oh Lord...' before the pillow descended on his face and the gunman with silencer fired another shot through the pillow, which exploded in a shower of reddened feathers.

Jim Earnshaw decided, after consuming another coke, to return to the ward. He was not looking forward to giving Elena the latest update. As he approached the room where Aleksei was housed, Elena appeared through the door, her eyes red from crying. She noticed her husband but said nothing. Jim swallowed hard and began to relate what he had been told, but Elena stopped him by raising her hand and shaking her head.

'I don't want to hear it just yet. I have had enough surprises already. I have a grandson as well as a daughter!'

'I know. Bill just told me. He apologised for not telling you earlier, but...' Jim struggled for the right words.

'But it would have hurt their secret plans, whatever *they* are.' Elena interrupted angrily. 'I have a few choice words to say to Bill Collins. Where is he?'

Jim looked down. 'He's not feeling too good. He's gone to his room for a rest.'

'He doesn't feel too well. What about me? What about that poor man in there with his body broken in two? Whose fault is it all anyway? This should never have happened, any of it. What kind of country are you running here? The Soviet Republic might appear a terrible place to you Westerners but I don't see Khrushchev being shot at. Perhaps I should take Aleksei back home to Russia after all.'

Her husband did not know how to reply. Here was the West producing propaganda about the threat of communism when Soviet Russia at least seemed able to protect its leadership. What had happened to his country? Where were the protecting heroes?

The commotion followed soon after. Men were dashing

around in all directions with weapons in their hands. Several hospital staff and some patients were shouting and screaming as they ran through corridors into wards and rooms. Jim and Elena watched silently as one young suited individual, obviously a security aide, ran past them and checked in Aleksei's room. Then he retreated in the opposite direction.

John Mackay appeared, his face taut and strained.

'What is going on?' Jim asked him.

'The world's gone mad. Bill's just been shot dead in his room. Jesus, are we in one sorry mess!'

'But why would anyone want to shoot Bill?' Jim was sickened.

'You could ask why would anyone want to shoot the President? Ain't it about the same? It's always the good guys. Here, you better guard the Russkie until we can make some sense of this. You never know, he might be on the hit list too.'

Mackay handed his revolver to Jim.

Elena glared first at Mackay and then at her husband.

'Give that to me please.'

Jim saw the steel in his wife's eyes and handed the weapon to her, remembering that this kind and lovable lady had once been a soldier in the Red Army and was probably more proficient with a gun than he would ever be.

32

Monsignor Venditti watched as his apprentice priests laboured at their tasks. Rudy was beginning to worry that everyone on the outside might have forgotten about him. He had been there only a matter of days but it seemed an eternity.

'What are you thinking, my child?'

Rudy looked up in surprise.

'I was thinking of home, where I should be and want to be right now. I never agreed to become a priest.'

Venditti's eyes began to glow again, increasing Rudy's discomfort.

'The agreement was for you to remain here and your mother would be safe. She *is* safe, I can assure you of that.'

Rudy looked suspiciously at him. 'She is safe? How do you know this? Where is she now?'

'Questions, questions, questions! I am not without influence, as you will appreciate, and I assure you I have managed to ensure your mother is in her rightful place, at home. She will remain safe as long as you obey your calling. You will grow to learn that the church can provide all kinds of rewards for those who show the right devotion.'

'But I did not agree to this. I was only supposed to be here until my mother came home safely.'

Rudy could see the monsignor was becoming irritated and winced as his eyes glared down on him.

'For the glory of God and the Saviour, his son, Jesus Christ, you are here to provide us all with your heavenly power and protection, which will enable us to create the power and glory required to carry out His great work on this damned earth.'

'I think you are mad!'

The words came from his mouth but the thought had not been in his mind. He felt a surge, something he hadn't experienced for a while.

The monsignor held his gaze as his eyes now formed again into red-hot coals, emitting a ferocious pressure on Rudy's body and soul. Rudy was about to cry out when he felt another surge inside him and the monsignor stepped back; his eyes no longer contained the menace they had before. He looked warily at Rudy, then smiled, revealing those teeth with gold fillings that Rudy had noticed on arrival.

'It seems you are already using your precocious powers in our domain. I hope you are willing to face the consequences of such actions. It might mean your mother will fall down the stairs and break her legs tonight.'

Rudy's eyes widened. 'You would not dare harm my mother. Those around me have already shown you what I am. She is within your sight.'

Again Rudy heard the words coming from his mouth but his mind was not engaged. Then he caught up with the situation and whispered, 'Liliya.'

Monsignor Venditti was glaring at him again but this time he felt afraid.

'What did you say? Whose name did you call?'

Rudy felt renewed confidence and said, 'You know well the name I spoke. Be aware that there are those who come to repay you for all the wickedness dealt out by your followers over time together with your own wicked past. Nothing is ever forgotten and we are here to remind you of the place you came from before you found this haven as a sanctuary.'

269

Monsignor Venditti's expression had changed but he remained calm.

'I have always expected this time to come and if it is to be now then so be it. But do not be fooled by my reticence for I am not without my own sources of power.'

He looked down on Rudy who again felt the same degree of discomfort he had earlier, but then another surge sent the monsignor staggering backwards a few paces. Venditti's face betrayed signs of fear.

He turned to go and as he did so realised that the whole episode had been witnessed. Others were now looking at him with curiosity. He barked orders at them and they all ducked down again and continued with their work.

He walked through a doorway on the other side of the old building where, being out of sight and hearing of the crowd, Venditti shouted obscenities and oaths at the empty walls that surrounded him. Here he stood in the oldest part of the monastery built many hundred years ago where he conducted many of his secret experiments. He remembered now the words of warning conveyed through Gustaf from Luis Suarez concerning the girl. He had not believed them. But at this precise moment he realised how wrong he had been and that he had to find another solution fast.

Whilst returning to his office on the other side of his living quarters, Venditti hid in the shadows as an aide rushed past. The monsignor guessed his purpose but was still feeling irritated and remained hidden until the monk disappeared; then he entered his office, picked up a bible and threw it across the desk. He looked at the telephone for a few long moments. It rang just as he had decided to pick it up. He recoiled and watched it until it rang off. The monk returned and burst into the office, out of breath.

'I apologise, Monsignor, I did not realise you were here.

I thought it might be Cardinal Medi again. He was most insistent that I find you and get you to contact him as soon as possible.'

Venditti waved his hand at the aide. 'No matter, Brother Stefano. I will ring him right now. There is no need for you to be concerned.'

The aide bowed and excused himself, leaving Venditti again looking at the telephone. It rang again and this time the monsignor answered it.

'Brother Luigi, I have been trying to contact you for over an hour now. We have the most worrying situation. The boy must be returned to the outside world immediately. However you arrange it, please ensure it is done today. His Holiness insists on this.'

'May I ask, Your Eminence, why this is necessary? I have only just begun his training.'

'There must be no delay and no argument. The boy must be returned today.'

The Cardinal's tone showed some frustration, which Venditti chose to ignore.

'If you would kindly remember, I offered myself as guarantor for this boy's entrance and education within this church. How can I now give him up when he is so willing a pupil?'

Cardinal Medi sighed heavily. 'You may believe that in your own heart, Brother Luigi, but I am afraid it is a misconception. The boy has no interest in the priesthood.'

'Who has said this? Let them come and face me and learn from the boy himself. I guarantee he will convince anyone that he wishes to stay within these walls and learn the glory of God's work on earth.'

Venditti was beginning to lose his composure, a fact that had not gone unnoticed by the Cardinal.

'Brother Luigi, please listen carefully. There have been accusations. It has been reported that you have kidnapped

271

the boy. He is there against his wishes. Release him immediately and arrange for his return whence he came.'

There followed a long silence.

'Monsignor, did you hear me? Please act immediately. That is the express wish of His Holiness. We must not be caught up in any scandal, do you hear?'

'I hear, Your Eminence. Good day to you, Cardinal Medi.'

At that Monsignor Venditti severed the call by pulling the wire out of the wall socket and furiously throwing the telephone across the room where it smashed against the wall.

A short distance away on a mountain road two men stood by their hire truck looking up at the imposing sight of the monastery. Further away, on another mountain pass, a lone figure trained a rifle on the pair. They were within range but the sniper waited, watching as the two men changed from civilian clothing into battle fatigues. They then unloaded a large wooden box and between them carried it up to the walls of the monastery. Apparently unseen by those inside the monastery, they began unloading weapons and explosives. Two shots suddenly rang out. They had been aimed at the weaponry but caught the explosives, causing a massive explosion. The armed men were sent flying into a drainage ditch. The sniper had sights on these two as they crawled slowly back out and headed back to their vehicle.

33

Bernadette Cullen and Helen Metthewson had decided to visit the church and speak to Father O'Flaherty but only after a lot of consideration, as both women were fast learning not to trust anyone in authority. They found that Father O'Flaherty had been promoted and had left the diocese.

'Whatever do we do next, Helen?' Bernadette asked as they made their way back to the bus stop.

Helen looked ahead as she replied, 'Find a way to contact my father. I am certain he will know what to do.'

Bernadette looked doubtful. 'But what if he is still too ill to be asked questions. He might not know of your existence anyway. He may think it a trick.'

'I am aware of that possibility but I am prepared to take the chance. What have I got to lose at the moment? My son's life might depend on it.'

Elena Earnshaw sat in a chair opposite her husband with her eyes trained on the door. Every now and then she would stretch her legs and peer outside for any signs of danger. Jim sat looking at the sleeping figure of the patient. Jim could not feel badly about him. Aleksei opened an eye and trained it on Elena's movements. He spoke quickly in Russian. She replied in the same tongue. Then, noticing her husband looking around him, she said. 'It's all right, Jim, Aleksei was asking me what was wrong and I have told him. He has asked me to give him the gun.'

'Him have the gun? But he can hardly move as it is?'

'Aleksei might not have his usual reflexes at the moment but he still has the determination to endure. That is what made him the feared sniper that he was. I would not wish to enter his territory as an enemy, even in the state he is in, eh Aleksei?'

Aleksei winked at her and spoke again in Russian.

This time Elena's face darkened and she hesitated to translate what he had said. But Aleksei nodded for her to proceed.

'Aleksei wishes to say that you have obviously looked after me with great care for I am as beautiful today as he remembered long ago.'

Jim was not sure how to react to this, so changed the subject.

'Bill said he was going to help you and Aleksei be reunited with your daughter and grandson. What will happen now he's gone?'

Before Elena could reply Aleksei said, 'Jim, I thank you for your concern. Take Elena away now, please. Go and find them and make them safe.'

Elena shook her head furiously at him. 'No, I will not leave you. *Niet!*'

Aleksei held up his right arm, still swathed in bandages over splints with only the fingers protruding.

'Look at me, Elena. If God wishes me to live until you return, I will live. But my wish now is for you to reunite yourself with our daughter and our grandson for he will be as special to me as I was to Stanislav. Please do this for me and do not look sad.'

Elena moved forward, kissed Aleksei on his cheek, then rushed from the room. Jim was about to follow but Aleksei called to him in that harsh whisper.

'Jim, I like you already. I know it is difficult for you. But please realise it is so for me too. She is one

hell of a woman. Please look after her, and God speed.'
Aleksei closed his eyes so he did not witness the tears in
Jim's.

34

General Guznischev had learned that Helen Metthewson had been set free and that she was, along with another woman, beginning a search for Rudy. He had also been told of the explosion near the monastery, together with the murder of Bill Collins. But the biggest bombshell was the news of Elena Zvadsky. The whole situation was becoming untenable and he had said as much to Khrushchev.

'We no longer have a choice in this matter. The mission must be aborted. Recall Captain Strashnikov immediately. It is not too late to do this?'

'No, comrade President. Captain Strashnikov had already anticipated this after witnessing the explosion at the monastery.'

'Not good, not good at all. With the news of Elena Zvadsky being reunited with Aleksei Vasiliy it will only be a matter of time before the boy becomes a major international incident. We cannot afford to be caught anywhere near all of this.'

John Mackay sat at his desk in the hotel that had been taken over by his team since they arrived. Mackay was assuming temporary control of the investigation after the murder of Bill Collins. He looked up as an aide entered his temporary office.

'I thought I told you I did not want to be disturbed unless it was urgent.'

Before the aide could reply another person walked in past him. The tall wiry man glared at Mackay.

'Still the same John, even in these circumstances. Ain't you ever learned any civility?'

Mackay glared back. 'What are you doing here, Doug? This is supposed to be off limits for anyone not officially connected.'

Doug James casually lit a cigarette and puffed the smoke towards the desk.

'Seems you haven't heard then. Can't say I'm surprised as your informants always seem to be one step behind all the others.'

'What are you on about?' asked Mackay angrily.

'Bill Collins wasn't the only one killed. Bill Turner and Harry also appear to have bit the dust. An explosion beside the monastery caused by a sniper firing into their weaponry by the looks of things.'

John Mackay looked at his aide, 'Why was I not told this?'

The aide looked awkwardly at Doug James who replied for him.

'It's all right, son, you go along and get on with that other matter I told you about, whilst I give your ex-boss the facts.'

'Ex-boss? What the hell are you talking about? Who is taking over from me?'

Doug James now had a grim smile on his face.

'Me, John. I am taking over this investigation.'

Mackay winced. 'Says who and why?'

'They called me and told me about Bill's death. Bill had asked me to take over if anything should happen to him, and I'd agreed. They already knew that and were all to happy to put me in charge. So here I am.'

Mackay took the news as badly as Doug James had expected. He knew he was completely out of the circle now.

'So what happens to me then?'

James eyed him for a moment. 'They want you back in your office a.s.a.p. – and you will be given your orders then.'

'You are loving this, aren't you, Doug?'

'I guess you will have to take your finger outta your ass and learn to be a little more polite now, John, beginning in future with how you address whoever is above you, huh?'

Doug James chuckled dryly as he watched John Mackay gathering up his papers from the desk and throwing them into his case before making an abrupt departure.

The aide returned a short while later, accompanied by John and Elena Earnshaw. By this time Doug had made himself comfortable at John Mackay's old desk.

'Hello Jim, and hello to you, Elena. Please come in and sit down. Terrible what happened to Bill, but I think deep down he was expecting it.'

Jim Earnshaw had met Doug James a couple of times at functions where he had been a guest of Bill's.

'You really think so, what makes you say that?'

'Just something in his demeanour since the Kennedy killing. I spoke to him a number of times over the phone and there was a certain edginess in his voice. I actually asked him if anyone else might be on the hit list and he replied that no-one was immune. He wouldn't be drawn on it any further but I detected it was his way of telling me something might happen. It was then he asked me to take over if anything happened to him and to make sure Martha was looked after. She is in a hell of state, as you can imagine.'

Jim nodded grimly. 'She was right all along. Bill should have got out earlier. I know he felt duty bound to carry out the investigation over Aleksei but I must admit that he looked and acted like a man waiting for his own execution. Are we any nearer finding out who might have done it?'

Doug shook his head slowly. 'Nothing as yet, but I am sure it must all be connected to the President's being shot.'

'And how safe is Aleksei?' Elena asked.

Doug replied. 'I know that he is a priority for you and I will do everything I can to ensure his safety, including moving him when the doctor gives permission.'

'Where will he be moved to and how can you ensure his safety?'

'What Doug is saying,' Jim interposed, 'is that there are other factors in play here and other people are equally in danger, isn't that right?'

Doug James nodded his head. 'But that doesn't detract from what I am saying. I will be putting my best men around him in a place that is more fortified than The Alamo.'

Elena still looked unimpressed. 'But they were all killed at the Alamo. Anyway, I want to be with him. Is that possible?'

Jim spoke again. 'Remember what Aleksei said. He wants you to find your daughter and grandson and bring them to safety.'

Elena glared at her husband. 'I know what he asked for, but did you hear me agree to that? He is being his usual self-effacing best, but I know deep down he does not want me to leave him again. What happened all that time ago is etched in his soul, as it is in mine, and I cannot bear the thought of being parted from him, even for a minute.'

Jim was about to argue further but Doug had other news.

'I have been informed that your daughter and grandson have been located. Bill was about to tell you more before

279

he died. Your daughter is Helen Metthewson and lives in Britain with her son, Rudy, who is fifteen, going on sixteen, years of age.'

Elena cried out with joy.

'I am afraid I have to tell you it hasn't all been plain sailing though. Your daughter was recently kidnapped in an attempt to persuade Rudy to subject himself to experimentation. But Helen managed to escape her captors.'

'What experimentation? What is going on here? Is that what this country had in mind for my Aleksei? But of course it was,' she said bitterly.

Doug James shifted uncomfortably in his chair. He was rarely stuck for words but on this occasion he just could not think of anything that would placate the angry woman sitting opposite.

Jim Earnshaw attempted to ease the situation.

'Come on, Elena, this is not solving anything. It's not Doug's fault. He is just filling us in. Those who were responsible for all of this mess are the ones we should be directing any flak at.'

Elena spoke a few words softly in Russian and then, to her and Jim's amazement, Doug James replied in her own language. He repeated his words in English for Jim's benefit.

'I know you are afraid. I was very afraid on the many times I entered your country; afraid I would be discovered. But I am still here and so are you – and so is Aleksei. Maybe God has a plan for us all.'

'You were a spy in Russia? Then you will have known all along that Aleksei was imprisoned there for experimentation?'

Elena eyed him with increasing suspicion. Doug James looked at her levelly.

'I never agreed to be involved in such things. In fact, the very thought of experimentation was abhorrent to me, and I finally shipped out. Left the company and went where the sun shines and the living is easy.' He looked across at Jim Earnshaw. 'I agreed to be called back because of what happened to Bill, because I liked and respected that man – as you did, Jim.'

Elena was still suspicious. 'That is all very well. But this country that is so proud of its tradition of democracy seems to be littered with the types I left Russian soil to get away from. What is it you hide? What have you hidden behind your masks? I am not convinced this capitalist world you live in is any different from the communist regime I left behind. For the rest of us, the ordinary people, it is always the same.'

Doug James was by now regretting opening up in such a frank manner as he had further bad news to impart.

'There is something else, however. A problem over locating Rudy.'

Elena sat perfectly still. 'Now what? What problem? Is he in danger too?'

'As you will appreciate, I can't apologise enough for what has happened to him in this country. I have been told that we, the United States, always wanted Aleksei to defect but we couldn't find a way to get near him. The irony of the situation that has developed over recent months is really beyond words. Rudy has special powers too, similar to Aleksei's. I gather this is a genetic thing passed through generations of his family. So there have been attempts to snatch Rudy. He was supposedly put under the protection of the church whilst Helen was located. Helen has been freed and I am arranging for her to be flown to this country. But we have yet to locate and secure your grandson, Rudy.'

Elena sat stony faced as she asked, 'He was put under the protection of the church? What church?'

'A Catholic priest arranged for him to be put under

281

the guardianship of a Monsignor Venditti with the blessing of the Vatican, Venditti has now gone renegade and is refusing to give Rudy up. The Vatican are asking for us to have patience and leave it in their hands as they negotiate the boy's release. There has always been some suspicion surrounding Venditti. I know Bill knew of him and that Venditti was indirectly involved with a failed attempt before to snatch Rudy, so it is of little surprise that this is how things have worked out.'

'So the happiness of my daughter's homecoming is shattered by the possibility of her son, our grandson, being in extreme danger?'

'All I can do is apologise again. I am sitting in the hot seat now and all I can do is tell you exactly what the position is at the moment. I will be completely frank and straightforward with you. No-one knows the capacity of this Monsignor Venditti. It is rumoured that he himself has mastered the arts of dark forces we are all unaware of, so we just cannot, at the moment, judge just what we are dealing with. It would appear, and this is completely my own assessment, that Venditti has some misguided idea of merging his power with Rudy's in order to become omnipotent.'

Jim Earnshaw whistled low as he listened. 'Now that is pure science fiction.'

Elena got up from her seat and made for the door.

'Where are you going, Elena?' Jim asked, also getting up.

'I am going to ask Aleksei for his advice. I trust no-one else, and can you blame me?'

35

A commotion was taking place outside the walls of the monastery. The explosion had brought a crowd of monks to the gates. A large hole had opened up in the ground about six feet from the wall, which, however, appeared to have withstood the impact of the explosion. The noise had also brought Luigi Venditti to the gateway, which was already opened wide allowing several monks who had been outside to rush back through, led by Brother Stefano.

'What in Heaven's name is the matter, Brother Stefano? What was that noise?' Venditti barked with irritation.

Brother Stefano was out of breath. 'We were going down to the vineyards on the lower slope and found a lorry on one of the roads. We heard two shots fired from the other hillside opposite the monastery and then the explosion by the wall alerted us. We ran back and discovered all kinds of weapons on the ground. Then we heard the groans and found two badly injured men crawling back towards the lorry.'

Venditti looked alarmed for a second then regained his calm composure. He followed the monks outside and surveyed the débris caused by the explosion, and the weaponry scattered over a wide area. Then he walked over to the two men who lay staring silently back at him.

'Brother Stefano, you say you found a vehicle on the lower road?'

'Yes, there is a truck on the lower path. That is obviously how they got here, Monsignor.'

'And the explosion? You say you heard shots fired from the other hillside?'

'Yes. Whoever it was must have aimed at, and detonated, the explosives.'

Venditti looked in the direction Brother Stefano indicated on the mountain slope, wondering who it was out there who had saved them.

'Brother Stefano, take some others. Go back and rid us of their transport. Push it into the ravine where no-one ever ventures.'

Brother Stefano bowed, then selected three monks for the task. They left at once.

Venditti looked down on the men again and his glare caused great discomfort to each, on top of their injuries.

'I will not waste my time asking who you are and who sent you. I know you are here to rescue the boy, but you have failed miserably. Whoever sent you would probably not want you to return after such a failure. I think we might be able to offer you an alternative.'

The monsignor chuckled dryly as he turned back and summoned a group of monks.

'Take these two miserable specimens inside, strip them, attend to their wounds and discover, if you can, who they are and where they came from. If they refuse to answer then take the course of action I have instructed you to do when dealing with such enemies.'

The monks each bowed to Monsignor Venditti and set about their task. Harry Swenson groaned as he was lifted up. He had a massive cut on the side of his head and his right arm, which was partially severed, hung loosely by his side.

However, Bill Turner was a different case altogether. He tried to fight off the monks despite his broken body. His left kneecap had been blown away and his right foot was also missing but it did not stop the powerful Turner

284

heaving two of the brothers onto their backs. Venditti approached, his eyes now like hot coals, and stood over the struggling man who spat back at the monsignor. But Turner began to yell in pain as the monsignor's glare intensified until he could no longer withstand it and passed out.

'Make sure he pays for that insolence,' Venditti ordered.

Later, he sat in his office deep in thought as Brother Stefano waited for him to give further orders. The monsignor raised a wicked smile.

'Brother Stefano, it would appear that we were right to be cautious over our acquisition of the boy. Is not the evidence now before our eyes?'

Brother Stefano was confused. 'Monsignor?'

'This boy will be our salvation, Brother Stefano. I can see you are confused over this but I will prepare what is necessary now for all of us. Have these two anything to identify them? Passports?'

'Yes, they were in their truck. I have them here.'

Brother Stefano handed them to the monsignor. 'Americans. Harry Swenson and Bill Turner. I have heard of them both and know what department they are from. Both are subjects of the American experimentation and, therefore, very dangerous indeed. But I think they are already sufficiently incapacitated not to pose a threat to our plans. These two came from America to plunder our treasures; others will follow in their footsteps.'

'What treasures, Monsignor? We have no riches here?'

'Not gold or jewels. Our riches will come from the boy. From what he can offer us in our search for complete enlightenment and an everlasting life filled with glorious spiritual gifts.'

Brother Stefano felt uneasy. 'You are convinced he will comply with our wishes?'

The monsignor nodded. 'Yes, I am certain he will assist

us in the end, especially after witnessing our next ceremony.'

Brother Stefano followed Monsignor Venditti back out to the yard where the monks were waiting for further orders.

'We will be conducting our usual ceremony. Please go and prepare yourselves for this. We will be initiating a new postulant into the wonders of our faith.'

Venditti scowled contemptuously as another voice piped up from behind, 'If you mean me, you are mistaken. I will never agree to be initiated into anything by you. You are totally mad. As you have seen, they are coming for me. To take me to safety.'

After the explosion Rudy had stood quietly in the background, horrified at what he had witnessed. At the same time his hopes rose and he began to believe that help was on its way.

The monsignor turned to face him. 'You are already in the safest place possible for someone with such demonic powers. It is here that you will have this power brought out of you and merged with the goodness I have created.' He began to laugh manically.

Rudy, however, stood his ground.

'You are a madman. My friends are all about you and will ensure you fail in whatever plans you have for me.'

Luigi Venditti's eyes began to glow with the red-hot coal effect and he felt himself beginning to wilt under the monsignor's gaze. Rudy finally fell to the ground in a semi-conscious state. He felt himself being lifted and carried inside and down a long stairway illuminated by flickering candles affixed to the walls. He was cold, as much from the atmosphere as from the fear building up inside of him. He was laid down on a slab of stone where he drowsily made out the sounds of muttering all round him. The mutterings were soon replaced by chanting, soft at first, then becoming louder in crescendo, rising up into the ceiling of the hall, situated in the bowels of the monastery.

Rudy opened his eyes and saw the sparkling eyes of many of the brotherhood looking down at him. In the distance on a raised dais Monsignor Luigi Venditti stood glaring at the youngster. He tried to glare back defiantly but his resolve had disappeared, leaving him at the mercy of the maniacal monsignor. Rudy tried to raise himself but his hands and feet were tied to rings fixed in the stone. He could not stop himself whimpering with terror as Venditti climbed down from the platform and began to approach him. Completely at the mercy of the mysterious monks, Rudy felt faint and finally lost consciousness.

Aleksei, half awake, felt the nurse fiddling with tubes, checking that all were working and generally ensuring he was comfortable. Then he heard her leave and opened one eye, watching the two agents positioned just outside of his room. He closed his eye again and began to recite all the things he wanted to tell Elena when she returned. His concentration was disturbed by a scuffling sound. He opened his eyes. He could no longer see the two agents. A figure wearing a white doctor's coat entered the room. Aleksei's vision was still poor over any distance but he noticed the man had something in his hand. As he came closer Aleksei saw it was a gun with silencer. It was aimed at him. Without hesitation, he fired the revolver he had been given. The shot hit its target. The figure dropped its own weapon and staggered forward, then fell to its knees beside the bed holding on to the covers.

'Too bad, my friend Aleksei, you were always that much faster in thought than me,' Oleg Chehovsky gasped.

'Why Oleg? Why?'

287

'Favours ... too many debts ... I am sorry, my friend...'
He let out a deep sigh and slid to the floor.

Elena found the journey back to the hospital slow and
kept asking the driver to go faster. His answer had been:
'In America, Ma'am, whoever we are we have to be real
careful of traffic violations.'

The hospital was full of other members of Doug James'
new team protecting Aleksei. That was clear to Elena as
she arrived and she was at least comforted by this fact.
Elena composed herself and walked down the familiar
route of corridors filled now with officers of the investigating
team. But as she approached the final corridor a shot
rang out and Elena froze. Her mind switched off for a
second and when she regained her senses she realised
others were running past her towards the scene. Elena
ran forward and saw the bodies of those who had been
protecting the patient lying outside the door to Aleksei's
room. Blood splattered the walls. Elena was prevented
from entering by two men.

'Do you know who I am? I am Elena.'

She pushed them aside and went in, only to witness
another bloody scene. There was a ragged hole in the
bed covers and blood splashed all over Aleksei who
had his eyes closed. Elena let out a cry of anguish but
then Aleksei opened his eyes. She rushed forward and
grabbed his arm. Looking now beyond him to other
side of the bed she saw the body of a man face down
on the floor. Aleksei spoke in Russian as others entered
the room.

Elena turned to them and simply said, 'This is the body
of Oleg Chehovsky. He came here to kill Aleksei. But
Aleksei was already armed with a gun and shot him. He
was his friend long ago – clearly not now.'

'He I trusted is now lying dead on the ground,' said Aleksei.

In the distant monastery Monsignor Luigi Venditti watched over his charge with diligence. The ceremony had been performed well and he hoped soon to feel its benefit.

36

Elena stood absolutely still as the mayhem went on around her. Nurses and doctors were moving the patient's bed through to another room whilst others were attending to the bodies. Throughout it all Aleksei remained silent. Elena followed the procession into a room further up the corridor where, for a moment, they were alone together. Aleksei and Elena spoke to each other quietly in Russian. A short while later a tall, wiry man with weather-beaten features entered the room. Aleksei looked at him with a suspicion. Elena immediately saw Aleksei's look and stood between the bed and the person who had just come in.

'It is all right, Aleksei, this is the new head of the investigation, Mr James.' She turned to Doug James and said, 'Mr James, from all we have discussed I think you should instruct anyone entering this room to announce themselves first. Aleksei is in no mood to ask questions, and do you blame him?'

Aleksei still had Mackay's gun as he had refused point-blank to give it up. No-one seemed to want to argue with him given the circumstances.

'Ok, I get the message loud and clear. Sorry about that. I am usually more careful but a lot of things have taken off all at the same time and I am running around trying to catch them before they fall. Whatever is going on elsewhere shouldn't concern either of you at this time. And, by the way, I am Doug. I like that better than "mister". Hope that's OK?'

Aleksei said quietly, 'That is fine with me. Elena has

told me you were a spy in my country. Please tell me what you saw and your experiences there.' Doug James hesitated for a moment and Aleksei chuckled. 'It is all right. I already know and trust you. Elena might take a little longer though.'

'Both Aleksei and myself are indebted to you for arranging for our daughter to be brought here, but we are very concerned over our grandson. Aleksei says he has heard bad things of this Venditti,' Elena said.

Aleksei again looked at the man standing in front of him and tried to remember exactly where he had seen him before in the Soviet Union.

'There are rumours about this man,' said Aleksei. 'It is said he seeks a power similar to my own. You do not live an existence in a laboratory devising all kinds of experiments without learning of others who do the same.'

Doug James had already heard that Venditti was thought to be practising many things to do with the occult and some were even saying he had mastered certain dark powers.

'So what do you think his aim is? Why does he want your grandson, Rudy, so badly?' he asked.

The look in Aleksei's eyes began to change as he felt a slight surge. Elena stood back in surprise, never having seen this in him before. The glow receded gradually and Aleksei looked around him. Seeing Elena's concerned expression he tried to reassure her with a further few quiet words in Russian, but she shook her head at him.

'I should leave you two alone together as you must have so much to catch up on. Whatever Venditti is up to I can assure you that everything possible is being done to gain Rudy's release. By the way, your husband said he would wait in the cafeteria as he was expecting a call from your son, Ben.' Doug James then left the room.

Elena, on being reminded of her other family, looked

291

awkwardly at Aleksei. She was wondering what to do. He watched her closely, able to read the situation.

'This is not a time for recriminations, my Elena. I know you feel badly about letting your husband and son down, but God put us back together after first blessing us with a daughter, who has since borne another child who has been called Rudy, but is yet another Aleksei. God will choose what is to happen next.'

Elena bent down and kissed him gently on his lips. 'I will do as God wills, but only if I am to be with you!'

Aleksei chuckled. 'That is the Elena I remember and held in my heart all these years. But, please, go and find our children safe. That is all I wish now, my Elena...'

She was about to protest when the nurse appeared and administered his medication. Aleksei drifted off into sleep.

The sniper watched the procession to the gates of the monastery being turned away. They were envoys sent by His Holiness with a personal request for the boy to be returned. They trudged sadly back to the bus that had brought them from the airport. Shortly after their departure a lone figure appeared trudging up the mountain slope towards the monastery. The sniper recognised him and set the rifle down, dismantling it expertly and replacing it in a black suitcase.

The man was now seated on a rock recovering from the arduous journey on foot. He had carried a large bag on his back, which was now on the ground in front of him and he rummaged through the contents, pulling out various garments which he put on. The clothes had been carefully chosen. His eyes now trained on the horizon, he saw the sleek figure dressed in black approaching him wearing a balaclava that hid the face. He smiled broadly.

'Welcome. It is our time now, yes?'

The figure in black nodded but said nothing.

The pair slowly approached the gates of the monastery where they were met with a shouted warning.

'You are not welcome. Be gone, and go with the safety of God's grace.'

The man replied, 'Please let us in so we can converse with your master.'

Brother Stefano immediately recognised the voice. 'Gustaf, is that you?'

'It is I, Gustaf, Brother Stefano. Will you please open the gates?'

A moment later the gates slowly opened, creaking heavily on worn hinges. Before Brother Stefano could say anything he heard Monsignor Venditti calling from the doorway.

'Brother, who is this you have allowed to enter without my permission? My express wishes were for no-one else to be allowed entry.'

'It is Gustaf, Monsignor. He wants to speak with you.'

Venditti at first looked surprised, then his eyes narrowed as he approached the visitors.

'Welcome back, Gustaf. But I am confused by your choice of clothing. If I am not mistaken these are the robes of the Russian Orthodox Church, are they not? And who is this other person who does not wish to show his face?'

Gustaf smiled at the man to whom he had devoted so many years of personal service.

'I am here to ask you to allow this person to take the boy, Rudy, back to where he belongs. I am here to explain why he must be returned.'

The monsignor scowled at the figure in black. 'And who, might I ask, are you to presume that I would give the boy up that easily?'

In reply the figure slowly pulled the balaclava off, revealing the face of Irina Dmitriev. Irina had been taught well how to use a rifle during the three years she had spent assisting the Chehovsky household.

Monsignor Venditti looked at her with disdain.

'So you bring a child along to do a man's work, eh Gustaf?'

'This girl is Irina Dmitriev and I must now admit my own true identity. I am Konstantin Zhirinovsky, a priest of the Russian Orthodox Church.'

Venditti looked furious. 'All of those years you were deceiving me.'

'I am sorry for that but the reasons I will make clear to you now. I was always aware that you dealt with matters of the occult and that you coveted the power of the boy, Rudy. But I am here to tell you that it is forbidden to tamper with a power source provided for one reason only. The source of the power derives from the special patriotic unity of Russian people past; it is purely for the benefit of Russian people present and future, working towards better times for all Soviet citizens. We believe that, with Rudy's assistance the present regime's attitude will thaw and we will be able to work towards peaceful co-existence with the rest of the world.'

Venditti snorted with derision. 'A pipe dream that will never be possible as long as you are all from a race of collective barbarians and lack the exquisite sophistication of our system of beliefs. The boy must remain here with the truth and within the sanctuary of the Roman Church.'

'I ask again, Monsignor Luigi, please offer him up.'

Venditti glared as he repeated, 'The boy stays here.'

'Is it not the case that the Vatican has asked you to return the boy whence he came? And that this came in a personal message from His Holiness?'

'Who told you this?'

'The party I passed on the road, the papal envoys. They halted to ask me if I required anything but I said I was not far from my destination. I told them who I was and that I was coming here and my intention. They wished me good fortune and said I would be in their prayers. They hoped I would be successful.'

'So Konstantin Zhirinovsky, Gustaf, you wish me to comply with your request? My answer will always be "no" for I have always believed my power would merge with His to ensure the protection of the Holy See.'

Konstantin shook his head slowly. 'But the Pope himself has asked you to give up on this. Monsignor Luigi, for the sake of all that we shared before and even though you may feel betrayed, I want to help you. Please reconsider. Give the boy to us and we will go in peace.'

Venditti looked curious. 'Go in peace? And what is the alternative?'

The Russian Orthodox priest looked around him and observed that there were several of the brotherhood watching and listening.

He raised his voice. 'The alternative you would not wish to witness, any of you. Monsignor Luigi I beg you not to incur the wrath of the power surrounding the boy.'

'Ha! An empty threat. I have already subjugated him. He is far less powerful than I was led to believe.'

Venditti was grinning demonically but his expression began to change as he felt a burning sensation in his left ear. He turned, noticed the fiery glare of the young woman and now recognised her for what she represented.

'You, it is you!'

Venditti fled towards the door to the underground vaults. Passing through, he slammed it shut and slipped the bolts securely. Konstantin and Irina arrived too late and hammered vainly on the door. They cried a warning to Rudy, and hoped he was able to hear them. Konstantin knew from his time there as Gustaf that there was no other way into the vaults – everywhere was sealed inside.

Rudy lay on the slab in a semi-conscious state. He heard a commotion above him but in his stupor he could not make out what was going on. Suddenly he was gripped by a massive surge that awoke him instantly. His eyes searched in the darkness for the danger he sensed. Luigi Venditti had not anticipated that most of the torches necessary to guide a safe path down the steep stairway would be extinguished. He took a lighted one from its holder and proceeded slowly down the stairway. There was a clear one-hundred-foot drop on one side to the lower vault, which housed the prisoner. Venditti put his back to the wall and inched down sideways. Rudy heard the slight scuffling above him and at the same time felt another even more powerful surge, which allowed him to wrench his arms free from their tethers. He bent forward, untied the knots binding his feet and stood up unsteadily. With another surge he found himself able to walk over to the stairway. As he did so he noticed two figures hanging from the far wall. He looked closer, then recoiled at the sight. Both had been skewered on hooks which left them dangling a foot from the ground. Their eyes had been gouged out. He recognised them as the two men who had arrived earlier and noted that their injuries had not been attended to. A large pool of blood lay beneath each body.

Rudy retched. Then, as he looked upwards, he saw the darkened shape of Monsignor Venditti slowly edging down the stairway. His face appeared white and ghoulish in the half-light afforded by the torch he was carrying. The monsignor felt a burning sensation in his right ear similar to what he had experienced outside when the girl had looked at him. He looked down to see Rudy, eyes burning like red-hot coals. Venditti felt faint and backed up against the wall, desperately trying to find something solid to hold onto. But it was sheer and his hands just slithered over the smooth surface. He found himself being slowly lured to the other edge of the stairway and reluctantly looked down on the massive drop to the lower vault. He struggled to right himself but suddenly an irresistible power propelled him off the stairway and he found himself plummeting downwards. His searing scream was silenced by the terrible thud of his body striking the stone slab from which Rudy had escaped earlier. Rudy walked over to the monsignor. The skull had fractured allowing brains and fluid to seep out over the stone. Venditti's eyes were still open and flickering – his mouth twitched. He suddenly raised a hand towards Rudy, who backed away. Venditti's arm then lowered as he gave a long, last sigh.

Rudy felt absolutely drained as he climbed the stairway. At the top he wrenched aside the bolts and opened the door. The daylight blinded him at first, then his sight improved and he beheld the beaming face of Irina Dmitriev. 'Liliya? Can it be you?'

Irina held out her hands and gently took his. 'Not Liliya, Rudy. I am Irina. But Liliya links us both. Do you understand?'

Rudy nodded, still feeling overwhelmed.

'And this is Konstantin. He has much to tell you of your power and how it can assist Russian peoples. Even if you decide never to go there, as long as you care for the people you descend from all will be well for the future. That is the power you have been given.'

37

Helen Metthewson felt nervous as her flight touched down onto the runway. Those guarding her had taken strategically planned places so as to offer the maximum protection, but at the same time left her comfortably in her own individual space. As she disembarked they were following at a safe distance. Aleksei had insisted that Jim drive Elena to the airport to meet her daughter, though Jim secretly wished he had been allowed to wait for the outcome at home.

Elena nervously smoked a cigarette in the arrivals lounge. Jim looked out of the window at the aeroplanes arriving and taking off, wishing he were on one flying a long way away. A crowd of people began to emerge from the gateway towards them. Elena stubbed out her cigarette and waited. Then she saw her; she knew it was her, the resemblance was too strong for it not to be. Helen noticed a lady with a fine bearing who was looking back at her. She suddenly felt overcome and stopped in her tracks. The aides that had been watching her also stopped. She approached her daughter, who had her eyes cast down. Elena spoke quietly to her in Russian and Helen looked up with tears in her eyes. Then both women hugged each other, weeping quietly.

On the drive back to the hospital Jim was grimly silent whilst Helen and Elena, now over their initial nervousness, chatted away, catching up on all that had happened to them. The subject of Rudy's disappearance was very much on Helen's mind but Elena told her that Aleksei, her father, had said he sensed Rudy would be safe soon. Helen had enquired as to how he sensed this and Elena had told her of the powers he had that she had only just discovered in him. Helen had then told her of the escapades involving Rudy and Elena sat back dumbfounded. Sitting in the driver's seat Jim did not hear anything that gave him any hope of saving his relationship and decided to depart as soon as he had dropped them off at the hospital. He would drive back to the hotel and pack his suitcase.

Elena had made a half-hearted attempt to change her husband's mind but he would not be moved on his decision. He gave her a quick hug and a kiss and departed.

Helen watched him go and said, 'It must be very difficult for him to accept all of this. What will you do? Ben must be missing you?'

'He is a good man but not the man I thought I had married, which probably is a good thing in the circumstances. He can be very irritating and sometimes act irrationally, as you see now. As for Ben, this is America where divorcees easily outnumber happily married couples. He will not feel alone amongst his peers.'

They both entered the hospital. Walking along the corridor Elena noticed that there was no sign of the aide that should have been guarding the room Aleksei was in. She walked quickly into the room and found the bed empty. Elena began swearing in Russian through gritted teeth. As she turned she gasped. In the doorway the aide had returned with Aleksei's arm clasped around his shoulder.

'You gave me such a shock. What are you doing out of bed? You are not well enough to be out of bed,' Elena said angrily.

'The doctor said I had healed beyond all his expectations. "A miracle" he called it,' Aleksei chuckled. 'Anyway I was fed up of using a bedpan. I wanted to feel the comfort of a toilet seat again!' He winked at the other woman standing quietly in the corner of the room. 'You see how the males of our family are determined to be a constant worry to you females with our awkward ways.'

The aide helped him over to his bed but he remained standing, holding a hand out to Helen. His expression had changed and a tear ran down his cheek as Helen held her father's hand at last. Aleksei wept quietly and held her in an awkward embrace for a few moments before releasing her and collapsing on the bed with a thud.

He cried out, 'Ouch! But it was worth it.'

Rudy sat in the front passenger seat of the hire car being driven by Irina. She glanced at him from time to time but there was little conversation because of the talkative soul in the back seat. Konstantin wanted to be assured that both knew of the consequences now that the matter had become so protracted with several different factions still showing an interest. But he also had to accept their view that once the news had been circulated of the demise of Monsignor Luigi Venditti no-one would relish crossing swords with either of them. Relief was evident in the pair when they had off-loaded the talkative priest at the railway station, his destination Kiev.

'Where will you take me now, Irina?' Rudy asked.

'I am tempted to take you home first to meet my family, even though I do not think they will be glad to see me.'

Rudy gave her a questioning look and Irina told him all of what had happened and her suspicions over her grandfather, Oleg.

'Do you think he is still alive?' Rudy asked after digesting the information.

Irina thought for what to Rudy seemed a long time.

'I don't really want to think about it Rudy. My feelings are so mixed up. I love my grandpapa but I just cannot get it out of my head that he may have betrayed us, and that thought upsets me no end.'

Rudy could see she was suffering so changed the subject. 'I will have to meet your family someday though, Irina.'

She looked at him curiously. 'Oh? And why would that be I wonder.'

He grinned. 'Liliya made a promise.'

Irina smiled back with a knowing expression. 'And what promise was that?'

'I think you know: that I would meet a beautiful Russian woman and immediately fall in love with her. We will be married and have children who will have children, one of which will be my grandson – and so it will go on.'

Irina feigned surprise. 'But Rudy, I am so much older than you. This cannot be right!'

Rudy grinned mischievously. 'I am as good as sixteen, and you eighteen. It might take me a little while to catch up with you but catch up I will. Then I will prove my manhood.'

Irina looked back at him with a strange look in her eyes, which Rudy found slightly disconcerting. He was about to apologise for his presumption when she pulled off the main road onto a track, heading up towards woodland at the top of a hill.

'Why wait that long? Let's test it out now!' she said casually.

Doug James put the telephone down and called an aide into his office. He told him to notify Aleksei, Elena and Helen that Rudy had been rescued and would be escorted to the U.S. by Irina Dmitriev and her brothers, Lev and Leonid.

301

When Irina and Rudy had arrived at the family home they were met by a relieved Nina and Nikolai. Irina had been overwhelmed by the welcome and the apologies that followed from both her parents and her brothers too. They had been informed that Oleg had been shot whilst trying to assassinate Aleksei and it took quite a while for Irina to take this in. She had fled to her room and wept whilst Rudy tried hard to make an impression and make himself understood with the rest of the family, who did not possess much English. Irina had eventually returned and, although a little sullen, had at least been able to act as an interpreter between Rudy and her family. Contact had been received from the Americans who were offering safe passage to the U.S. and it had finally been decided that Lev and Leonid would act as their guardians on the journey. The visas for all four were organised through Doug James. Little did they appreciate that there was also considerable backup on each stage of their journey. Doug had made sure of this.

John Mackay sat in the bath of his hotel room. He had been drinking heavily and did not realise anyone else was in the room until a bullet hit him in the throat. Blood oozed from the wound through his fingers as he gasped for breath. He looked up and his eyes widened in terror. The next shot went through his temple exiting through the back of his head. The bath of water slowly turned crimson.

In Britain, Graham Digby had received a warning to disappear and was hastily packing his suitcase at home. His wife had left to do some shopping, but when he heard movement downstairs he thought she had returned. He called out to her but did not receive any reply. A cold sweat ran over him as he descended the stairs. The gunman appeared from the front room and Digby turned to run up the stairs but made only two more steps before being hit by three bullets, two in the back and the other in his buttock. Groaning, Digby slid down the stairs, turning with great effort toward his assassin. He recognised him and tried to speak, but two more bullets, fired at point blank range into his head, killed him instantly.

General Guznischev sat in a chair sipping a glass of brandy. He was in good spirits after hearing that Aleksei was recovering and that Elena, Helen and Rudy were at last united. But the best news of all was that the clean-up campaign had been completed in a thoroughly efficient manner, removing all those who might have become an embarrassment in the future.

Aleksei watched silently as all around him chattered away happily. From time to time some would look across at him and he knew they were talking about him. Lev and Leonid had felt intimidated when they had first arrived, but Aleksei had warned them that if they did not enjoy their trip to the United States he would personally ensure they were flown straight back to Siberia. Elena felt so proud of him. Eventually Irina approached him again, Elena watching closely as she had already seen the intimacy between them when Irina had arrived. Aleksei saw Elena staring and winked at her, but received a glare in return. Irina whispered something in his ear, then turned and walked back to the others. Elena could not help herself and approached Aleksei who closed his eyes and pretended to be resting.

'Have I competition here, Comrade Rudikov?' Elena said formally.

Aleksei opened his eyes. 'No,' he whispered, 'she is to be your future grand-daughter-in-law.' He chuckled.

Elena looked across at her grandson and smiled at him. He grinned cheekily back at her.

'Babushka!'

'Another Aleksei, my Aleksei,' she muttered.

Aleksei listened and responded. 'God is still with us then!'

38

1964 was a very eventful year in the lives of Aleksei and Elena and for all those closely connected to them. Doug James had been as good as his word and kept his promise to provide a safe haven in which to allow for Aleksei's recuperation. A ranch house deep in the heart of Texas had been provided together with an army of agents patrolling the perimeters. This allowed for ample space and privacy. Aleksei had made such a good recovery that he was able to move around freely, but often overdid things and had to rest. Elena kept a strict eye on him and complained frequently at his excesses. Aleksei would always promise to be good, until the next time!

Medical assistance was always on hand and a regular team of doctor and nurses arrived at the ranch every few days to check on the patient's progress.

Irina Dmitriev and her brothers had returned to their home just outside West Berlin. Doug James had assured them they would be allowed to stay indefinitely in the United States if they wished to do so and that they could bring their parents back with them. Irina thought that her parents, Nina and Nikolai, would feel intimidated by such a move, but she herself had not ruled out the possibility of returning, perhaps even with her brothers. Rudy had said a sad farewell to Irina, but they had agreed to be together again as soon as was practicable.

Aleksei had been granted diplomatic immunity. Doug James had also been instrumental in closing down the department he had been attached to for so many years.

This meant that the experimentation into phenomena had been abandoned, much to the relief of Aleksei and Elena.

Helen Metthewson was still coming to terms with everything, but each day that passed in the company of her parents she grew more confident and decided to take up her Russian name, Elena, immediately. To avoid confusion her mother decided to be known as Elena R for Rudikov and Helen as Elena Z for Zvadsky.

Rudy, however, had decided to keep his name for the time being. Aleksei and Elena had felt so proud of their grandson on learning of his experiences with Luis Suarez and Luigi Venditti. Aleksei had also noticed the power around Rudy and could not wait to impart what he had been told by Stanislav all those years ago. He would walk some small distance with his grandson and sit down to rest under a tree on a hill looking down on the ranch house. There they would talk for an hour or so, then return to the house, where Elena would chide him for overdoing things. On one particular day Aleksei appeared with a rifle he had found in one of the back rooms. He had also managed to persuade one of the agents to find him some ammunition.

'Where the hell did you get that, Aleksei?' Elena said sharply.

'Found it in the back. It's in good shape. Thought I would go catch us a rabbit. Show Rudy here how to use it.'

Elena shook her head at him. 'I don't think that is a good idea. People are still jumpy around here and you shooting a rifle might just start another battle. Anyway I would have thought you would have been sick of such weapons after all your experiences.'

'Firing it in wartime is another matter altogether. No pleasure then. But for sport and to catch a rabbit, much pleasure!' At that Aleksei led Rudy out of the house and up the hill. 'Have you ever fired a gun, Rudy?'

Rudy shook his head.

'Pity. But your life in Britain was much different from my childhood. I learned to shoot when I was eight years old. Old Stanislav, my grandpapa, he taught me well. He said I had a natural sight and a knack for being precise. I learned some years later that he too was a sniper like me. It was a tremendous shock but made a lot of sense to me when I thought it over.' He then handed the rifle to Rudy. 'Here, get a feel for it. The safety catch is on so it will not fire by mistake.'

Rudy took the weapon from Aleksei and held it as if to shoot. Aleksei watched him with an experienced eye.

'Ok, I take the safety catch off now and you shoot that tin can over there.'

Rudy felt a little nervous realising he had such a powerful weapon under his control.

'Which can? I can't see it.'

Aleksei smiled. 'Look through the sights and move a little to your right. Do you see it now?'

Rudy moved the weapon to the right and saw the tin can in the distance. 'Yes, I see it now.'

'Good. So when you think your aim is right just gently squeeze the trigger.'

Rudy concentrated and at the same time felt a slight surge that made him feel calm and confident. He fired off a shot and the tin can left the ground and spun in the air.

Agents appeared running towards the sounds but were halted by a radio message from the agent who had supplied the ammunition and who was standing by admiring Rudy's prowess with a rifle. Both Elenas also came racing out of the house and stood glaring up disapprovingly at Aleksei and Rudy who had huge grins on their faces. Aleksei slapped Rudy on the back.

'Come, we find that tin can and put it in a glass case as your first trophy.'

Jim Earnshaw had decided to remain in their Californian home and wait for his wife to return, but each week that passed without her caused him to believe that the best thing would be to ask for a divorce. At first Elena was upset and angry over the suddeness of her husband's request, but she realised how he had suffered and agreed to have the matter sorted out as quickly as possible. Initially, Ben had been terribly upset, but, as Elena had astutely remarked a while previously, American kids were used to such things happening and Ben had the resilience of youth. He appeared to get over it fairly quickly – so much so that he agreed to stay at the ranch for a week at a time, getting along with everyone, especially Rudy. Ben was intrigued by the fact that although he and Rudy were similar ages Rudy's mum was, in fact, his stepsister.

Doug James would pass by from time to time, especially around mealtimes and fill them in over what was happening in the world. Nikita Khrushchev had sought the repatriation of Aleksei and had even sent for the Russian Orthodox priest, Konstantin Zhirinovsky, to ask him if he would persuade Aleksei Rudikov to return, even offering a full pardon. Konstantin had agreed to try but on 14th October 1964 Khrushchev had been deposed. He had returned from a vacation in the Crimea to be greeted with news that his resignation had been accepted and his protégé, Leonid Brezhnev, had become the Party First Secretary.

Aleksei sat at the dinner table having just consumed his meal. Elena could see he was mulling the situation over. Doug James was also looking closely at him for a reaction. Rudy felt something inside him as he sensed the tension in the room. He had not seen his grandfather in such a serious mood before and he found it quite disconcerting.

'So it is back to the old days.' Aleksei's face darkened as he whispered this.

Doug James enquired, 'The old days. As bad as that?'

Aleksei looked first at Elena who did not like this change of mood in him, and then across at Doug.

'Brezhnev is a Stalinist. He aligned himself with Khrushchev only as long as it was convenient. I know why they have got rid of him. They were afraid he would go too far with his ideas. He denounced Stalin and all he stood for and I admired him for that. Elena and I know well what the years under Stalin felt like. I still feel it, right inside my soul.' Aleksei had tears in his eyes. Elena looked away from him biting back her own grief. 'So we seem to be heading backwards, I am afraid. The world watches better now than in those dark days when Stalin did as he pleased, so Brezhnev and his co-conspirators will have to take a little more care. Inside me I have a strange desire to visit my country once again and I was looking forward to that possibility, but not now. I do not trust that lot an inch.'

Elena shook her head at him. 'No, Aleksei, you are a dreamer and it has never been better, never. Khrushchev was not averse to carrying out Stalin's orders. There is no-one from those times who hasn't got the blood of our poor people on his hands.'

Aleksei sighed. 'I know you are right Elena, but maybe a dream will come true – sometime?' Rudy felt that strangeness that visited him from time to time. Liliya was here with him. He found himself talking but, as before, a lot of what he was saying wasn't present in his own mind.

'Dreams are important, especially positive dreams. One day the dream of Russian people will become reality, if we all dream together. That day is not so far away. There will come another who will cause things to change for Mother Russia, and create a better existence for all.'

Rudy looked down as Aleksei's face lit up again. 'You see this, Rudy? You really see this?'

Rudy nodded his head then looked up with a strange glow in his eyes that everyone, apart from Aleksei, found disconcerting.

Aleksei looked around at the rest and whispered, 'It is his power of sight. They are connecting with him. Stanislav spoke of such things. Rudy is surely more powerful than I ever was.'

Elena held her hand out to her daughter who clasped it. Both women were shaking now. Even Doug James, who thought he had seen everything in life, was awestruck.

'I have just to concentrate on where I came from and wish everyone a better existence and then it will happen. Not overnight, but sometime in the future.' Rudy shuddered as he looked down. A moment later he looked up again and smiled. 'I have been told that one day we all will go back together. You, Grandpapa – and you, Babushka – and you, Mama – and me. It is a promise.'